CANE

JEAN TOOMER

CANE

AUTHORITATIVE TEXT

LIVERIGHT

New York | London

For information about permission to reproduce selections from this book,
write to Permissions, W. W. Norton & Company, Inc.,
500 Fifth Avenue, New York, NY 10110

For information about special discounts for bulk purchases, please contact
W. W. Norton Special Sales at specialsales@wwnorton.com or 800-233-4830

Manufacturing by Courier Westford
Book design by Chris Welch
Production managers: Devon Zahn and Louise Mattarelliano

Library of Congress Cataloging-in-Publication Data

Toomer, Jean, 1894–1967.
Cane : authoritative text / Jean Toomer.
p. cm.
ISBN 978-0-87140-210-3 (pbk.)
1. African Americans—Fiction. 2. Southern States—Fiction. I. Title.
PS3539.O478C3 2011
813'.52—dc22

2011014913

Liveright Publishing Corporation
500 Fifth Avenue, New York, N.Y. 10110
www.wwnorton.com

W. W. Norton & Company Ltd.
Castle House, 75/76 Wells Street, London W1T 3QT

4 5 6 7 8 9 0

CONTENTS

CANE

▼▼▼

TO MY GRANDMOTHER . . .

Karíntha

Her skin is like dusk on the eastern horizon,
O cant you see it, O cant you see it,
Her skin is like dusk on the eastern horizon
. . . When the sun goes down.

Men had always wanted her, this Karintha, even as a child, Karintha carrying beauty, perfect as dusk when the sun goes down. Old men rode her hobby-horse upon their knees. Young men danced with her at frolics when they should have been dancing with their grown-up girls. God grant us youth, secretly prayed the old men. The young fellows counted the time to pass before she would be old enough to mate with them. This interest of the male, who wishes to ripen a growing thing too soon, could mean no good to her.

Karintha, at twelve, was a wild flash that told the other folks just what it was to live. At sunset, when there was no wind, and the pine-smoke from over by the sawmill hugged the earth, and you couldnt see more than a few feet in front, her sudden darting past you was a bit of vivid color, like a black bird that flashes in light. With the other children one could hear, some distance off, their feet flopping in the two-inch dust. Karintha's running was a whir. It had the sound of the red dust that sometimes makes a spiral in the road. At dusk, during the hush just after the sawmill had closed down, and before any of the women had started their supper-getting-ready songs, her voice, high-pitched, shrill, would put one's ears to itching. But no one ever thought to make her stop because of it. She stoned the cows, and beat her dog, and fought the other children . . . Even the preacher, who caught her at mischief, told himself that she was as innocently lovely as a November cotton flower. Already, rumors were out about her. Homes in Georgia are most often built on the two-room plan. In one, you cook and eat, in the other you sleep, and there love goes on. Karintha had seen or heard, perhaps she had felt her parents loving. One could but imitate one's parents, for to follow them was the way of God. She played "home" with a small boy who was not afraid to do her bidding. That started the whole thing. Old men could no longer ride her hobby-horse upon their knees. But young men counted faster.

> Her skin is like dusk,
> O cant you see it,
> Her skin is like dusk,
> When the sun goes down.

Karintha is a woman. She who carries beauty, perfect as dusk when the sun goes down. She has been married many times. Old men remind her that a few years back they rode her hobby-horse upon their knees. Karintha smiles, and indulges them when she is in the mood for it. She has contempt for them. Karintha is a woman. Young men run stills to make her money. Young men go to the big cities and run on the road. Young men go away to college. They all want to bring her money. These are the young men who thought that all they had to do was to count time. But Karintha is a woman, and she has had a child. A child fell out of her womb onto a bed of pine-needles in the forest. Pine-needles are smooth and sweet. They are elastic to the feet of rabbits . . . A sawmill was nearby. Its pyramidal sawdust pile smouldered. It is a year before one completely burns. Meanwhile, the smoke curls up and hangs in odd wraiths about the trees, curls up, and spreads itself out over the valley . . . Weeks after Karintha returned home the smoke was so heavy you tasted it in water. Some one made a song:

> Smoke is on the hills. Rise up.
> Smoke is on the hills, O rise
> And take my soul to Jesus.

Karintha is a woman. Men do not know that the soul of her was a growing thing ripened too soon. They will bring their money; they will die not having found it out . . . Karintha at twenty, carrying beauty, perfect as dusk when the sun goes down. Karintha . . .

> Her skin is like dusk on the eastern horizon,
> O cant you see it, O cant you see it,
> Her skin is like dusk on the eastern horizon
> . . . When the sun goes down.

Goes down . . .

Reapers

Black reapers with the sound of steel on stones
Are sharpening scythes. I see them place the hones
In their hip-pockets as a thing that's done,
And start their silent swinging, one by one.
Black horses drive a mower through the weeds,
And there, a field rat, startled, squealing bleeds,
His belly close to ground. I see the blade,
Blood-stained, continue cutting weeds and shade.

November Cotton Flower

Boll-weevil's coming, and the winter's cold,
Made cotton-stalks look rusty, seasons old,
And cotton, scarce as any southern snow,
Was vanishing; the branch, so pinched and slow,
Failed in its function as the autumn rake;
Drouth fighting soil had caused the soil to take
All water from the streams; dead birds were found
In wells a hundred feet below the ground—
Such was the season when the flower bloomed.
Old folks were startled, and it soon assumed
Significance. Superstition saw
Something it had never seen before:
Brown eyes that loved without a trace of fear,
Beauty so sudden for that time of year.

Becky

Becky was the white woman who had two Negro sons.
She's dead; they've gone away. The pines whisper to
Jesus. The Bible flaps its leaves with an aimless rustle
on her mound.

Becky had one Negro son. Who gave it to her? Damn buck
nigger, said the white folks' mouths. She wouldnt tell. Common, God-forsaken, insane white shameless wench, said the
white folks' mouths. Her eyes were sunken, her neck stringy, her
breasts fallen, till then. Taking their words, they filled her, like a
bubble rising—then she broke. Mouth setting in a twist that held
her eyes, harsh, vacant, staring . . . Who gave it to her? Low-
down nigger with no self-respect, said the black folks' mouths.
She wouldnt tell. Poor Catholic poor-white crazy woman, said the
black folks' mouths. White folks and black folks built her cabin,
fed her and her growing baby, prayed secretly to God who'd put
His cross upon her and cast her out.

When the first was born, the white folks said they'd have no
more to do with her. And black folks, they too joined hands to cast
her out . . . The pines whispered to Jesus . . . The railroad boss
said not to say he said it, but she could live, if she wanted to, on
the narrow strip of land between the railroad and the road. John
Stone, who owned the lumber and the bricks, would have shot
the man who told he gave the stuff to Lonnie Deacon, who stole

out there at night and built the cabin. A single room held down to earth . . . O fly away to Jesus . . . by a leaning chimney . . .

Six trains each day rumbled past and shook the ground under her cabin. Fords, and horse- and mule-drawn buggies went back and forth along the road. No one ever saw her. Trainmen, and passengers who'd heard about her, threw out papers and food. Threw out little crumpled slips of paper scribbled with prayers, as they passed her eye-shaped piece of sandy ground. Ground islandized between the road and railroad track. Pushed up where a blue-sheen God with listless eyes could look at it. Folks from the town took turns, unknown, of course, to each other, in bringing corn and meat and sweet potatoes. Even sometimes snuff . . . O thank y Jesus . . . Old David Georgia, grinding cane and boiling syrup, never went her way without some sugar sap. No one ever saw her. The boy grew up and ran around. When he was five years old as folks reckoned it, Hugh Jourdon saw him carrying a baby. "Becky has another son," was what the whole town knew. But nothing was said, for the part of man that says things to the likes of that had told itself that if there was a Becky, that Becky now was dead.

The two boys grew. Sullen and cunning . . . O pines, whisper to Jesus; tell Him to come and press sweet Jesus-lips against their lips and eyes . . . It seemed as though with those two big fellows there, there could be no room for Becky. The part that prayed wondered if perhaps she'd really died, and they had buried her. No one dared ask. They'd beat and cut a man who meant nothing at all in mentioning that they lived along the road. White or colored? No one knew, and least of all themselves. They drifted around from job to job. We, who had cast out their mother because of them, could we take them in? They answered black and white folks by shooting up two men and leaving town. "Godam the white folks; godam the niggers," they shouted as they left town. Becky? Smoke curled up from her chimney; she must be there. Trains passing shook the ground. The ground shook the leaning chimney. Nobody noticed it. A creepy feeling came over all who saw that thin wraith of smoke and felt the trembling of the ground. Folks began to take her food again. They quit it soon because they had a fear. Becky if dead might be a hant, and if alive—it took some nerve even to mention it . . . O pines, whisper to Jesus . . .

It was Sunday. Our congregation had been visiting at Pulverton, and were coming home. There was no wind. The autumn sun, the bell from Ebenezer Church, listless and heavy. Even the pines were stale, sticky, like the smell of food that makes you sick. Before we turned the bend of the road that would show us the Becky cabin, the horses stopped stock-still, pushed back their ears, and nervously whinnied. We urged, then whipped them on. Quarter of a mile away thin smoke curled up from the leaning chimney . . . O pines, whisper to Jesus . . . Goose-flesh came on my skin though there still was neither chill nor wind. Eyes left their sockets for the cabin. Ears burned and throbbed. Uncanny eclipse! fear closed my mind. We were just about to pass . . . Pines shout to Jesus! . . . the ground trembled as a ghost train rumbled by. The chimney fell into the cabin. Its thud was like a hollow report, ages having passed since it went off. Barlo and I were pulled out of our seats. Dragged to the door that had swung open. Through the dust we saw the bricks in a mound upon the floor. Becky, if she was there, lay under them. I thought I heard a groan. Barlo, mumbling something, threw his Bible on the pile. (No one has ever touched it.) Somehow we got away. My buggy was still on the road. The last thing that I remember was whipping old Dan like fury; I remember nothing after that—that is, until I reached town and folks crowded round to get the true word of it.

> Becky was the white woman who had two Negro sons.
> She's dead; they've gone away. The pines whisper to
> Jesus. The Bible flaps its leaves with an aimless rustle
> on her mound.

Face

Hair—
silver-gray,
like streams of stars,
Brows—
recurved canoes
quivered by the ripples blown by pain,
Her eyes—
mist of tears
condensing on the flesh below
And her channeled muscles
are cluster grapes of sorrow
purple in the evening sun
nearly ripe for worms.

Cotton Song

Come, brother, come. Lets lift it;
Come now, hewit! roll away!
Shackles fall upon the Judgment Day
But lets not wait for it.

God's body's got a soul,
Bodies like to roll the soul,
Cant blame God if we dont roll,
Come, brother, roll, roll!

Cotton bales are the fleecy way
Weary sinner's bare feet trod,
Softly, softly to the throne of God,
"We aint agwine t wait until th Judgment Day!

Nassur; nassur,
Hump.
Eoho, eoho, roll away!
We aint agwine t wait until th Judgment Day!"

God's body's got a soul,
Bodies like to roll the soul,
Cant blame God if we dont roll,
Come, brother, roll, roll!

Carma

Wind is in the cane. Come along.
Cane leaves swaying, rusty with talk,
Scratching choruses above the guinea's squawk,
Wind is in the cane. Come along.

Carma, in overalls, and strong as any man, stands behind the old brown mule, driving the wagon home. It bumps, and groans, and shakes as it crosses the railroad track. She, riding it easy. I leave the men around the stove to follow her with my eyes down the red dust road. Nigger woman driving a Georgia chariot down an old dust road. Dixie Pike is what they call it. Maybe she feels my gaze, perhaps she expects it. Anyway, she turns. The sun, which has been slanting over her shoulder, shoots primitive rockets into her mangrove-gloomed, yellow flower face. Hi! Yip! God has left the Moses-people for the nigger. "Gedap." Using reins to slap the mule, she disappears in a cloudy rumble at some indefinite point along the road.

(The sun is hammered to a band of gold. Pine-needles, like mazda, are brilliantly aglow. No rain has come to take the rustle from the falling sweet-gum leaves. Over in the forest, across the swamp, a sawmill blows its closing whistle. Smoke curls up. Marvelous web spun by the spider sawdust pile. Curls up and spreads itself pine-high above the branch, a single silver band along the eastern valley. A black boy . . . you are the most sleepiest man

I ever seed, Sleeping Beauty . . . cradled on a gray mule, guided by the hollow sound of cowbells, heads for them through a rusty cotton field. From down the railroad track, the chug-chug of a gas engine announces that the repair gang is coming home. A girl in the yard of a whitewashed shack not much larger than the stack of worn ties piled before it, sings. Her voice is loud. Echoes, like rain, sweep the valley. Dusk takes the polish from the rails. Lights twinkle in scattered houses. From far away, a sad strong song. Pungent and composite, the smell of farmyards is the fragrance of the woman. She does not sing; her body is a song. She is in the forest, dancing. Torches flare . . . juju men, greegree, witch-doctors . . . torches go out . . . The Dixie Pike has grown from a goat path in Africa.

Night.

Foxie, the bitch, slicks back her ears and barks at the rising moon.)

> Wind is in the cane. Come along.
> Cane leaves swaying, rusty with talk,
> Scratching choruses above the guinea's squawk,
> Wind is in the cane. Come along.

Carma's tale is the crudest melodrama. Her husband's in the gang. And its her fault he got there. Working with a contractor, he was away most of the time. She had others. No one blames her for that. He returned one day and hung around the town where he picked up week-old boasts and rumors . . . Bane accused her. She denied. He couldnt see that she was becoming hysterical. He would have liked to take his fists and beat her. Who was strong as a man. Stronger. Words, like corkscrews, wormed to her strength. It fizzled out. Grabbing a gun, she rushed from the house and plunged across the road into a canebrake . . . There, in quarter heaven shone the crescent moon . . . Bane was afraid to follow till he heard the gun go off. Then he wasted half an hour gathering the neighbor men. They met in the road where lamp-light showed tracks dissolving in the loose earth about the cane. The search began. Moths flickered the lamps. They put them out. Really, because she still might be live enough to shoot. Time and space have no meaning in a canefield. No more than the interminable stalks . . . Some one stumbled over her. A cry went up. From the road, one would have thought that they were cornering a rabbit or a skunk . . . It is difficult carrying dead weight through cane. They placed her on the sofa. A curious, nosey somebody looked for the wound. This fussing with her clothes aroused her. Her eyes were weak and pitiable for so strong a woman. Slowly, then like a flash, Bane came to know that the shot she fired, with averted head, was aimed to whistle like a dying hornet through the cane. Twice deceived, and one deception proved the other. His head went off. Slashed one of the men who'd helped, the man who'd stumbled over her. Now he's in the gang. Who was her husband. Should she not take others, this Carma, strong as a man, whose tale as I have told it is the crudest melodrama?

> Wind is in the cane. Come along.
> Cane leaves swaying, rusty with talk,
> Scratching choruses above the guinea's squawk,
> Wind is in the cane. Come along.

Song of the Son

Pour O pour that parting soul in song,
O pour it in the sawdust glow of night,
Into the velvet pine-smoke air to-night,
And let the valley carry it along.
And let the valley carry it along.

O land and soil, red soil and sweet-gum tree,
So scant of grass, so profligate of pines,
Now just before an epoch's sun declines
Thy son, in time, I have returned to thee,
Thy son, I have in time returned to thee.

In time, for though the sun is setting on
A song-lit race of slaves, it has not set;
Though late, O soil, it is not too late yet
To catch thy plaintive soul, leaving, soon gone,
Leaving, to catch thy plaintive soul soon gone.

O Negro slaves, dark purple ripened plums,
Squeezed, and bursting in the pine-wood air,
Passing, before they stripped the old tree bare
One plum was saved for me, one seed becomes

An everlasting song, a singing tree,
Caroling softly souls of slavery,
What they were, and what they are to me,
Caroling softly souls of slavery.

Georgia Dusk

The sky, lazily disdaining to pursue
    The setting sun, too indolent to hold
    A lengthened tournament for flashing gold,
Passively darkens for night's barbecue,

A feast of moon and men and barking hounds,
    An orgy for some genius of the South
    With blood-hot eyes and cane-lipped scented mouth,
Surprised in making folk-songs from soul sounds.

The sawmill blows its whistle, buzz-saws stop,
    And silence breaks the bud of knoll and hill,
    Soft settling pollen where plowed lands fulfill
Their early promise of a bumper crop.

Smoke from the pyramidal sawdust pile
    Curls up, blue ghosts of trees, tarrying low
    Where only chips and stumps are left to show
The solid proof of former domicile.

Meanwhile, the men, with vestiges of pomp,
    Race memories of king and caravan,
    High-priests, an ostrich, and a juju-man,
Go singing through the footpaths of the swamp.

Their voices rise . . . the pine trees are guitars,
   Strumming, pine-needles fall like sheets of rain . . .
   Their voices rise . . . the chorus of the cane
Is caroling a vesper to the stars . . .

O singers, resinous and soft your songs
   Above the sacred whisper of the pines,
   Give virgin lips to cornfield concubines,
Bring dreams of Christ to dusky cane-lipped throngs.

Fern

ace flowed into her eyes. Flowed in soft cream foam and plaintive ripples, in such a way that wherever your glance may momentarily have rested, it immediately thereafter wavered in the direction of her eyes. The soft suggestion of down slightly darkened, like the shadow of a bird's wing might, the creamy brown color of her upper lip. Why, after noticing it, you sought her eyes, I cannot tell you. Her nose was aquiline, Semitic. If you have heard a Jewish cantor sing, if he has touched you and made your own sorrow seem trivial when compared with his, you will know my feeling when I follow the curves of her profile, like mobile rivers, to their common delta. They were strange eyes. In this, that they sought nothing—that is, nothing that was obvious and tangible and that one could see, and they gave the impression that nothing was to be denied. When a woman seeks, you will have observed, her eyes deny. Fern's eyes desired nothing that you could give her; there was no reason why they should withhold. Men saw her eyes and fooled themselves. Fern's eyes said to them that she was easy. When she was young, a few men took her, but got no joy from it. And then, once done, they felt bound to her (quite unlike their hit and run with other girls), felt as though it would take them a lifetime to fulfill an obligation which they could find no name for. They became attached to her, and hungered after finding the barest trace of what she might desire. As she grew up, new men who came to town felt as almost everyone

21

did who ever saw her: that they would not be denied. Men were everlastingly bringing her their bodies. Something inside of her got tired of them, I guess, for I am certain that for the life of her she could not tell why or how she began to turn them off. A man in fever is no trifling thing to send away. They began to leave her, baffled and ashamed, yet vowing to themselves that some day they would do some fine thing for her: send her candy every week and not let her know whom it came from, watch out for her wedding-day and give her a magnificent something with no name on it, buy a house and deed it to her, rescue her from some unworthy fellow who had tricked her into marrying him. As you know, men are apt to idolize or fear that which they cannot understand, especially if it be a woman. She did not deny them, yet the fact was that they were denied. A sort of superstition crept into their consciousness of her being somehow above them. Being above them meant that she was not to be approached by anyone. She became a virgin. Now a virgin in a small southern town is by no means the usual thing, if you will believe me. That the sexes were made to mate is the practice of the South. Particularly, black folks were made to mate. And it is black folks whom I have been talking about thus far. What white men thought of Fern I can arrive at only by analogy. They let her alone.

Anyone, of course, could see her, could see her eyes. If you walked up the Dixie Pike most any time of day, you'd be most like to see her resting listless-like on the railing of her porch, back propped against a post, head tilted a little forward because there was a nail in the porch post just where her head came which for some reason or other she never took the trouble to pull out. Her eyes, if it were sunset, rested idly where the sun, molten and glorious, was pouring down between the fringe of pines. Or maybe they gazed at the gray cabin on the knoll from which an evening folk-song was coming. Perhaps they followed a cow that had been turned loose to roam and feed on cotton-stalks and corn leaves. Like as not they'd settle on some vague spot above the horizon, though hardly a trace of wistfulness would come to them. If it were dusk, then they'd wait for the search-light of the evening train which you could see miles up the track before it flared across the Dixie Pike, close to her home. Wherever they looked, you'd follow them and then waver back. Like her face, the whole countryside seemed to flow into her eyes. Flowed into them with the soft listless cadence of Georgia's South. A young Negro, once, was looking at her, spellbound, from the road. A white man passing in a buggy had to flick him with his whip if he was to get by without running him over. I first saw her on her porch. I was passing with a fellow whose crusty numbness (I was from the North and suspected of being prejudiced and stuck-up) was melting as he found me warm. I asked him who she was. "That's Fern," was all that I could get from him. Some folks already thought that I was given to nosing around; I let it go at that, so far as questions were concerned. But at first sight of her I felt as if I heard a Jewish cantor sing. As if his singing rose above the unheard chorus of a folk-song. And I felt bound to her. I too had my dreams: something I would do for her. I have knocked about from town to town too much not to know the futility of mere change of place. Besides, picture if you can, this cream-colored solitary girl sitting at a tenement window looking down on the indifferent throngs of Harlem. Better that she listen to folk-songs at dusk in Georgia, you would say, and so would I. Or, suppose she came up North and married. Even a doctor or a lawyer, say, one who would be sure to get along—that is, make money. You and I know, who have had experience in such things, that love is not a thing like prejudice which can be bettered by changes of town. Could men in Washington, Chicago, or New York, more than the men of Georgia, bring her something left vacant by the bestowal of their bodies? You and I who know men in these cities will have to say, they could not. See her out and out a prostitute along State Street in Chicago. See her move into a southern town where white men are more aggressive. See her become a white man's concubine . . . Something I must do for her. There was myself. What could I do for her? Talk, of course. Push back the fringe of pines upon new horizons. To what purpose? and what for? Her? Myself? Men in her case seem to lose their selfishness. I lost mine before I touched her. I ask you, friend (it makes no difference if you sit in the Pullman or the Jim Crow as the train crosses her road), what thoughts would come to you—that is, after you'd finished with the thoughts that leap into men's minds at the sight of a pretty woman who will not deny them; what thoughts would come to you, had you seen her in a quick flash, keen and intuitively, as she sat there on her porch when your train thundered by? Would you have got off at the next station and come back for her to take her where? Would you have completely forgotten her as soon as you reached Macon, Atlanta, Augusta, Pasadena, Madison, Chicago, Boston, or New Orleans? Would you tell your wife or sweetheart about a girl you saw? Your thoughts can help me, and I would like to know. Something I would do for her . . .

One evening I walked up the Pike on purpose, and stopped to say hello. Some of her family were about, but they moved away to make room for me. Damn if I knew how to begin. Would you? Mr. and Miss So-and-So, people, the weather, the crops, the new preacher, the frolic, the church benefit, rabbit and possum hunting, the new soft drink they had at old Pap's store, the schedule of the trains, what kind of town Macon was, Negro's migration north, bollweevils, syrup, the Bible—to all these things she gave a yassur or nassur, without further comment. I began to wonder if perhaps my own emotional sensibility had played one of its tricks on me. "Lets take a walk," I at last ventured. The suggestion, coming after so long an isolation, was novel enough, I guess, to surprise. But it wasnt that. Something told me that men before me had said just that as a prelude to the offering of their bodies. I tried to tell her with my eyes. I think she understood. The thing from her that made my throat catch, vanished. Its passing left her visible in a way I'd thought, but never seen. We walked down the Pike with people on all the porches gaping at us. "Doesnt it make you mad?" She meant the row of petty gossiping people. She meant the world. Through a canebrake that was ripe for cutting, the branch was reached. Under a sweet-gum tree, and where reddish leaves had dammed the creek a little, we sat down. Dusk, suggesting the almost imperceptible procession of giant trees, settled with a purple haze about the cane. I felt strange, as I always do in Georgia, particularly at dusk. I felt that things unseen to men were tangibly immediate. It would not have surprised me had I had vision. People have them in Georgia more often than you would suppose. A black woman once saw the mother of Christ and drew her in charcoal on the courthouse wall . . . When one is on the soil of one's ancestors, most anything can come to one . . . From force of habit, I suppose, I held Fern in my arms—that is, without at first noticing it. Then my mind came back to her. Her eyes, unusually weird and open, held me. Held God. He flowed in as I've seen the countryside flow in. Seen men. I must have done something—what, I dont know, in the confusion of my emotion. She sprang up. Rushed some distance from me. Fell to her knees, and began swaying, swaying. Her body was tortured with something it could not let out. Like boiling sap it flooded arms and fingers till she shook them as if they burned her. It found her throat, and spattered inarticulately in plaintive, convulsive sounds, mingled with calls to Christ Jesus. And then she sang, brokenly. A Jewish cantor singing with a broken voice. A child's voice, uncertain, or an old man's. Dusk hid her; I could hear only her song. It seemed to me as though she were pounding her head in anguish upon the ground. I rushed to her. She fainted in my arms.

There was talk about her fainting with me in the canefield. And I got one or two ugly looks from town men who'd set themselves up to protect her. In fact, there was talk of making me leave town. But they never did. They kept a watch-out for me, though. Shortly after, I came back North. From the train window I saw her as I crossed her road. Saw her on her porch, head tilted a little forward where the nail was, eyes vaguely focused on the sunset. Saw her face flow into them, the countryside and something that I call God, flowing into them . . . Nothing ever really happened. Nothing ever came to Fern, not even I. Something I would do for her. Some fine unnamed thing . . . And, friend, you? She is still living, I have reason to know. Her name, against the chance that you might happen down that way, is Fernie May Rosen.

Nullo

A spray of pine-needles,
Dipped in western horizon gold,
Fell onto a path.
Dry moulds of cow-hoofs.
In the forest.
Rabbits knew not of their falling,
Nor did the forest catch aflame.

Evening Song

Full moon rising on the waters of my heart,
Lakes and moon and fires,
Cloine tires,
Holding her lips apart.

Promises of slumber leaving shore to charm the moon,
Miracle made vesper-keeps,
Cloine sleeps,
And I'll be sleeping soon.

Cloine, curled like the sleepy waters where the
     moon-waves start,
Radiant, resplendently she gleams,
Cloine dreams,
Lips pressed against my heart.

Esther

I

Nine.

Esther's hair falls in soft curls about her high-cheek-boned chalk-white face. Esther's hair would be beautiful if there were more gloss to it. And if her face were not prematurely serious, one would call it pretty. Her cheeks are too flat and dead for a girl of nine. Esther looks like a little white child, starched, frilled, as she walks slowly from her home towards her father's grocery store. She is about to turn in Broad from Maple Street. White and black men loafing on the corner hold no interest for her. Then a strange thing happens. A clean-muscled, magnificent, black-skinned Negro, whom she had heard her father mention as King Barlo, suddenly drops to his knees on a spot called the Spittoon. White men, unaware of him, continue squirting tobacco juice in his direction. The saffron fluid splashes on his face. His smooth black face begins to glisten and to shine. Soon, people notice him, and gather round. His eyes are rapturous upon the heavens. Lips and nostrils quiver. Barlo is in a religious trance. Town folks know it. They are not startled. They are not afraid. They gather round. Some beg boxes from the grocery stores. From old McGregor's notion shop. A coffin-case is pressed into use. Folks line the curb-stones. Business men close shop. And Banker Warply parks his car close by. Silently, all await the prophet's voice. The sheriff, a great florid fellow whose leggings never meet around his bulging calves, swears in three deputies. "Wall, y cant never tell what a nigger like King Barlo might be up t." Soda bottles, five fingers full of shine, are passed to those who want them. A couple of stray dogs start a fight. Old Goodlow's cow comes flopping up the street. Barlo, still as an Indian fakir, has not moved. The town bell strikes six. The sun slips in behind a heavy mass of horizon cloud. The crowd is hushed and expectant. Barlo's under jaw relaxes, and his lips begin to move.

"Jesus has been awhisperin strange words deep down, O way down deep, deep in my ears."

Hums of awe and of excitement.

"He called me to His side an said, 'Git down on your knees beside me, son, Ise gwine t whisper in your ears.'"

An old sister cries, "Ah, Lord."

"'Ise agwine t whisper in your ears,' he said, an I replied, 'Thy will be done on earth as it is in heaven.'"

"Ah, Lord. Amen. Amen."

"An Lord Jesus whispered strange good words deep down, O way down deep, deep in my ears. An He said, 'Tell em till you feel your throat on fire.' I saw a vision. I saw a man arise, an he was big an black an powerful—"

Some one yells, "Preach it, preacher, preach it!"

"—but his head was caught up in th clouds. An while he was agazin at th heavens, heart filled up with th Lord, some little white-ant biddies came an tied his feet to chains. They led him t th coast, they led him t th sea, they led him across th ocean an they didnt set him free. The old coast didnt miss him, an th new coast wasnt free, he left the old-coast brothers, t give birth t you an me. O Lord, great God Almighty, t give birth t you an me."

Barlo pauses. Old gray mothers are in tears. Fragments of melodies are being hummed. White folks are touched and curiously awed. Off to themselves, white and black preachers confer as to how best to rid themselves of the vagrant, usurping fellow. Barlo looks as though he is struggling to continue. People are hushed. One can hear weevils work. Dusk is falling rapidly, and the customary store lights fail to throw their feeble glow across the gray dust and flagging of the Georgia town. Barlo rises to his full height. He is immense. To the people he assumes the outlines of his visioned African. In a mighty voice he bellows:

"Brothers an sisters, turn your faces t th sweet face of the Lord, an fill your hearts with glory. Open your eyes an see th dawnin of th mornin light. Open your ears—"

Years afterwards Esther was told that at that very moment a great, heavy, rumbling voice actually was heard. That hosts of angels and of demons paraded up and down the streets all night. That King Barlo rode out of town astride a pitch-black bull that had a glowing gold ring in its nose. And that old Limp Underwood, who hated niggers, woke up next morning to find that he held a black man in his arms. This much is certain: an inspired Negress, of wide reputation for being sanctified, drew a portrait of a black madonna on the courthouse wall. And King Barlo left town. He left his image indelibly upon the mind of Esther. He became the starting point of the only living patterns that her mind was to know.

2

Sixteen.

Esther begins to dream. The low evening sun sets the windows of McGregor's notion shop aflame. Esther makes believe that they really are aflame. The town fire department rushes madly down the road. It ruthlessly shoves black and white idlers to one side. It whoops. It clangs. It rescues from the second-story window a dimpled infant which she claims for her own. How had she come by it? She thinks of it immaculately. It is a sin to think of it immaculately. She must dream no more. She must repent her sin. Another dream comes. There is no fire department. There are no heroic men. The fire starts. The loafers on the corner form a circle, chew their tobacco faster, and squirt juice just as fast as they can chew. Gallons on top of gallons they squirt upon the flames. The air reeks with the stench of scorched tobacco juice. Women, fat chunky Negro women, lean scrawny white women, pull their skirts up above their heads and display the most ludicrous underclothes. The women scoot in all directions from the danger zone. She alone is left to take the baby in her arms. But what a baby! Black, singed, woolly, tobacco-juice baby—ugly as sin. Once held to her breast, miraculous thing: its breath is sweet and its lips can nibble. She loves it frantically. Her joy in it changes the town folks' jeers to harmless jealousy, and she is left alone.

Twenty-two.

Esther's schooling is over. She works behind the counter of her father's grocery store. "To keep the money in the family," so he said. She is learning to make distinctions between the business and the social worlds. "Good business comes from remembering that the white folks dont divide the niggers, Esther. Be just as black as any man who has a silver dollar." Esther listlessly forgets that she is near white, and that her father is the richest colored man in town. Black folk who drift in to buy lard and snuff and flour of her, call her a sweet-natured, accommodating girl. She learns their names.

She forgets them. She thinks about men. "I dont appeal to them. I wonder why." She recalls an affair she had with a little fair boy while still in school. It had ended in her shame when he as much as told her that for sweetness he preferred a lollipop. She remembers the salesman from the North who wanted to take her to the movies that first night he was in town. She refused, of course. And he never came back, having found out who she was. She thinks of Barlo. Barlo's image gives her a slightly stale thrill. She spices it by telling herself his glories. Black. Magnetically so. Best cotton picker in the county, in the state, in the whole world for that matter. Best man with his fists, best man with dice, with a razor. Promoter of church benefits. Of colored fairs. Vagrant preacher. Lover of all the women for miles and miles around. Esther decides that she loves him. And with a vague sense of life slipping by, she resolves that she will tell him so, whatever people say, the next time he comes to town. After the making of this resolution which becomes a sort of wedding cake for her to tuck beneath her pillow and go to sleep upon, she sees nothing of Barlo for five years. Her hair thins. It looks like the dull silk on puny corn ears. Her face pales until it is the color of the gray dust that dances with dead cotton leaves.

3

Esther is twenty-seven.

Esther sells lard and snuff and flour to vague black faces that drift in her store to ask for them. Her eyes hardly see the people to whom she gives change. Her body is lean and beaten. She rests listlessly against the counter, too weary to sit down. From the street some one shouts, "King Barlo has come back to town." He passes her window, driving a large new car. Cut-out open. He veers to the curb, and steps out. Barlo has made money on cotton during the war. He is as rich as anyone. Esther suddenly is animate. She goes to her door. She sees him at a distance, the center of a group of credulous men. She hears the deep-bass rumble of his talk. The sun swings low. McGregor's windows are aflame again. Pale flame. A sharply dressed white girl passes by. For a moment Esther wishes that she might be like her. Not white; she has no need for being that. But sharp, sporty, with get-up about her. Barlo is connected with that wish. She mustnt wish. Wishes only make you restless. Emptiness is a thing that grows by being moved. "I'll not think. Not wish. Just set my mind against it." Then the thought comes to her that those purposeless, easy-going men will possess him, if she doesnt. Purpose is not dead in her, now that she comes to think of it. That loose women will have their arms around him at Nat Bowle's place to-night. As if her veins are full of fired sun-bleached southern shanties, a swift heat sweeps them. Dead dreams, and a forgotten resolution are carried upward by the flames. Pale flames. "They shant have him. Oh, they shall not. Not if it kills me they shant have him." Jerky, aflutter, she closes the store and starts home. Folks lazing on store windowsills wonder what on earth can be the matter with Jim Crane's gal, as she passes them. "Come to remember, she always was a little off, a little crazy, I reckon." Esther seeks her own room, and locks the door. Her mind is a pink meshbag filled with baby toes.

Using the noise of the town clock striking twelve to cover the creaks of her departure, Esther slips into the quiet road. The town, her parents, most everyone is sound asleep. This fact is a stable thing that comforts her. After sundown a chill wind came up from the west. It is still blowing, but to her it is a steady, settled thing like the cold. She wants her mind to be like that. Solid, contained, and blank as a sheet of darkened ice. She will not permit herself to notice the peculiar phosphorescent glitter of the sweet-gum leaves. Their movement would excite her. Exciting too, the recession of the dull familiar homes she knows so well. She doesnt know them at all. She closes her eyes, and holds them tightly. Wont do. Her being aware that they are closed recalls her purpose. She does not want to think of it. She opens them. She turns now into the deserted business street. The corrugated iron canopies and mule- and horse-gnawed hitching posts bring her a strange composure. Ghosts of the commonplaces of her daily life take stride with her and become her companions. And the echoes of her heels upon the flagging are rhythmically monotonous and soothing. Crossing the street at the corner of McGregor's notion shop, she thinks that the windows are a dull flame. Only a fancy. She walks faster. Then runs. A turn into a side street brings her abruptly to Nat Bowle's place. The house is squat and dark. It is always dark. Barlo is within. Quietly she opens the outside door and steps in. She passes through a small room. Pauses before a flight of stairs down which people's voices, muffled, come. The air is heavy with fresh tobacco smoke. It makes her sick. She wants to turn back. She goes up the steps. As if she were mounting to some great height, her head spins. She is violently dizzy. Blackness rushes to her eyes. And then she finds that she is in a large room. Barlo is before her.

"Well, I'm sholy damned—skuse me, but what, what brought you here, lil milk-white gal?"

"You." Her voice sounds like a frightened child's that calls homeward from some point miles away.

"Me?"

"Yes, you Barlo."

"This aint th place fer y. This aint th place fer y."

"I know. I know. But I've come for you."

"For me for what?"

She manages to look deep and straight into his eyes. He is slow at understanding. Guffaws and giggles break out from all around the room. A coarse woman's voice remarks, "So thats how th dictie niggers does it." Laughs. "Mus give em credit fo their gall."

Esther doesnt hear. Barlo does. His faculties are jogged. She sees a smile, ugly and repulsive to her, working upward through thick licker fumes. Barlo seems hideous. The thought comes suddenly, that conception with a drunken man must be a mighty sin. She draws away, frozen. Like a somnambulist she wheels around and walks stiffly to the stairs. Down them. Jeers and hoots pelter bluntly upon her back. She steps out. There is no air, no street, and the town has completely disappeared.

Conversion

African Guardian of Souls,
Drunk with rum,
Feasting on a strange cassava,
Yielding to new words and a weak palabra
Of a white-faced sardonic god—
Grins, cries
Amen,
Shouts hosanna.

Portrait in Georgia

Hair—braided chestnut,
    coiled like a lyncher's rope,
Eyes—fagots,
Lips—old scars, or the first red blisters,
Breath—the last sweet scent of cane,
And her slim body, white as the ash
    of black flesh after flame.

Blood-Burning Moon

I

Up from the skeleton stone walls, up from the rotting floor boards and the solid hand-hewn beams of oak of the pre-war cotton factory, dusk came. Up from the dusk the full moon came. Glowing like a fired pine-knot, it illumined the great door and soft showered the Negro shanties aligned along the single street of factory town. The full moon in the great door was an omen. Negro women improvised songs against its spell.

Louisa sang as she came over the crest of the hill from the white folks' kitchen. Her skin was the color of oak leaves on young trees in fall. Her breasts, firm and up-pointed like ripe acorns. And her singing had the low murmur of winds in fig trees. Bob Stone, *white man*, younger son of the people she worked for, loved her. By the way the world reckons things, he had won her. By measure of that warm glow which came into her mind at thought of him, he had won her. Tom Burwell, whom the whole town called Big Boy, also loved her. But working in the fields all day, and far away from her gave him no chance to show it. Though often enough of evenings he had tried to. Somehow, he never got along. Strong as he was with hands upon the ax or plow, he found it difficult to hold her. Or so he thought. But the fact was that he held her to factory town more firmly than he thought for. His black balanced, and pulled against, the white of Stone, when she thought of them. And her mind was vaguely upon them as she came over the crest of the hill,

about Louisa

39

coming from the white folks' kitchen. As she sang softly at the evil face of the full moon.

A strange stir was in her. Indolently, she tried to fix upon Bob or Tom as the cause of it. To meet Bob in the canebrake, as she was going to do an hour or so later, was nothing new. And Tom's proposal which she felt on its way to her could be indefinitely put off. Separately, there was no unusual significance to either one. But for some reason, they jumbled when her eyes gazed vacantly at the rising moon. And from the jumble came the stir that was strangely within her. Her lips trembled. The slow rhythm of her song grew agitant and restless. Rusty black and tan spotted hounds, lying in the dark corners of porches or prowling around back yards, put their noses in the air and caught its tremor. They began plaintively to yelp and howl. Chickens woke up and cackled. Intermittently, all over the countryside dogs barked and roosters crowed as if heralding a weird dawn or some ungodly awakening. The women sang lustily. Their songs were cotton-wads to stop their ears. Louisa came down into factory town and sank wearily upon the step before her home. The moon was rising towards a thick cloud-bank which soon would hide it.

> Red nigger moon. Sinner!
> Blood-burning moon. Sinner!
> Come out that fact'ry door.

2

Up from the deep dusk of a cleared spot on the edge of the forest a mellow glow arose and spread fan-wise into the low-hanging heavens. And all around the air was heavy with the scent of boil-

ing cane. A large pile of cane-stalks lay like ribboned shadows
upon the ground. A mule, harnessed to a pole, trudged lazily
round and round the pivot of the grinder. Beneath a swaying oil
lamp, a Negro alternately whipped out at the mule, and fed cane-
stalks to the grinder. A fat boy waddled pails of fresh ground juice
between the grinder and the boiling stove. Steam came from the
copper boiling pan. The scent of cane came from the copper pan
and drenched the forest and the hill that sloped to factory town,
beneath its fragrance. It drenched the men in circle seated around
the stove. Some of them chewed at the white pulp of stalks, but
there was no need for them to, if all they wanted was to taste the
cane. One tasted it in factory town. And from factory town one
could see the soft haze thrown by the glowing stove upon the low-
hanging heavens.

Old David Georgia stirred the thickening syrup with a long
ladle, and ever so often drew it off. Old David Georgia tended
his stove and told tales about the white folks, about moonshining
and cotton picking, and about sweet nigger gals, to the men who
sat there about his stove to listen to him. Tom Burwell chewed
cane-stalk and laughed with the others till some one mentioned
Louisa. Till some one said something about Louisa and Bob Stone,
about the silk stockings she must have gotten from him. Blood ran
up Tom's neck hotter than the glow that flooded from the stove.
He sprang up. Glared at the men and said, "She's my gal." Will
Manning laughed. Tom strode over to him. Yanked him up and
knocked him to the ground. Several of Manning's friends got up
to fight for him. Tom whipped out a long knife and would have
cut them to shreds if they hadnt ducked into the woods. Tom had
had enough. He nodded to Old David Georgia and swung down
the path to factory town. Just then, the dogs started barking and
the roosters began to crow. Tom felt funny. Away from the fight,

41

away from the stove, chill got to him. He shivered. He shuddered when he saw the full moon rising towards the cloud-bank. He who didnt give a godam for the fears of old women. He forced his mind to fasten on Louisa. Bob Stone. Better not be. He turned into the street and saw Louisa sitting before her home. He went towards her, ambling, touched the brim of a marvelously shaped, spotted, felt hat, said he wanted to say something to her, and then found that he didnt know what he had to say, or if he did, that he couldnt say it. He shoved his big fists in his overalls, grinned, and started to move off.

"Youall want me, Tom?"

"Thats what us wants, sho, Louisa."

"Well, here I am—"

"An here I is, but that aint ahelpin none, all th same."

"You wanted to say something? . . ."

"I did that, sho. But words is like th spots on dice: no matter how y fumbles em, there's times when they jes wont come. I dunno why. Seems like th love I feels fo yo done stole m tongue. I got it now. Whee! Louisa, honey, I oughtnt tell y, I feel I oughtnt cause yo is young an goes t church an I has had other gals, but Louisa I sho do love y. Lil gal, Ise watched y from them first days when youall sat right here befo yo door befo th well an sang sometimes in a way that like t broke m heart. Ise carried y with me into th fields, day after day, an after that, an I sho can plow when yo is there, an I can pick cotton. Yassur! Come near beatin Barlo yesterday. I sho did. Yassur! An next year if ole Stone'll trust me, I'll have a farm. My own. My bales will buy yo what y gets from white folks now. Silk stockings an purple dresses—course I dont believe what some folks been whisperin as t how y gets them things now. White folks always did do for niggers what they likes. An they jes cant help alikin yo, Louisa. Bob Stone likes y. Course he does. But not th way folks is awhisperin. Does he, hon?"

"I dont know what you mean, Tom." *language is so different*

"Course y dont. Ise already cut two niggers. Had t hon, t tell em so. Niggers always tryin t make somethin out a nothin. An then besides, white folks aint up t them tricks so much nowadays. Godam better not be. Leastawise not with yo. Cause I wouldnt stand f it. Nassur."

"What would you do, Tom?"

"Cut him jes like I cut a nigger."

"No, Tom—"

"I said I would an there aint no mo to it. But that aint th talk f now. Sing, honey Louisa, an while I'm listenin t y I'll be makin love."

Tom took her hand in his. Against the tough thickness of his own, hers felt soft and small. His huge body slipped down to the step beside her. The full moon sank upward into the deep purple of the cloud-bank. An old woman brought a lighted lamp and hung it on the common well whose bulky shadow squatted in the middle of the road, opposite Tom and Louisa. The old woman lifted the well-lid, took hold the chain, and began drawing up the heavy bucket. As she did so, she sang. Figures shifted, restlesslike, between lamp and window in the front rooms of the shanties. Shadows of the figures fought each other on the gray dust of the road. Figures raised the windows and joined the old woman in song. Louisa and Tom, the whole street, singing:

> Red nigger moon. Sinner!
> Blood-burning moon. Sinner!
> Come out that fact'ry door.

3

Bob Stone sauntered from his veranda out into the gloom of fir trees and magnolias. The clear white of his skin paled, and the flush of his cheeks turned purple. As if to balance this outer change, his mind became consciously a white man's. He passed the house with its huge open hearth which, in the days of slavery, was the plantation cookery. He saw Louisa bent over that hearth. He went in as a master should and took her. Direct, honest, bold. None of this sneaking that he had to go through now. The contrast was repulsive to him. His family had lost ground. Hell no, his family still owned the niggers, practically. Damned if they did, or he wouldnt have to duck around so. What would they think if they knew? His mother? His sister? He shouldnt mention them, shouldnt think of them in this connection. There in the dusk he blushed at doing so. Fellows about town were all right, but how about his friends up North? He could see them incredible, repulsed. They didnt know. The thought first made him laugh. Then, with their eyes still upon him, he began to feel embarrassed. He felt the need of explaining things to them. Explain hell. They wouldnt understand, and moreover, who ever heard of a Southerner getting on his knees to any Yankee, or anyone. No sir. He was going to see Louisa tonight, and love her. She was lovely—in her way. Nigger way. What way was that? Damned if he knew. Must know. He'd known her long enough to know. Was there something about niggers that you couldnt know? Listening to them at church didnt tell you anything. Looking at them didnt tell you anything. Talking to them didnt tell you anything—unless it was gossip, unless they wanted to talk. Of course, about farming, and licker, and craps—but those werent nigger. Nigger was something more. How much more? Something to be afraid of, more? Hell no. Who ever heard of being afraid of a nigger? Tom Burwell. Cartwell had told him that Tom went with Louisa after she reached home. No sir. No nigger had ever been with his girl. He'd like to see one try. Some position for him to be in. Him, Bob Stone, of the old Stone family, in a scrap with a nigger over a nigger girl. In the good old days . . . Ha! Those were the days. His family had lost ground. Not so much, though. Enough for him to have to cut through old Lemon's canefield by way of the woods, that he might meet her. She was worth it. Beautiful nigger gal. Why nigger? Why not, just gal? No, it was because she was nigger that he went to her. Sweet . . . The scent of boiling cane came to him. Then he saw the rich glow of the stove. He heard the voices of the men circled around it. He was about to skirt the clearing when he heard his own name mentioned. He stopped. Quivering. Leaning against a tree, he listened.

"Bad nigger. Yassur, he sho is one bad nigger when he gets started."

"Tom Burwell's been on th gang three times fo cuttin men."

"What y think he's agwine t do t Bob Stone?"

"Dunno yet. He aint found out. When he does—Baby!"

"Aint no tellin."

"Young Stone aint no quitter an I ken tell y that. Blood of th old uns in his veins."

"Thats right. He'll scrap, sho."

"Be gettin too hot f niggers round this away."

"Shut up, nigger. Y dont know what y talkin bout."

Bob Stone's ears burned as though he had been holding them over the stove. Sizzling heat welled up within him. His feet felt as if they rested on red-hot coals. They stung him to quick movement. He circled the fringe of the glowing. Not a twig cracked beneath his feet. He reached the path that led to factory town. Plunged furiously down it. Halfway along, a blindness within him veered him aside. He crashed into the bordering canebrake. Cane leaves cut his face and lips. He tasted blood. He threw himself down and dug his fingers in the ground. The earth was cool. Cane-roots took the fever from his hands. After a long while, or so it seemed to him, the thought came to him that it must be time to see Louisa. He got to his feet and walked calmly to their meeting place. No Louisa. Tom Burwell had her. Veins in his forehead bulged and distended. Saliva moistened the dried blood on his lips. He bit down on his lips. He tasted blood. Not his own blood; Tom Burwell's blood. Bob drove through the cane and out again upon the road. A hound swung down the path before him towards factory town. Bob couldnt see it. The dog loped aside to let him pass. Bob's blind rushing made him stumble over it. He fell with a thud that dazed him. The hound yelped. Answering yelps came from all over the countryside. Chickens cackled. Roosters crowed, heralding the bloodshot eyes of southern awakening. Singers in the town were silenced. They shut their windows down. Palpitant between the rooster crows, a chill hush settled upon the huddled forms of Tom and Louisa. A figure rushed from the shadow and stood before them. Tom popped to his feet.

"Whats y want?"

"I'm Bob Stone."

"Yassur—an I'm Tom Burwell. Whats y want?"

Bob lunged at him. Tom side-stepped, caught him by the shoulder, and flung him to the ground. Straddled him.

"Let me up."

"Yassur—but watch yo doins, Bob Stone."

A few dark figures, drawn by the sound of scuffle, stood about them. Bob sprang to his feet.

"Fight like a man, Tom Burwell, an I'll lick y."

Again he lunged. Tom side-stepped and flung him to the ground. Straddled him.

"Get off me, you godam nigger you."

"Yo sho has started somethin now. Get up."

Tom yanked him up and began hammering at him. Each blow sounded as if it smashed into a precious, irreplaceable soft something. Beneath them, Bob staggered back. He reached in his pocket and whipped out a knife.

"Thats my game, sho."

Blue flash, a steel blade slashed across Bob Stone's throat. He had a sweetish sick feeling. Blood began to flow. Then he felt a sharp twitch of pain. He let his knife drop. He slapped one hand against his neck. He pressed the other on top of his head as if to hold it down. He groaned. He turned, and staggered towards the crest of the hill in the direction of white town. Negroes who had seen the fight slunk into their homes and blew the lamps out. Louisa, dazed, hysterical, refused to go indoors. She slipped, crumbled, her body loosely propped against the woodwork of the well. Tom Burwell leaned against it. He seemed rooted there.

Bob reached Broad Street. White men rushed up to him. He collapsed in their arms.

"Tom Burwell. . . ."

White men like ants upon a forage rushed about. Except for the taut hum of their moving, all was silent. Shotguns, revolvers, rope, kerosene, torches. Two high-powered cars with glaring searchlights. They came together. The taut hum rose to a low roar. Then nothing could be heard but the flop of their feet in the thick dust of the road. The moving body of their silence preceded them over the crest of the hill into factory town. It flattened the Negroes beneath it. It rolled to the wall of the factory, where it stopped. Tom knew that they were coming. He couldnt move. And then he saw the search-lights of the two cars glaring down on him. A quick shock went through him. He stiffened. He started to run. A yell went up from the mob. Tom wheeled about and faced them. They poured down on him. They swarmed. A large man with dead-white face and flabby cheeks came to him and almost jabbed a gun-barrel through his guts.

"Hands behind y, nigger."

Tom's wrists were bound. The big man shoved him to the well. Burn him over it, and when the woodwork caved in, his body would drop to the bottom. Two deaths for a godam nigger. Louisa was driven back. The mob pushed in. Its pressure, its momentum was too great. Drag him to the factory. Wood and stakes already there. Tom moved in the direction indicated. But they had to drag him. They reached the great door. Too many to get in there. The mob divided and flowed around the walls to either side. The big man shoved him through the door. The mob pressed in from the sides. Taut humming. No words. A stake was sunk into the ground. Rotting floor boards piled around it. Kerosene poured on the rotting floor boards. Tom bound to the stake. His breast was bare. Nails' scratches let little lines of blood trickle down and mat into the hair. His face, his eyes were set and stony. Except for irregular breathing, one would have thought him already dead. Torches were flung onto the pile. A great flare muffled in black smoke shot upward. The mob yelled. The mob was silent. Now Tom could be seen within the flames. Only his head, erect, lean, like a blackened stone. Stench of burning flesh soaked the air. Tom's eyes popped. His head settled downward. The mob yelled. Its yell echoed against the skeleton stone walls and sounded like a hundred yells. Like a hundred mobs yelling. Its yell thudded against the thick front wall and fell back. Ghost of a yell slipped

opposition (margin annotation)

through the flames and out the great door of the factory. It fluttered like a dying thing down the single street of factory town. Louisa, upon the step before her home, did not hear it, but her eyes opened slowly. They saw the full moon glowing in the great door. The full moon, an evil thing, an omen, soft showering the homes of folks she knew. Where were they, these people? She'd sing, and perhaps they'd come out and join her. Perhaps Tom Burwell would come. At any rate, the full moon in the great door was an omen which she must sing to:

> Red nigger moon. Sinner!
> Blood-burning moon. Sinner!
> Come out that fact'ry door.

Seventh Street

Money burns the pocket, pocket hurts,
Bootleggers in silken shirts,
Ballooned, zooming Cadillacs,
Whizzing, whizzing down the street-car tracks.

Seventh Street is a bastard of Prohibition and the War. A crude-boned, soft-skinned wedge of nigger life breathing its loafer air, jazz songs and love, thrusting unconscious rhythms, black reddish blood into the white and whitewashed wood of Washington. Stale soggy wood of Washington. Wedges rust in soggy wood . . . Split it! In two! Again! Shred it! . . . the sun. Wedges are brilliant in the sun; ribbons of wet wood dry and blow away. Black reddish blood. Pouring for crude-boned soft-skinned life, who set you flowing? Blood suckers of the War would spin in a frenzy of dizziness if they drank your blood. Prohibition would put a stop to it. Who set you flowing? White and whitewash disappear in blood. Who set you flowing? Flowing down the smooth asphalt of Seventh Street, in shanties, brick office buildings, theaters, drug stores, restaurants, and cabarets? Eddying on the corners? Swirling like a blood-red smoke up where the buzzards fly in heaven? God would not dare to suck black red blood. A Nigger God! He would duck his head in shame and call for the Judgment Day. Who set you flowing?

Money burns the pocket, pocket hurts,
Bootleggers in silken shirts,
Ballooned, zooming Cadillacs,
Whizzing, whizzing down the street-car tracks.

Rhobert

Rhobert wears a house, like a monstrous diver's helmet, on his head. His legs are banty-bowed and shaky because as a child he had rickets. He is way down. Rods of the house like antennae of a dead thing, stuffed, prop up in the air. He is way down. He is sinking. His house is a dead thing that weights him down. He is sinking as a diver would sink in mud should the water be drawn off. Life is a murky, wiggling, microscopic water that compresses him. Compresses his helmet and would crush it the minute that he pulled his head out. He has to keep it in. Life is water that is being drawn off.

Brother, life is water that is being drawn off.
Brother, life is water that is being drawn off.

The dead house is stuffed. The stuffing is alive. It is sinful to draw one's head out of live stuffing in a dead house. The propped-up antennæ would cave in and the stuffing be strewn . . . shredded life-pulp . . . in the water. It is sinful to have one's own head crushed. Rhobert is an upright man whose legs are banty-bowed and shaky because as a child he had rickets. The earth is round. Heaven is a sphere that surrounds it. Sink where you will. God is a Red Cross man with a dredge and a respiration-pump who's waiting for you at the opposite periphery. God built the house.

He blew His breath into its stuffing. It is good to die obeying Him who can do these things.

A futile something like the dead house wraps the live stuffing of the question: how long before the water will be drawn off? Rhobert does not care. [Like most men who wear monstrous helmets, the pressure it exerts is enough to convince him of its practical infinity.] And he cares not two straws as to whether or not he will ever see his wife and children again. Many a time he's seen them drown in his dreams and has kicked about joyously in the mud for days after. One thing about him goes straight to the heart. He has an Adam's-apple which strains sometimes as if he were painfully gulping great globules of air . . . air floating shredded life-pulp. It is a sad thing to see a banty-bowed, shaky, ricket-legged man straining the raw insides of his throat against smooth air. Holding furtive thoughts about the glory of pulp-heads strewn in water . . . He is way down. Down. Mud, coming to his banty knees, almost hides them. Soon people will be looking at him and calling him a strong man. No doubt he is for one who has had rickets. Lets give it to him. Lets call him great when the water shall have been all drawn off. Lets build a monument and set it in the ooze where he goes down. A monument of hewn oak, carved in nigger-heads. Lets open our throats, brother, and sing "Deep River" when he goes down.

> Brother, Rhobert is sinking.
> Lets open our throats, brother,
> Lets sing Deep River when he goes down.

Avey

or a long while she was nothing more to me than one of those skirted beings whom boys at a certain age disdain to play with. Just how I came to love her, timidly, and with secret blushes, I do not know. But that I did was brought home to me one night, the first night that Ned wore his long pants. Us fellers were seated on the curb before an apartment house where she had gone in. The young trees had not outgrown their boxes then. V Street was lined with them. When our legs grew cramped and stiff from the cold of the stone, we'd stand around a box and whittle it. I like to think now that there was a hidden purpose in the way we hacked them with our knives. I like to feel that something deep in me responded to the trees, the young trees that whinnied like colts impatient to be let free . . . On the particular night I have in mind, we were waiting for the top-floor light to go out. We wanted to see Avey leave the flat. This night she stayed longer than usual and gave us a chance to complete the plans of how we were going to stone and beat that feller on the top floor out of town. Ned especially had it in for him. He was about to throw a brick up at the window when at last the room went dark. Some minutes passed. Then Avey, as unconcerned as if she had been paying an old-maid aunt a visit, came out. I dont remember what she had on, and all that sort of thing. But I do know that I turned hot as bare pavements in the summertime at Ned's boast: "Hell, bet I could get her too if you little niggers weren't always spying and crabbing everything." I didnt say a word to him. It wasnt my way then. I just stood there like the others, and something like a fuse burned up inside of me. She never noticed us, but swung along lazy and easy as anything. We sauntered to the corner and watched her till her door banged to. Ned repeated what he'd said. I didnt seem to care. Sitting around old Mush-Head's bread box, the discussion began. "Hang if I can see how she gets away with it," Doc started. Ned knew, of course. There was nothing he didnt know when it came to women. He dilated on the emotional needs of girls. Said they werent much different from men in that respect. And concluded with the solemn avowal: "It does em good." None of us liked Ned much. We all talked dirt; but it was the way he said it. And then too, a couple of the fellers had sisters and had caught Ned playing with them. But there was no disputing the superiority of his smutty wisdom. Bubs Sanborn, whose mother was friendly with Avey's, had overheard the old ladies talking. "Avey's mother's ont her," he said. We thought that only natural and began to guess at what would happen. Some one said she'd marry that feller on the top floor. Ned called that a lie because Avey was going to marry nobody but him. We had our doubts about that, but we did agree that she'd soon leave school and marry some one. The gang broke up, and I went home, picturing myself as married.

Nothing I did seemed able to change Avey's indifference to me. I played basket-ball, and when I'd make a long clean shot she'd clap with the others, louder than they, I thought. I'd meet her on the street, and there'd be no difference in the way she said hello. She never took the trouble to call me by my name. On the days for drill, I'd let my voice down a tone and call for a complicated maneuver when I saw her coming. She'd smile appreciation, but it was an impersonal smile, never for me. It was on a summer excursion down to Riverview that she first seemed to take me into account. The day had been spent riding merry-go-rounds, scenic-railways, and shoot-the-chutes. We had been in swimming and we had danced. I was a crack swimmer then. She didnt know how. I held her up and showed her how to kick her legs and draw her arms. Of course she didnt learn in one day, but she thanked me for bothering with her. I was also somewhat of a dancer. And I had already noticed that love can start on a dance floor. We danced. But though I held her tightly in my arms, she was way away. That college feller who lived on the top floor was somewhere making money for the next year. I imagined that she was thinking, wishing for him. Ned was along. He treated her until his money gave out. She went with another feller. Ned got sore. One by one the boys' money gave out. She left them. And they got sore. Every one of them but me got sore. This is the reason, I guess, why I had her to myself on the top deck of the *Jane Mosely* that night as we puffed up the Potomac, coming home. The moon was brilliant. The air was sweet like clover. And every now and then, a salt tang, a stale drift of sea-weed. It was not my mind's fault if it went romancing. I should have taken her in my arms the minute we were stowed in that old lifeboat. I dallied, dreaming. She took me in hers. And I could feel by the touch of it that it wasnt a man-to-woman love. It made me restless. I felt chagrined. I didnt know what it was, but I did know that I couldnt handle it. She ran her fingers through my hair and kissed my forehead. I itched to break through her tenderness to passion. I wanted her to take me in her arms as I knew she had that college feller. I wanted her to love me passionately as she did him. I gave her one burning kiss. Then she laid me in her lap as if I were a child. Helpless. I got sore when she started to hum a lullaby. She wouldnt let me go. I talked. I knew damned well that I could beat her at that. Her eyes were soft and misty, the curves of her lips were wistful, and her smile seemed indulgent of the irrelevance of my remarks. I gave up at last and let her love me, silently, in her own way. The moon was brilliant. The air was sweet like clover, and every now and then, a salt tang, a stale drift of sea-weed . . .

The next time I came close to her was the following summer at Harpers Ferry. We were sitting on a flat projecting rock they give the name of Lover's Leap. Some one is supposed to have jumped off it. The river is about six hundred feet beneath. A railroad track runs up the valley and curves out of sight where part of the mountain rock had to be blasted away to make room for it. The engines of this valley have a whistle, the echoes of which sound like iterated gasps and sobs. I always think of them as crude music from the soul of Avey. We sat there holding hands. Our palms were soft and warm against each other. Our fingers were not tight. She would not let them be. She would not let me twist them. I wanted to talk. To explain what I meant to her. Avey was as silent as those great trees whose tops we looked down upon. She has always been like that. At least, to me. I had the notion that if I really wanted to, I could do with her just what I pleased. Like one can strip a tree. I did kiss her. I even let my hands cup her breasts. When I was through, she'd seek my hand and hold it till my pulse cooled down. Evening after evening we sat there. I tried to get her to talk about that college feller. She never would. There was no set time to go home. None of my family had come down. And as for hers, she didnt give a hang about them. The general gossips could hardly say more than they had. The boarding-house porch was always deserted when we returned. No one saw us enter, so the time was set conveniently for scandal. This worried me a little, for I thought it might keep Avey from getting an appointment in the schools.

She didnt care. She had finished normal school. They could give her a job if they wanted to. As time went on, her indifference to things began to pique me; I was ambitious. I left the Ferry earlier than she did. I was going off to college. The more I thought of it, the more I resented, yes, hell, thats what it was, her downright laziness. Sloppy indolence. There was no excuse for a healthy girl taking life so easy. Hell! she was no better than a cow. I was certain that she was a cow when I felt an udder in a Wisconsin stock-judging class. Among those energetic Swedes, or whatever they are, I decided to forget her. For two years I thought I did. When I'd come home for the summer she'd be away. And before she returned, I'd be gone. We never wrote; she was too damned lazy for that. But what a bluff I put up about forgetting her. The girls up that way, at least the ones I knew, havent got the stuff: they dont know how to love. Giving themselves completely was tame beside just the holding of Avey's hand. One day I received a note from her. The writing, I decided, was slovenly. She wrote on a torn bit of note-book paper. The envelope had a faint perfume that I remembered. A single line told me she had lost her school and was going away. I comforted myself with the reflection that shame held no pain for one so indolent as she. Nevertheless, I left Wisconsin that year for good. Washington had seemingly forgotten her. I hunted Ned. Between curses, I caught his opinion of her. She was no better than a whore. I saw her mother on the street. The same old pinch-beck, jerky-gaited creature that I'd always known.

Perhaps five years passed. The business of hunting a job or something or other had bruised my vanity so that I could recognize it. I felt old. Avey and my real relation to her, I thought I came to know. I wanted to see her. I had been told that she was in New York. As I had no money, I hiked and bummed my way there. I got work in a ship-yard and walked the streets at night, hoping to meet her. Failing in this, I saved enough to pay my fare back home. One evening in early June, just at the time when dusk is most lovely on the eastern horizon, I saw Avey, indolent as ever, leaning on the arm of a man, strolling under the recently lit arclights of U Street. She had almost passed before she recognized me. She showed no surprise. The puff over her eyes had grown heavier. The eyes themselves were still sleepy-large, and beautiful. I had almost concluded—indifferent. "You look older," was what she said. I wanted to convince her that I was, so I asked her to walk with me. The man whom she was with, and whom she never took the trouble to introduce, at a nod from her, hailed a taxi, and drove away. That gave me a notion of what she had been used to. Her dress was of some fine, costly stuff. I suggested the park, and then added that the grass might stain her skirt. Let it get stained, she said, for where it came from there are others.

I have a spot in Soldier's Home to which I always go when I want the simple beauty of another's soul. Robins spring about the lawn all day. They leave their footprints in the grass. I imagine that the grass at night smells sweet and fresh because of them. The ground is high. Washington lies below. Its light spreads like a blush against the darkened sky. Against the soft dusk sky of Washington. And when the wind is from the South, soil of my homeland falls like a fertile shower upon the lean streets of the city. Upon my hill in Soldier's Home. I know the policeman who watches the place of nights. When I go there alone, I talk to him. I tell him I come there to find the truth that people bury in their hearts. I tell him that I do not come there with a girl to do the thing he's paid to watch out for. I look deep in his eyes when I say these things, and he believes me. He comes over to see who it is on the grass. I say hello to him. He greets me in the same way and goes off searching for other black splotches upon the lawn. Avey and I went there. A band in one of the buildings a fair distance off was playing a march. I wished they would stop. Their playing was like a tin spoon in one's mouth. I wanted the Howard Glee Club to sing "Deep River," from the road. To sing "Deep River, Deep River," from the road . . . Other than the first comments, Avey had been silent. I started to hum a folk-tune. She slipped her hand in mine. Pillowed her head as best she could upon my arm. Kissed the hand that she was holding and listened, or so I thought, to what I had to say. I traced my development from the early days up to the present time, the phase in which I could understand her. I described her own nature and temperament. Told how they needed a larger life for their expression. How incapable Washington was of understanding that need. How it could not meet it. I pointed out that in lieu of proper channels, her emotions had overflowed into paths that dissipated them. I talked, beautifully I thought, about an art that would be born, an art that would open the way for women the likes of her. I asked her to hope, and build up an inner life against the coming of that day. I recited some of my own things to her. I sang, with a strange quiver in my voice, a promise-song. And then I began to wonder why her hand had not once returned a single pressure. My old-time feeling about her laziness came back. I spoke sharply. My policeman friend passed by. I said hello to him. As he went away, I began to visualize certain possibilities. An immediate and urgent passion swept over me. Then I looked at Avey. Her heavy eyes were closed. Her breathing was as faint and regular as a child's in slumber. My passion died. I was afraid to move lest I disturb her. Hours and hours, I guess it was, she lay there. My body grew numb. I shivered. I coughed. I wanted to get up and whittle at the boxes of young trees. I withdrew my hand. I raised her head to waken her. She did not stir. I got up and walked around. I found my policeman friend and talked to him. We both came up, and bent over her. He said it would be all right for her to stay there just so long as she got away before the workmen came at dawn. A blanket was borrowed from a neighbor house. I sat beside her through the night. I saw the dawn steal over Washington. The Capitol dome looked like a gray ghost ship drifting in from sea. Avey's face was pale, and her eyes were heavy. She did not have the gray crimson-splashed beauty of the dawn. I hated to wake her. Orphan-woman . . .

Beehíve

Within this black hive to-night
There swarm a million bees;
Bees passing in and out the moon,
Bees escaping out the moon,
Bees returning through the moon,
Silver bees intently buzzing,
Silver honey dripping from the swarm of bees
Earth is a waxen cell of the world comb,
And I, a drone,
Lying on my back,
Lipping honey,
Getting drunk with silver honey,
Wish that I might fly out past the moon
And curl forever in some far-off farmyard flower.

Storm Ending

Thunder blossoms gorgeously above our heads,
Great, hollow, bell-like flowers,
Rumbling in the wind,
Stretching clappers to strike our ears . . .
Full-lipped flowers
Bitten by the sun
Bleeding rain
Dripping rain like golden honey—
And the sweet earth flying from the thunder.

Theater

ife of nigger alleys, of pool rooms and restaurants and near-beer saloons soaks into the walls of Howard Theater and sets them throbbing jazz songs. Black-skinned, they dance and shout above the tick and trill of white-walled buildings. At night, they open doors to people who come in to stamp their feet and shout. At night, road-shows volley songs into the mass-heart of black people. Songs soak the walls and seep out to the nigger life of alleys and near-beer saloons, of the Poodle Dog and Black Bear cabarets. Afternoons, the house is dark, and the walls are sleeping singers until rehearsal begins. Or until John comes within them. Then they start throbbing to a subtle syncopation. And the space-dark air grows softly luminous.

John is the manager's brother. He is seated at the center of the theater, just before rehearsal. Light streaks down upon him from a window high above. One half his face is orange in it. One half his face is in shadow. The soft glow of the house rushes to and compacts about, the shaft of light. John's mind coincides with the shaft of light. Thoughts rush to, and compact about it. Life of the house and of the slowly awakening stage swirls to the body of John, and thrills it. John's body is separate from the thoughts that pack his mind.

Stage-lights, soft, as if they shine through clear pink fingers. Beneath them, hid by the shadow of a set, Dorris. Other chorus girls drift in. John feels them in the mass. And as if his own body were the mass-heart of a black audience listening to them singing, he wants to stamp his feet and shout. His mind, contained above desires of his body, singles the girls out, and tries to trace origins and plot destinies.

A pianist slips into the pit and improvises jazz. The walls awake. Arms of the girls, and their limbs, which . . . jazz, jazz . . . by lifting up their tight street skirts they set free, jab the air and clog the floor in rhythm to the music. (Lift your skirts, Baby, and talk t papa!) Crude, individualized, and yet . . . monotonous . . .

John: Soon the director will herd you, my full-lipped, distant beauties, and tame you, and blunt your sharp thrusts in loosely suggestive movements, appropriate to Broadway. (O dance!) Soon the audience will paint your dusk faces white, and call you beautiful. (O dance!) Soon I . . . (O dance!) I'd like . . .

Girls laugh and shout. Sing discordant snatches of other jazz songs. Whirl with loose passion into the arms of passing show-men.

John: Too thick. Too easy. Too monotonous. Her whom I'd love I'd leave before she knew that I was with her. Her? Which? (O dance!) I'd like to . . .

Girls dance and sing. Men clap. The walls sing and press inward. They press the men and girls, they press John towards a center of physical ecstasy. Go to it, Baby! Fan yourself, and feed your papa! Put . . . nobody lied . . . and take . . . when they said I cried over you. No lie! The glitter and color of stacked scenes, the gilt and brass and crimson of the house, converge towards a center of physical ecstasy. John's feet and torso and his blood press in. He wills thought to rid his mind of passion.

"All right, girls. Alaska. Miss Reynolds, please."

The director wants to get the rehearsal through with.

The girls line up. John sees the front row: dancing ponies. The rest are in shadow. The leading lady fits loosely in the front. Lack-life, monotonous. "One, two, three——" Music starts. The song is somewhere where it will not strain the leading lady's throat. The dance is somewhere where it will not strain the girls. Above the staleness, one dancer throws herself into it. Dorris. John sees her. Her hair, crisp-curled, is bobbed. Bushy, black hair bobbing about her lemon-colored face. Her lips are curiously full, and very red. Her limbs in silk purple stockings are lovely. John feels them. Desires her. Holds off.

John: Stage-door johnny; chorus-girl. No, that would be all right. Dictie, educated, stuck-up; show-girl. Yep. Her suspicion would be stronger than her passion. It wouldnt work. Keep her loveliness. Let her go.

Dorris sees John and knows that he is looking at her. Her own glowing is too rich a thing to let her feel the slimness of his diluted passion.

"Who's that?" she asks her dancing partner.

"Th manager's brother. Dictie. Nothin doin, hon."

Dorris tosses her head and dances for him until she feels she has him. Then, withdrawing disdainfully, she flirts with the director.

Dorris: Nothin doin? How come? Aint I as good as him? Couldnt I have got an education if I'd wanted one? Dont I know respectable folks, lots of em, in Philadelphia and New York and Chicago? Aint I had men as good as him? Better. Doctors an lawyers. Whats a manager's brother, anyhow?

Two steps back, and two steps front.

"Say, Mame, where do you get that stuff?"

"Whatshmean, Dorris?"

"If you two girls cant listen to what I'm telling you, I know where I can get some who can. Now listen."

Mame: Go to hell, you black bastard.

Dorris: Whats eatin at him, anyway?

69

"Now follow me in this, you girls. Its three counts to the right, three counts to the left, and then you shimmy—"

John:—and then you shimmy. I'll bet she can. Some good cabaret, with rooms upstairs. And what in hell do you think you'd get from it? Youre going wrong. Here's right: get her to herself— (Christ, but how she'd bore you after the first five minutes)—not if you get her right she wouldnt. Touch her, I mean. To herself—in some room perhaps. Some cheap, dingy bedroom. Hell no. Cant be done. But the point is, brother John, it can be done. Get her to herself somewhere, anywhere. Go down in yourself—and she'd be calling you all sorts of asses while you were in the process of going down. Hold em, bud. Cant be done. Let her go. (Dance and I'll love you!) And keep her loveliness.

"All right now, Chicken Chaser. Dorris and girls. Where's Dorris? I told you to stay on the stage, didnt I? Well? Now thats enough. All right. All right there, Professor? All right. One, two, three—"

Dorris swings to the front. The line of girls, four deep, blurs within the shadow of suspended scenes. Dorris wants to dance. The director feels that and steps to one side. He smiles, and picks her for a leading lady, one of these days. Odd ends of stage-men emerge from the wings, and stare and clap. A crap game in the alley suddenly ends. Black faces crowd the rear stage doors. The girls, catching joy from Dorris, whip up within the footlights' glow. They forget set steps; they find their own. The director forgets to bawl them out. Dorris dances.

John: Her head bobs to Broadway. Dance from yourself. Dance! O just a little more.

Dorris' eyes burn across the space of seats to him.

Dorris: I bet he can love. Hell, he cant love. He's too skinny. His lips are too skinny. He wouldnt love me anyway, only for

that. But I'd get a pair of silk stockings out of it. Red silk. I got
purple. Cut it, kid. You cant win him to respect you that away.
He wouldnt anyway. Maybe he would. Maybe he'd love. I've
heard em say that men who look like him (what does he look
like?) will marry if they love. O will you love me? And give me
kids, and a home, and everything? (I'd like to make your nest,
and honest, hon, I wouldnt run out on you.) You will if I make
you. Just watch me.

Dorris dances. She forgets her tricks. She dances.

Glorious songs are the muscles of her limbs.

And her singing is of canebrake loves and mangrove feastings.

The walls press in, singing. Flesh of a throbbing body, they press
close to John and Dorris. They close them in. John's heart beats
tensely against her dancing body. Walls press his mind within his
heart. And then, the shaft of light goes out the window high above
him. John's mind sweeps up to follow it. Mind pulls him upward
into dream.   Dorris dances . . .

John dreams:

Dorris is dressed in a loose black gown splashed with lemon ribbons. Her feet taper long and slim from trim ankles. She waits for
him just inside the stage door. John, collar and tie colorful and flaring, walks towards the stage door. There are no trees in the alley.
But his feet feel as though they step on autumn leaves whose rustle
has been pressed out of them by the passing of a million satin slippers. The air is sweet with roasting chestnuts, sweet with bonfires
of old leaves. John's melancholy is a deep thing that seals all senses
but his eyes, and makes him whole.

Dorris knows that he is coming. Just at the right moment she
steps from the door, as if there were no door. Her face is tinted like
the autumn alley. Of old flowers, or of a southern canefield, her

perfume. "Glorious Dorris." So his eyes speak. And their sadness is too deep for sweet untruth. She barely touches his arm. They glide off with footfalls softened on the leaves, the old leaves powdered by a million satin slippers.

They are in a room. John knows nothing of it. Only, that the flesh and blood of Dorris are its walls. Singing walls. Lights, soft, as if they shine through clear pink fingers. Soft lights, and warm.

John reaches for a manuscript of his, and reads. Dorris, who has no eyes, has eyes to understand him. He comes to a dancing scene. The scene is Dorris. She dances. Dorris dances. Glorious Dorris. Dorris whirls, whirls, dances . . .

Dorris dances. The pianist crashes a bumper chord. The whole stage claps. Dorris, flushed, looks quick at John. His whole face is in shadow. She seeks for her dance in it. She finds it a dead thing in the shadow which is his dream. She rushes from the stage. Falls down the steps into her dressing-room. Pulls her hair. Her eyes, over a floor of tears, stare at the whitewashed ceiling. (Smell of dry paste, and paint, and soiled clothing.) Her pal comes in Dorris flings herself into the old safe arms, and cries bitterly.

"I told you nothin doin," is what Mame says to comfort her.

into atmosphere → contrasts w/ southern imagery

Her Lips Are Copper Wire

whisper of yellow globes
gleaming on lamp-posts that sway
like bootleg licker drinkers in the fog

and let your breath be moist against me
like bright beads on yellow globes

telephone the power-house
that the main wires are insulate

(her words play softly up and down
dewy corridors of billboards)

then with your tongue remove the tape
and press your lips to mine
till they are incandescent

Calling Jesus

er soul is like a little thrust-tailed dog that follows her, whimpering. She is large enough, I know, to find a warm spot for it. But each night when she comes home and closes the big outside storm door, the little dog is left in the vestibule, filled with chills till morning. Some one . . . eoho Jesus . . . soft as a cotton boll brushed against the milk-pod cheek of Christ, will steal in and cover it that it need not shiver, and carry it to her where she sleeps upon clean hay cut in her dreams.

When you meet her in the daytime on the streets, the little dog keeps coming. Nothing happens at first, and then, when she has forgotten the streets and alleys, and the large house where she goes to bed of nights, a soft thing like fur begins to rub your limbs, and you hear a low, scared voice, lonely, calling, and you know that a cool something nozzles moisture in your palms. Sensitive things like nostrils, quiver. Her breath comes sweet as honeysuckle whose pistils bear the life of coming song. And her eyes carry to where builders find no need for vestibules, for swinging on iron hinges, storm doors.

Her soul is like a little thrust-tailed dog, that follows her, whimpering. I've seen it tagging on behind her, up streets where chestnut trees flowered, where dusty asphalt had been freshly sprinkled with clean water. Up alleys where niggers sat on low door-steps before tumbled shanties and sang and loved. At night, when she comes home, the little dog is left in the vestibule, nosing the crack beneath the big storm door, filled with chills till morning. Some one . . . eoho Jesus . . . soft as the bare feet of Christ moving across bales of southern cotton, will steal in and cover it that it need not shiver, and carry it to her where she sleeps: cradled in dream-fluted cane.

Box Seat

I

Houses are shy girls whose eyes shine reticently upon the dusk body of the street. Upon the gleaming limbs and asphalt torso of a dreaming nigger. Shake your curled wool-blossoms, nigger. Open your liver lips to the lean, white spring. Stir the root-life of a withered people. Call them from their houses, and teach them to dream.

Dark swaying forms of Negroes are street songs that woo virginal houses.

Dan Moore walks southward on Thirteenth Street. The low limbs of budding chestnut trees recede above his head. Chestnut buds and blossoms are wool he walks upon. The eyes of houses faintly touch him as he passes them. Soft girl-eyes, they set him singing. Girl-eyes within him widen upward to promised faces. Floating away, they dally wistfully over the dusk body of the street. Come on, Dan Moore, come on. Dan sings. His voice is a little hoarse. It cracks. He strains to produce tones in keeping with the houses' loveliness. Cant be done. He whistles. His notes are shrill. They hurt him. Negroes open gates, and go indoors, perfectly. Dan thinks of the house he's going to. Of the girl. Lips, flesh-notes of a forgotten song, plead with him . . .

Dan turns into a side-street, opens an iron gate, bangs it to. Mounts the steps, and searches for the bell. Funny, he cant find it. He fumbles around. The thought comes to him that some one passing by might see him, and not understand. Might think that he is trying to sneak, to break in.

Dan: Break in. Get an ax and smash in. Smash in their faces. I'll show em. Break into an engine-house, steal a thousand horse-power fire truck. Smash in with the truck. I'll show em. Grab an ax and brain em. Cut em up. Jack the Ripper. Baboon from the zoo. And then the cops come. "No, I aint a baboon. I aint Jack the Ripper. I'm a poor man out of work. Take your hands off me, you bull-necked bears. Look into my eyes. I am Dan Moore. I was born in a canefield. The hands of Jesus touched me. I am come to a sick world to heal it. Only the other day, a dope fiend brushed against me—Dont laugh, you mighty, juicy, meat-hook men. Give me your fingers and I will peel them as if they were ripe bananas."

Some one might think he is trying to break in. He'd better knock. His knuckles are raw bone against the thick glass door. He waits. No one comes. Perhaps they havent heard him. He raps again. This time, harder. He waits. No one comes. Some one is surely in. He fancies that he sees their shadows on the glass. Shadows of gorillas. Perhaps they saw him coming and dont want to let him in. He knocks. The tension of his arms makes the glass rattle. Hurried steps come towards him. The door opens.

"Please, you might break the glass—the bell—oh, Mr. Moore! I thought it must be some stranger. How do you do? Come in, wont you? Muriel? Yes. I'll call her. Take your things off, wont you? And have a seat in the parlor. Muriel will be right down. Muriel! Oh Muriel! Mr. Moore to see you. She'll be right down. You'll pardon me, wont you? So glad to see you."

Her eyes are weak. They are bluish and watery from reading newspapers. The blue is steel. It gimlets Dan while her mouth flaps amiably to him.

Dan: Nothing for you to see, old mussel-head. Dare I show you? If I did, delirium would furnish you headlines for a month. Now look here. Thats enough. Go long, woman. Say some nasty thing and I'll kill you. Huh. Better damned sight not. Ta-ta, Mrs. Pribby.

Mrs. Pribby retreats to the rear of the house. She takes up a newspaper. There is a sharp click as she fits into her chair and draws it to the table. The click is metallic like the sound of a bolt being shot into place. Dan's eyes sting. Sinking into a soft couch, he closes them. The house contracts about him. It is a sharp-edged, massed, metallic house. Bolted. About Mrs. Pribby. Bolted to the endless rows of metal houses. Mrs. Pribby's house. The rows of houses belong to other Mrs. Pribbys. No wonder he couldn't sing to them.

Dan: What's Muriel doing here? God, what a place for her. Whats she doing? Putting her stockings on? In the bathroom. Come out of there, Dan Moore. People must have their privacy, Peeping-toms. I'll never peep. I'll listen. I like to listen.

Dan goes to the wall and places his ear against it. A passing street car and something vibrant from the earth sends a rumble to him. That rumble comes from the earth's deep core. It is the mut-ter of powerful underground races. Dan has a picture of all the people rushing to put their ears against walls, to listen to it. The next world-savior is coming up that way. Coming up. A continent sinks down. The new-world Christ will need consummate skill to walk upon the waters where huge bubbles burst . . . Thuds of Muriel coming down. Dan turns to the piano and glances through a stack of jazz music sheets. Ji-ji-bo, JI-JI-BO! . . .

"Hello, Dan, stranger, what brought you here?"

Muriel comes in, shakes hands, and then clicks into a high-armed seat under the orange glow of a floor-lamp. Her face is

fleshy. It would tend to coarseness but for the fresh fragrant something which is the life of it. Her hair like an Indian's. But more
curly and bushed and vagrant. Her nostrils flare. The flushed gin-
ger of her cheeks is touched orange by the shower of color from
the lamp.

"Well, you havent told me, you havent answered my question,
stranger. What brought you here?"

Dan feels the pressure of the house, of the rear room, of the
rows of houses, shift to Muriel. He is light. He loves her. He is
doubly heavy.

"Dont know, Muriel—wanted to see you—wanted to talk
to you—to see you and tell you that I know what you've been
through—what pain the last few months must have been—"

"Lets dont mention that."

"But why not, Muriel? I—"

"Please."

"But Muriel, life is full of things like that. One grows strong
and beautiful in facing them. What else is life?"

"I dont know, Dan. And I dont believe I care. Whats the use?
Lets talk about something else. I hear there's a good show at the
Lincoln this week."

"Yes, so Harry was telling me. Going?"

"To-night."

Dan starts to rise.

"I didnt know. I dont want to keep you."

"Its all right. You dont have to go till Bernice comes. And she
wont be here till eight. I'm all dressed. I'll let you know."

"Thanks."

Silence. The rustle of a newspaper being turned comes from
the rear room.

Muriel: Shame about Dan. Something awfully good and fine

about him. But he dont fit in. In where? Me? Dan, I could love you if I tried. I dont have to try. I do. O Dan, dont you know I do? Timid lover, brave talker that you are. Whats the good of all you know if you dont know that? I wont let myself. I? Mrs. Pribby who reads newspapers all night wont. What has she got to do with me? She *is* me, somehow. No she's not. Yes she is. She is the town, and the town wont let me love you, Dan. Dont you know? You could make it let me if you would. Why wont you? Youre selfish. I'm not strong enough to buck it. Youre too selfish to buck it, for me. I wish you'd go. You irritate me. Dan, please go.

"What are you doing now, Dan?"

"Same old thing, Muriel. Nothing, as the world would have it. Living, as I look at things. Living as much as I can without——"

"But you cant live without money, Dan. Why dont you get a good job and settle down?"

Dan: Same old line. Shoot it at me, sister. Hell of a note, this loving business. For ten minutes of it youve got to stand the torture of an intolerable heaviness and a hundred platitudes. Well, damit, shoot on.

"To what? my dear. Rustling newspapers?"

"You mustnt say that, Dan. It isnt right. Mrs. Pribby has been awfully good to me."

"Dare say she has. Whats that got to do with it?"

"Oh, Dan, youre so unconsiderate and selfish. All you think of is yourself."

"I think of you."

"Too much—I mean, you ought to work more and think less. Thats the best way to get along."

"Mussel-heads get along, Muriel. There is more to you than that——"

"Sometimes I think there is, Dan. But I dont know. I've tried.

I've tried to do something with myself. Something real and beautiful, I mean. But whats the good of trying? I've tried to make
people, every one I come in contact with, happy—"

Dan looks at her, directly. Her animalism, still unconquered
by zoo-restrictions and keeper-taboos, stirs him. Passion tilts
upward, bringing with it the elements of an old desire. Muriel's
lips become the flesh-notes of a futile, plaintive longing. Dan's
impulse to direct her is its fresh life.

"Happy, Muriel? No, not happy. Your aim is wrong. There is no
such thing as happiness. Life bends joy and pain, beauty and ugliness, in such a way that no one may isolate them. No one should
want to. Perfect joy, or perfect pain, with no contrasting element
to define them, would mean a monotony of consciousness, would
mean death. Not happy, Muriel. Say that you have tried to make
them create. Say that you have used your own capacity for life to
cradle them. To start them upward-flowing. Or if you cant say
that you have, then say that you will. My talking to you will make
you aware of your power to do so. Say that you will love, that you
will give yourself in love—"

"To you, Dan?"

Dan's consciousness crudely swerves into his passions. They
flare up in his eyes. They set up quivers in his abdomen. He is suddenly over-tense and nervous.

"Muriel—"

The newspaper rustles in the rear room.

"Muriel—"

Dan rises. His arms stretch towards her. His fingers and his
palms, pink in the lamplight, are glowing irons. Muriel's chair
is close and stiff about her. The house, the rows of houses locked
about her chair. Dan's fingers and arms are fire to melt and bars
to wrench and force and pry. Her arms hang loose. Her hands are

hot and moist. Dan takes them. He slips to his knees before her.

"Dan, you mustnt."

"Muriel—"

"Dan, really you mustnt. No, Dan. No."

"Oh, come, Muriel. Must I—"

"Shhh. Dan, please get up. Please. Mrs. Pribby is right in the next room. She'll hear you. She may come in. Dont, Dan. She'll see you—"

"Well then, lets go out."

"I cant. Let go, Dan. Oh, wont you please let go."

Muriel tries to pull her hands away. Dan tightens his grip. He feels the strength of his fingers. His muscles are tight and strong. He stands up. Thrusts out his chest. Muriel shrinks from him. Dan becomes aware of his crude absurdity. His lips curl. His passion chills. He has an obstinate desire to possess her.

"Muriel, I love you. I want you, whatever the world of Pribby says. Damn your Pribby. Who is she to dictate my love? I've stood enough of her. Enough of you. Come here."

Muriel's mouth works in and out. Her eyes flash and waggle. She wrenches her hands loose and forces them against his breast to keep him off. Dan grabs her wrists. Wedges in between her arms. Her face is close to him. It is hot and blue and moist. Ugly.

"Come here now."

"Dont, Dan. Oh, dont. What are you killing?"

"Whats weak in both of us and a whole litter of Pribbys. For once in your life youre going to face whats real, by God—"

A sharp rap on the newspaper in the rear room cuts between them. The rap is like cool thick glass between them. Dan is hot on one side. Muriel, hot on the other. They straighten. Gaze fearfully at one another. Neither moves. A clock in the rear room, in the rear room, the rear room, strikes eight. Eight slow, cool sounds.

Bernice. Muriel fastens on her image. She smooths her dress. She adjusts her skirt. She becomes prim and cool. Rising, she skirts Dan as if to keep the glass between them. Dan, gyrating nervously above the easy swing of his limbs, follows her to the parlor door. Muriel retreats before him till she reaches the landing of the steps that lead upstairs. She smiles at him. Dan sees his face in the hall mirror. He runs his fingers through his hair. Reaches for his hat and coat and puts them on. He moves towards Muriel. Muriel steps backward up one step. Dan's jaw shoots out. Muriel jerks her arm in warning of Mrs. Pribby. She gasps and turns and starts to run. Noise of a chair scraping as Mrs. Pribby rises from it, ratchets down the hall. Dan stops. He makes a wry face, wheels round, goes out, and slams the door.

2

People come in slowly . . . mutter, laughs, flutter, whishadwash, "I've changed my work-clothes—" . . . and fill vacant seats of Lincoln Theater. Muriel, leading Bernice who is a cross between a washerwoman and a blue-blood lady, a washer-blue, a washer-lady, wanders down the right aisle to the lower front box. Muriel has on an orange dress. Its color would clash with the crimson box-draperies, its color would contradict the sweet rose smile her face is bathed in, should she take her coat off. She'll keep it on. Pale purple shadows rest on the planes of her cheeks. Deep purple comes from her thick-shocked hair. Orange of the dress goes well with these. Muriel presses her coat down from around her shoulders. Teachers are not supposed to have bobbed hair. She'll keep her hat on. She takes the first chair, and indicates that Bernice is to take the one directly behind her. Seated thus, her eyes are level with, and near to, the face of an imaginary man upon the stage. To speak to Berny she must turn. When she does, the audience is square upon her.

People come in slowly . . . "—for my Sunday-go-to-meeting dress. O glory God! O shout Amen!" . . . and fill vacant seats of Lincoln Theater. Each one is a bolt that shoots into a slot, and is locked there. Suppose the Lord should ask, where was Moses when the light went out? Suppose Gabriel should blow his trumpet! The seats are slots. The seats are bolted houses. The mass grows denser. Its weight at first is impalpable upon the box. Then Muriel begins to feel it. She props her arm against the brass box-rail, to ward it off. Silly. These people are friends of hers: a parent of a child she teaches, an old school friend. She smiles at them. They return her courtesy, and she is free to chat with Berny. Berny's tongue, started, runs on, and on. O washer-blue! O washer-lady!

Muriel: Never see Dan again. He makes me feel queer. Starts things he doesnt finish. Upsets me. I am not upset. I am perfectly calm. I am going to enjoy the show. Good show. I've had some show! This damn tame thing. O Dan. Wont see Dan again. Not alone. Have Mrs. Pribby come in. She *was* in. Keep Dan out. If I love him, can I keep him out? Well then, I dont love him. Now he's out. Who is that coming in? Blind as a bat. Ding-bat. Looks like Dan. He mustnt see me. Silly. He cant reach me. He wont dare come in here. He'd put his head down like a goring bull and charge me. He'd trample them. He'd gore. He'd rape! Berny! He wont dare come in here.

"Berny, who was that who just came in? I havent my glasses."

"A friend of yours, a *good* friend so I hear. Mr. Daniel Moore, Lord."

"Oh. He's no friend of mine."

"No? I hear he is."

"Well, he isnt."

Dan is ushered down the aisle. He has to squeeze past the knees of seated people to reach his own seat. He treads on a man's corns. The man grumbles, and shoves him off. He shrivels close beside a portly Negress whose huge rolls of flesh meet about the bones of seat-arms. A soil-soaked fragrance comes from her. Through the cement floor her strong roots sink down. They spread under the asphalt streets. Dreaming, the streets roll over on their bellies, and suck their glossy health from them. Her strong roots sink down and spread under the river and disappear in blood-lines that waver south. Her foots shoot down. Dan's hands follow them. Roots throb. Dan's heart beats violently. He places his palms upon the earth to cool them. Earth throbs. Dan's heart beats violently. He sees all the people in the house rush to the walls to listen to the rumble. A new-world Christ is coming up. Dan comes up. He is startled. The eyes of the woman dont belong to her. They look at him unpleasantly. From either aisle, bolted masses press in. He doesnt fit. The mass grows agitant. For an instant, Dan's and Muriel's eyes meet. His weight there slides the weight on her. She braces an arm against the brass rail, and turns her head away.

Muriel: Damn fool; dear Dan, what did you want to follow me here for? Oh cant you ever do anything right? Must you always pain me, and make me hate you? I do hate you. I wish some one would come in with a horse-whip and lash you out. I wish some one would drag you up a back alley and brain you with the whip-butt.

Muriel glances at her wrist-watch.

"Quarter of nine. Berny, what time have you?"

"Eight-forty. Time to begin. Oh, look Muriel, that woman with the plume; doesnt she look good! They say she's going with, oh, whats his name. You know. Too much powder. I can see it from here. Here's the orchestra now. O fine! Jim Clem at the piano!"

The men fill the pit. Instruments run the scale and tune. The saxophone moans and throws a fit. Jim Clem, poised over the piano, is ready to begin. His head nods forward. Opening crash. The house snaps dark. The curtain recedes upward from the blush of the footlights. Jazz overture is over. The first act is on.

Dan: Old stuff. Muriel—bored. Must be. But she'll smile and she'll clap. Do what youre bid, you she-slave. Look at her. Sweet, tame woman in a brass box seat. Clap, smile, fawn, clap. Do what youre bid. Drag me in with you. Dirty me. Prop me in your brass box seat. I'm there, am I not? because of you. He-slave. Slave of a woman who is a slave. I'm a damned sight worse than you are. I sing your praises, Beauty! I exalt thee, O Muriel! A slave, thou art greater than all Freedom because I love thee.

Dan fidgets, and disturbs his neighbors. His neighbors glare at him. He glares back without seeing them. The man whose corns have been trod upon speaks to him.

"Keep quiet, cant you, mister. Other people have paid their money besides yourself to see the show."

The man's face is a blur about two sullen liquid things that are his eyes. The eyes dissolve in the surrounding vagueness. Dan suddenly feels that the man is an enemy whom he has long been looking for.

Dan bristles. Glares furiously at the man.

"All right. All right then. Look at the show. I'm not stopping you."

"Shhh," from some one in the rear.

Dan turns around.

"Its that man there who started everything. I didnt say a thing to him until he tried to start something. What have I got to do with whether he has paid his money or not? Thats the manager's business. Do I look like the manager?"

"Shhhh. Youre right. Shhhh."

"Dont tell me to shhh. Tell him. That man there. He started everything. If what he wanted was to start a fight, why didnt he say so?"

The man leans forward.

"Better be quiet, sonny. I aint said a thing about fight, yet."

"Its a good thing you havent."

"Shhhh."

Dan grips himself. Another act is on. Dwarfs, dressed like prizefighters, foreheads bulging like boxing gloves, are led upon the stage. They are going to fight for the heavyweight championship. Gruesome. Dan glances at Muriel. He imagines that she shudders. His mind curves back into himself, and picks up tailends of experiences. His eyes are open, mechanically. The dwarfs pound and bruise and bleed each other, on his eyeballs.

Dan: Ah, but she was some baby! And not vulgar either. Funny how some women can do those things. Muriel dancing like that! Hell. She rolled and wabbled. Her buttocks rocked. She pulled up her dress and showed her pink drawers. Baby! And then she caught my eyes. Dont know what my eyes had in them. Yes I do. God, dont I though! Sometimes I think, Dan Moore, that your eyes could burn clean . . . burn clean . . . BURN CLEAN! . . .

The gong rings. The dwarfs set to. They spar grotesquely, playfully, until one lands a stiff blow. This makes the other sore. He commences slugging. A real scrap is on. Time! The dwarfs go to their corners and are sponged and fanned off. Gloves bulge from their wrists. Their wrists are necks for the tight-faced gloves. The fellow to the right lets his eyes roam over the audience. He sights Muriel. He grins.

Dan: Those silly women arguing feminism. Here's what I should have said to them. "It should be clear to you women, that the proposition must be stated thus:

> Me, horizontally above her.
> Action: perfect strokes downward oblique.
> Hence, man dominates because of limitation.
> Or, so it shall be until women learn their stuff.

So framed, the proposition is a mental-filler, Dentist, I want gold teeth. It should become cherished of the technical intellect. I hereby offer it to posterity as one of the important machine-age designs. P. S. It should be noted, that because it *is* an achievement of this age, its growth and hence its causes, up to the point of maturity, antedate machinery. Ery . . ."

The gong rings. No fooling this time. The dwarfs set to. They clinch. The referee parts them. One swings a cruel upper-cut and knocks the other down. A huge head hits the floor. Pop! The house roars. The fighter, groggy, scrambles up. The referee whispers to the contenders not to fight so hard. They ignore him. They charge. Their heads jab like boxing-gloves. They kick and spit and bite. They pound each other furiously. Muriel pounds. The house pounds. Cut lips. Bloody noses. The referee asks for the gong. Time! The house roars. The dwarfs bow, are made to bow. The house wants more. The dwarfs are led from the stage.

Dan: Strange I never really noticed him before. Been sitting there for years. Born a slave. Slavery not so long ago. He'll die in his chair. Swing low, sweet chariot. Jesus will come and roll him down the river Jordan. Oh, come along, Moses, you'll get lost; stretch out your rod and come across. LET MY PEOPLE GO! Old man. Knows everyone who passes the corners. Saw the first horse-cars. The first Oldsmobile. And he was born in slavery. I did see his eyes. Never miss eyes. But they were bloodshot and watery. It hurt to look at them. It hurts to look in most people's eyes. He saw Grant and Lincoln. He saw Walt—old man, did you see Walt Whitman? Did you see Walt Whitman! Strange force that drew me to him. And I went up to see. The woman thought I saw crazy. I told him to look into the heavens. He did, and smiled. I asked him if he knew what that rumbling is that comes up from the ground. Christ, what a stroke that was. And the jabbering idiots crowding around. And the crossing-cop leaving his job to come over and wheel him away . . .

The house applauds. The house wants more. The dwarfs are led back. But no encore. Must give the house something. The attendant comes out and announces that Mr. Barry, the champion, will sing one of his own songs, "for your approval." Mr. Barry grins at Muriel as he wabbles from the wing. He holds a fresh white rose, and a small mirror. He wipes blood from his nose. He signals Jim Clem. The orchestra starts. A sentimental love song, Mr. Barry sings, first to one girl, and then another in the audience. He holds the mirror in such a way that it flashes in the face of each one he sings to. The light swings around.

Dan: I am going to reach up and grab the girders of this building and pull them down. The crash will be a signal. Hid by the smoke and dust Dan Moore will arise. In his right hand will be a dynamo. In his left, a god's face that will flash white light from ebony. I'll grab a girder and swing it like a walking-stick. Lightning will flash. I'll grab its black knob and swing it like a crippled cane. Lightning . . . Some one's flashing . . . some one's flashing . . . Who in hell is flashing that mirror? Take it off me, godam you.

Dan's eyes are half blinded. He moves his head. The light follows. He hears the audience laugh. He hears the orchestra. A

man with a high-pitched, sentimental voice is singing. Dan sees
the dwarf. Along the mirror flash the song comes. Dan ducks his
head. The audience roars. The light swings around to Muriel. Dan
looks. Muriel is too close. Mr. Barry covers his mirror. He sings
to her. She shrinks away. Nausea. She clutches the brass box-rail.
She moves to face away. The audience is square upon her. Its eyes
smile. Its hands itch to clap. Muriel turns to the dwarf and forces a
smile at him. With a showy blare of orchestration, the song comes
to its close. Mr. Barry bows. He offers Muriel the rose, first having kissed it. Blood of his battered lips is a vivid stain upon its petals. Mr. Barry offers Muriel the rose. The house applauds. Muriel
flinches back. The dwarf steps forward, diffident; threatening.
Hate pops from his eyes and crackles like a brittle heat about the
box. The thick hide of his face is drawn in tortured wrinkles.
Above his eyes, the bulging, tight-skinned brow. Dan looks at it.
It grows calm and massive. It grows profound. It is a thing of wisdom and tenderness, of suffering and beauty. Dan looks down.
The eyes are calm and luminous. Words come from them . . .
Arms of the audience reach out, grab Muriel, and hold her there.
Claps are steel fingers that manacle her wrists and move them for-
ward to acceptance. Berny leans forward and whispers:

"Its all right. Go on—take it."

Words form in the eyes of the dwarf:

Do not shrink. Do not be afraid of me.
Jesus
See how my eyes look at you.
the Son of God
I too was made in His image.
was once—
I give you the rose.

Muriel, tight in her revulsion, sees black, and daintily reaches for the offering. As her hand touches it, Dan springs up in his seat and shouts:

"JESUS WAS ONCE A LEPER!"

Dan steps down.

He is as cool as a green stem that has just shed its flower.

Rows of gaping faces strain towards him. They are distant, beneath him, impalpable. Squeezing out, Dan again treads upon the corn-foot man. The man shoves him.

"Watch where youre going, mister. Crazy or no, you aint going to walk over me. Watch where youre going there."

Dan turns, and serenely tweaks the fellow's nose. The man jumps up. Dan is jammed against a seat-back. A slight swift anger flicks him. His fist hooks the other's jaw.

"Now you have started something. Aint no man living can hit me and get away with it. Come on on the outside."

The house, tumultuously stirring, grabs its wraps and follows the men.

The man leads Dan up a black alley. The alley-air is thick and moist with smells of garbage and wet trash. In the morning, singing niggers will drive by and ring their gongs . . . Heavy with the scent of rancid flowers and with the scent of fight. The crowd, pressing forward, is a hollow roar. Eyes of houses, soft girl-eyes, glow reticently upon the hubbub and blink out. The man stops. Takes off his hat and coat. Dan, having forgotten him, keeps going on.

Prayer

My body is opaque to the soul.
Driven of the spirit, long have I sought to temper it unto the
      spirit's longing,
But my mind, too, is opaque to the soul.
A closed lid is my soul's flesh-eye.
O Spirits of whom my soul is but a little finger,
Direct it to the lid of its flesh-eye.
I am weak with much giving.
I am weak with the desire to give more.
(How strong a thing is the little finger!)
So weak that I have confused the body with the soul,
And the body with its little finger.
(How frail is the little finger.)
My voice could not carry to you did you dwell in stars,
O Spirits of whom my soul is but a little finger . . .

Harvest Song

I am a reaper whose muscles set at sundown. All my oats are
    cradled.
But I am too chilled, and too fatigued to bind them. And I
    hunger.

I crack a grain between my teeth. I do not taste it.
I have been in the fields all day. My throat is dry. I hunger.

My eyes are caked with dust of oatfields at harvest-time.
I am a blind man who stares across the hills, seeking stack'd
    fields of other harvesters.

It would be good to see them . . . crook'd, split, and iron-ring'd
    handles of the scythes. It would be good to see them, dust-
    caked and blind. I hunger.

(Dusk is a strange fear'd sheath their blades are dull'd in.)
My throat is dry. And should I call, a cracked grain like the oats
    . . . eoho—

I fear to call. What should they hear me, and offer me their
    grain, oats, or wheat, or corn? I have been in the fields
    all day. I fear I could not taste it. I fear knowledge of my
    hunger.

My ears are caked with dust of oatfields at harvest-time.
I am a deaf man who strains to hear the calls of other harvesters
    whose throats are also dry.

It would be good to hear their songs . . . reapers of the sweet-
    stalk'd cane, cutters of the corn . . . even though their
    throats cracked and the strangeness of their voices deafened
    me.

I hunger. My throat is dry. Now that the sun has set and I am
    chilled, I fear to call. (Eoho, my brothers!)

I am a reaper. (Eoho!) All my oats are cradled. But I am too
    fatigued to bind them. And I hunger. I crack a grain. It has
    no taste to it. My throat is dry . . .

O my brothers, I beat my palms, still soft, against the stubble of
    my harvesting. (You beat your soft palms, too.) My pain is
    sweet. Sweeter than the oats or wheat or corn. It will not
    bring me knowledge of my hunger.

Bona and Paul

O n the school gymnasium floor, young men and women are drilling. They are going to be teachers, and go out into the world . . . thud, thud . . . and give precision to the movements of sick people who all their lives have been drilling. One man is out of step. In step. The teacher glares at him. A girl in bloomers, seated on a mat in the corner because she has told the director that she is sick, sees that the footfalls of the men are rhythmical and syncopated. The dance of his blue-trousered limbs thrills her.

Bona: He is a candle that dances in a grove swung with pale balloons.

Columns of the drillers thud towards her. He is in the front row. He is in no row at all. Bona can look close at him. His red-brown face—

Bona: He is a harvest moon. He is an autumn leaf. He is a nigger. Bona! But dont all the dorm girls say so? And dont you, when you are sane, say so? Thats why I love—Oh, nonsense. You have never loved a man who didnt first love you. Besides—

Columns thud away from her. Come to a halt in line formation. Rigid. The period bell rings, and the teacher dismisses them.

A group collects around Paul. They are choosing sides for basket-ball. Girls against boys. Paul has his. He is limbering up beneath the basket. Bona runs to the girl captain and asks to be chosen. The girls fuss. The director comes to quiet them. He hears what Bona wants.

"But, Miss Hale, you were excused—"

"So I was, Mr. Boynton, but—"

"—you can play basket-ball, but you are too sick to drill."

"If you wish to put it that way."

She swings away from him to the girl captain.

"Helen, I want to play, and you must let me. This is the first time I've asked and I dont see why—"

"Thats just it, Bona. We have our team."

"Well, team or no team, I want to play and thats all there is to it."

She snatches the ball from Helen's hands, and charges down the floor.

Helen shrugs. One of the weaker girls says that she'll drop out. Helen accepts this. The team is formed. The whistle blows. The game starts. Bona, in center, is jumping against Paul. He plays with her. Out-jumps her, makes a quick pass, gets a quick return, and shoots a goal from the middle of the floor. Bona burns crimson. She fights, and tries to guard him. One of her team-mates advises her not to play so hard. Paul shoots his second goal.

Bona begins to feel a little dizzy and all in. She drives on. Almost hugs Paul to guard him. Near the basket, he attempts to shoot, and Bona lunges into his body and tries to beat his arms. His elbow, going up, gives her a sharp crack on the jaw. She whirls. He catches her. Her body stiffens. Then becomes strangely vibrant, and bursts to a swift life within her anger. He is about to give way before her hatred when a new passion flares at him and makes his stomach fall. Bona squeezes him. He suddenly feels stifled, and wonders why in hell the ring of silly gaping faces that's caked about him doesnt make way and give him air. He has a swift illusion that it is himself who has been struck. He looks at Bona. Whir. Whir. They seem to be human distortions spinning tensely in a fog. Spinning . . . dizzy . . . spinning . . . Bona jerks herself free, flushes a startling crimson, breaks through the bewildered teams, and rushes from the hall.

2

Paul is in his room of two windows.

Outside, the South-Side L track cuts them in two.

Bona is one window. One window, Paul.

Hurtling Loop-jammed L trains throw them in swift shadow.

Paul goes to his. Gray slanting roofs of houses are tinted lavender in the setting sun. Paul follows the sun, over the stock-yards where a fresh stench is just arising, across wheat lands that are still waving above their stubble, into the sun. Paul follows the sun to a pine-matted hillock in Georgia. He sees the slanting roofs of gray unpainted cabins tinted lavender. A Negress chants a lullaby beneath the mate-eyes of a southern planter. Her breasts are ample for the suckling of a song. She weans it, and sends it, curiously weaving, among lush melodies of cane and corn. Paul follows the sun into himself in Chicago.

He is at Bona's window.

With his own glow he looks through a dark pane.

Paul's room-mate comes in.

"Say, Paul, I've got a date for you. Come on. Shake a leg, will you?"

His blond hair is combed slick. His vest is snug about him.

He is like the electric light which he snaps on.

"Whatdoysay, Paul? Get a wiggle on. Come on. We havent got much time by the time we eat and dress and everything."

His bustling concentrates on the brushing of his hair.

Art: What in hell's getting into Paul of late, anyway? Christ, but he's getting moony. Its his blood. Dark blood: moony. Doesnt get anywhere unless you boost it. You've got to keep it going—

"Say, Paul!"

—or it'll go to sleep on you. Dark blood; nigger? Thats what those jealous she-hens say. Not Bona though, or she . . . from the South . . . wouldnt want me to fix a date for him and her. Hell of a thing, that Paul's dark: youve got to always be answering questions.

"Say, Paul, for Christ's sake leave that window, cant you?"

"Whats it, Art?"

"Hell, I've told you about fifty times. Got a date for you. Come on."

"With who?"

Art: He didnt use to ask; now he does. Getting up in the air. Getting funny.

"Heres your hat. Want a smoke? Paul! Here. I've got a match. Now come on and I'll tell you all about it on the way to supper."

Paul: He's going to Life this time. No doubt of that. Quit your kidding. Some day, dear Art, I'm going to kick the living slats out of you, and you wont know what I've done it for. And your slats will bring forth Life . . . beautiful woman . . .

Pure Food Restaurant.

"Bring me some soup with a lot of crackers, understand? And then a roast-beef dinner. Same for you, eh, Paul? Now as I was saying, you've got a swell chance with her. And she's game. Best proof: she dont give a damn what the dorm girls say about you and her in the gym, or about the funny looks that Boynton gives her, or about what they say about, well, hell, you know, Paul. And say, Paul, she's a sweetheart. Tall, not puffy and pretty, more serious and deep—the kind you like these days. And they say she's got a car. And say, she's on fire. But you know all about that. She got Helen to fix it up with me. The four of us—remember the last party? Crimson Gardens! Boy!"

Paul's eyes take on a light that Art can settle in.

3

Art has on his patent-leather pumps and fancy vest. A loose fall coat is swung across his arm. His face has been massaged, and over a close shave, powdered. It is a healthy pink the blue of evening tints a purple pallor. Art is happy and confident in the good looks that his mirror gave him. Bubbling over with a joy he must spend now if the night is to contain it all. His bubbles, too, are curiously tinted purple as Paul watches them. Paul, contrary to what he had thought he would be like, is cool like the dusk, and like the dusk, detached. His dark face is a floating shade in evening's shadow. He sees Art, curiously. Art is a purple fluid, carbon-charged, that effervesces beside him. He loves Art. But is it not queer, this pale purple facsimile of a red-blooded Norwegian friend of his? Perhaps for some reason, white skins are not supposed to live at night. Surely, enough nights would transform them fantastically, or kill them. And their red passion? Night paled that too, and made it moony. Moony. Thats what Art thought of him. Bona didnt, even in the daytime. Bona, would she be pale? Impossible. Not that red glow. But the conviction did not set his emotion flowing.

"Come right in, wont you? The young ladies will be right down.

Oh, Mr. Carlstrom, do play something for us while you are wait-ing. We just love to listen to your music. You play so well."

Houses, and dorm sitting-rooms are places where white faces seclude themselves at night. There is a reason . . .

Art sat on the piano and simply tore it down. Jazz. The picture of Our Poets hung perilously.

Paul: I've got to get the kid to play that stuff for me in the day-time. Might be different. More himself. More nigger. Different? There is. Curious, though.

The girls come in. Art stops playing, and almost immediately takes up a petty quarrel, where he had last left it, with Helen.

Bona, black-hair curled staccato, sharply contrasting with Hel-en's puffy yellow, holds Paul's hand. She squeezes it. Her own emotion supplements the return pressure. And then, for no tan-gible reason, her spirits drop. Without them, she is nervous, and slightly afraid. She resents this. Paul's eyes are critical. She resents Paul. She flares at him. She flares to poise and security.

"Shall we be on our way?"

"Yes, Bona, certainly."

The Boulevard is sleek in asphalt, and, with arc-lights and lim-ousines, aglow. Dry leaves scamper behind the whir of cars. The scent of exploded gasoline that mingles with them is faintly sweet. Mellow stone mansions overshadow clapboard homes which now resemble Negro shanties in some southern alley. Bona and Paul, and Art and Helen, move along an island-like, far-stretching strip of leaf-soft ground. Above them, worlds of shadow-planes and sol-ids, silently moving. As if on one of these, Paul looks down on Bona. No doubt of it: her face is pale. She is talking. Her words have no feel to them. One sees them. They are pink petals that fall upon velvet cloth. Bona is soft, and pale, and beautiful.

"Paul, tell me something about yourself—or would you rather wait?"

"I'll tell you anything you'd like to know."

"Not what I want to know, Paul; what you want to tell me."

"You have the beauty of a gem fathoms under sea."

"I feel that, but I dont want to be. I want to be near you. Perhaps I will be if I tell you something. Paul, I love you."

The sea casts up its jewel into his hands, and burns them furiously. To tuck her arm under his and hold her hand will ease the burn.

"What can I say to you, brave dear woman—I cant talk love. Love is a dry grain in my mouth unless it is wet with kisses."

"You would dare? right here on the Boulevard? before Arthur and Helen?"

"Before myself? I dare."

"Here then."

Bona, in the slim shadow of a tree trunk, pulls Paul to her. Suddenly she stiffens. Stops.

"But you have not said you love me."

"I cant—yet—Bona."

"Ach, you never will. Youre cold. Cold."

Bona: Colored; cold. Wrong somewhere.

She hurries and catches up with Art and Helen.

4

Crimson Gardens. Hurrah! So one feels. People . . . University of Chicago students, members of the stock exchange, a large Negro in crimson uniform who guards the door . . . had watched them enter. Had leaned towards each other over ash-smeared tablecloths and highballs and whispered: What is he, a Spaniard, an Indian, an Italian, a Mexican, a Hindu, or a Japanese? Art had at first fidgeted under their stares . . . what are *you* looking at, you godam pack of owl-eyed hyenas? . . . but soon settled into his fuss with Helen, and forgot them. A strange thing happened to Paul. Suddenly he knew that he was apart from the people around him. Apart from the pain which they had unconsciously caused. Suddenly he knew that people saw, not attractiveness in his dark skin, but difference. Their stares, giving him to himself, filled something long empty within him, and were like green blades sprouting in his consciousness. There was fullness, and strength and peace about it all. He saw himself, cloudy, but real. He saw the faces of the people at the tables round him. White lights, or as now, the pink lights of the Crimson Gardens gave a glow and immediacy to white faces. The pleasure of it, equal to that of love or dream, of seeing this. Art and Bona and Helen? He'd look. They were wonderfully flushed and beautiful. Not for himself; because they were. Distantly. Who were they, anyway? God, if he knew them. He'd come in with them. Of that he was sure. Come where? Into life? Yes. No. Into the Crimson Gardens. A part of life. A carbon bubble. Would it look purple if he went out into the night and looked at it? His sudden starting to rise almost upset the table.

"What in hell—pardon—whats the matter, Paul?"

"I forgot my cigarettes—"

"Youre smoking one."

"So I am. Pardon me."

The waiter straightens them out. Takes their order.

Art: What in hell's eating Paul? Moony aint the word for it. From bad to worse. And those godam people staring so. Paul's a queer fish. Doesnt seem to mind . . . He's my pal, let me tell you,

you horn-rimmed owl-eyed hyena at that table, and a lot better
than you whoever you are . . . Queer about him. I could stick up
for him if he'd only come out, one way or the other, and tell a
feller. Besides, a room-mate has a right to know. Thinks I wont
understand. Said so. He's got a swell head when it comes to brains,
all right. God, he's a good straight feller, though. Only, moony.
Nut. Nuttish. Nuttery. Nutmeg . . . "What'd you say, Helen?"

"I was talking to Bona, thank you."

"Well, its nothing to get spiffy about."

"What? Oh, of course not. Please lets dont start some silly
argument all over again."

"Well."

"Well."

"Now thats enough. Say, waiter, whats the matter with our
order? Make it snappy, will you?"

Crimson Gardens. Hurrah! So one feels. The drinks come.
Four highballs. Art passes cigarettes. A girl dressed like a bare-
back rider in flaming pink, makes her way through tables to the
dance floor. All lights are dimmed till they seem a lush afterglow
of crimson. Spotlights the girl. She sings. "Liza, Little Liza Jane."

Paul is rosy before his window.

He moves, slightly, towards Bona.

With his own glow, he seeks to penetrate a dark pane.

Paul: From the South. What does that mean, precisely, except
that you'll love or hate a nigger? Thats a lot. What does it mean
except that in Chicago you'll have the courage to neither love or
hate. A priori. But it would seem that you have. Queer words,
arent these, for a man who wears blue pants on a gym floor in the
daytime. Well, never matter. You matter. I'd like to know you
whom I look at. Know, not love. Not that knowing is a greater
pleasure; but that I have just found the joy of it. You came just a

month too late. Even this afternoon I dreamed. To-night, along the Boulevard, you found me cold. Paul Johnson, cold! Thats a good one, eh, Art, you fine old stupid fellow, you! But I feel good! The color and the music and the song . . . A Negress chants a lullaby beneath the mate-eyes of a southern planter. O song . . . And those flushed faces. Eager brilliant eyes. Hard to imagine them as unawakened. Your own. Oh, they're awake all right. "And you know it too, dont you Bona?"

"What, Paul?"

"The truth of what I was thinking."

"I'd like to know I know—something of you."

"You will—before the evening's over. I promise it."

Crimson Gardens. Hurrah! So one feels. The bare-back rider balances agilely on the applause which is the tail of her song. Orchestral instruments warm up for jazz. The flute is a cat that ripples its fur against the deep-purring saxophone. The drum throws sticks. The cat jumps on the piano keyboard. Hi diddle, hi diddle, the cat and the fiddle. Crimson Gardens . . . hurrah! . . . jumps over the moon. Crimson Gardens! Helen . . . O Eliza . . . rabbit-eyes sparkling, plays up to, and tries to placate what she considers to be Paul's contempt. She always does that . . . Little Liza Jane . . . Once home, she burns with the thought of what she's done. She says all manner of snidy things about him, and swears that she'll never go out again when he is along. She tries to get Art to break with him, saying, that if Paul, whom the whole dormitory calls a nigger, is more to him than she is, well, she's through. She does not break with Art. She goes out as often as she can with Art and Paul. She explains this to herself by a piece of information which a friend of hers had given her: men like him (Paul) can fascinate. One is not responsible for fascination. Not one girl had really loved Paul; he fascinated them. Bona didnt;

only thought she did. Time would tell. And of course, *she* didn't.
Liza . . . She plays up to, and tries to placate, Paul.

"Paul is so deep these days, and I'm so glad he's found some one
to interest him."

"I dont believe I do."

The thought escapes from Bona just a moment before her anger
at having said it.

Bona: You little puffy cat, I do. I do!

Dont I, Paul? her eyes ask.

Her answer is a crash of jazz from the palm-hidden orchestra.
Crimson Gardens is a body whose blood flows to a clot upon the
dance floor. Art and Helen clot. Soon, Bona and Paul. Paul finds
her a little stiff, and his mind, wandering to Helen (silly little kid
who wants every highball spoon her hands touch, for a souvenir),
supple, perfect little dancer, wishes for the next dance when he
and Art will exchange.

Bona knows that she must win him to herself.

"Since when have men like you grown cold?"

"The first philosopher."

"I thought you were a poet—or a gym director."

"Hence, your failure to make love."

Bona's eyes flare. Water. Grow red about the rims. She would
like to tear away from him and dash across the clotted floor.

"What do you mean?"

"Mental concepts rule you. If they were flush with mine—
good. I dont believe they are."

"How do you know, Mr. Philosopher?"

"Mostly a priori."

"You talk well for a gym director."

"And you—"

"I hate you. Ou!"

She presses away. Paul, conscious of the convention in it, pulls her to him. Her body close. Her head still strains away. He nearly crushes her. She tries to pinch him. Then sees people staring, and lets her arms fall. Their eyes meet. Both, contemptuous. The dance takes blood from their minds and packs it, tingling, in the torsos of their swaying bodies. Passionate blood leaps back into their eyes. [They are a dizzy blood clot on a gyrating floor.] They know that the pink-faced people have no part in what they feel. Their instinct leads them away from Art and Helen, and towards the big uniformed black man who opens and closes the gilded exit door. The cloak-room girl is tolerant of their impatience over such trivial things as wraps. And slightly superior. As the black man swings the door for them, his eyes are knowing. Too many couples have passed out, flushed and fidgety, for him not to know. The chill air is a shock to Paul. A strange thing happens. He sees the Gardens purple, as if he were way off. And a spot is in the purple. The spot comes furiously towards him. Face of the black man. It leers. It smiles sweetly like a child's. Paul leaves Bona and darts back so quickly that he doesnt give the door-man a chance to open. He swings in. Stops. Before the huge bulk of the Negro.

"Youre wrong."

"Yassur."

"Brother, youre wrong.

"I came back to tell you, to shake your hand, and tell you that you are wrong. That something beautiful is going to happen. That the Gardens are purple like a bed of roses would be at dusk. That I came into the Gardens, into life in the Gardens with one whom I did not know. That I danced with her, and did not know her. That I felt passion, contempt and passion for her whom I did not know. That I thought of her. That my thoughts were matches thrown into a dark window. And all the while the Gardens were purple like a bed of roses would be at dusk. I came back to tell you, brother, that white faces are petals of roses. That dark faces are petals of dusk. That I am going out and gather petals. That I am going out and know her whom I brought here with me to these Gardens which are purple like a bed of roses would be at dusk."

Paul and the black man shook hands.

When he reached the spot where they had been standing, Bona was gone.

to *Waldo Frank.*

Kabnís

I

Ralph Kabnis, propped in his bed, tries to read. To read himself
to sleep. An oil lamp on a chair near his elbow burns unsteadily.
The cabin room is spaced fantastically about it. Whitewashed
hearth and chimney, black with sooty saw-teeth. Ceiling, patterned by the fringed globe of the lamp. The walls, unpainted, are
seasoned a rosin yellow. And cracks between the boards are black.
These cracks are the lips the night winds use for whispering. Night
winds in Georgia are vagrant poets, whispering. Kabnis, against
his will, lets his book slip down, and listens to them. The warm
whiteness of his bed, the lamp-light, do not protect him from the
weird chill of their song:

> White-man's land.
> Niggers, sing.
> Burn, bear black children
> Till poor rivers bring
> Rest, and sweet glory
> In Camp Ground.

Kabnis' thin hair is streaked on the pillow. His hand strokes
the slim silk of his mustache. His thumb, pressed under his chin,
seems to be trying to give squareness and projection to it. Brown
eyes stare from a lemon face. Moisture gathers beneath his arm-
pits. He slides down beneath the cover, seeking release.

Kabnis: Near me. Now. Whoever you are, my warm glowing sweetheart, do not think that the face that rests beside you is the real Kabnis. Ralph Kabnis is a dream. And dreams are faces with large eyes and weak chins and broad brows that get smashed by the fists of square faces. The body of the world is bull-necked. A dream is a soft face that fits uncertainly upon it . . . God, if I could develop that in words. Give what I know a bull-neck and a heaving body, all would go well with me, wouldnt it, sweetheart? If I could feel that I came to the South to face it. If I, the dream (not what is weak and afraid in me) could become the face of the South. How my lips would sing for it, my songs being the lips of its soul. Soul. Soul hell. There aint no such thing. What in hell was that?

A rat had run across the thin boards of the ceiling. Kabnis thrusts his head out from the covers. Through the cracks, a powdery faded red dust sprays down on him. Dust of slavefields, dried, scattered . . . No use to read. Christ, if he only could drink himself to sleep. Something as sure as fate was going to happen. He couldnt stand this thing much longer. A hen, perched on a shelf in the adjoining room begins to tread. Her nails scrape the soft wood. Her feathers ruffle.

"Get out of that, you egg-laying bitch."

Kabnis hurls a slipper against the wall. The hen flies from her perch and cackles as if a skunk were after her.

"Now cut out that racket or I'll wring your neck for you."

Answering cackles arise in the chicken yard.

"Why in Christ's hell cant you leave me alone? Damn it, I wish your cackle would choke you. Choke every mother's son of them in this God-forsaken hole. Go away. By God I'll wring your neck for you if you dont. Hell of a mess I've got in: even the poultry is hostile. Go way. Go way. By God, I'll . . ."

Kabnis jumps from his bed. His eyes are wild. He makes for the door. Bursts through it. The hen, driving blindly at the window-pane, screams. Then flies and flops around trying to elude him. Kabnis catches her.

"Got you now, you she-bitch."

With his fingers about her neck, he thrusts open the outside door and steps out into the serene loveliness of Georgian autumn moon-light. Some distance off, down in the valley, a band of pine-smoke, silvered gauze, drifts steadily. The half-moon is a white child that sleeps upon the tree-tops of the forest. White winds croon its sleep-song:

> rock a-by baby . . .
> Black mother sways, holding a white child on her bosom.
> when the bough bends . . .
> Her breath hums through pine-cones.
> cradle will fall . . .
> Teat moon-children at your breasts,
> down will come baby . . .
> Black mother.

Kabnis whirls the chicken by its neck, and throws the head away. Picks up the hopping body, warm, sticky, and hides it in a clump of bushes. He wipes blood from his hands onto the coarse scant grass.

Kabnis: Thats done. Old Chromo in the big house there will wonder whats become of her pet hen. Well, it'll teach her a lesson: not to make a hen-coop of my quarters. Quarters. Hell of a fine quarters, I've got. Five years ago; look at me now. Earth's child. The earth my mother. God is a profligate red-nosed man about town. Bastardy; me. A bastard son has got a right to curse his maker. God . . .

Kabnis is about to shake his fists heavenward. He looks up, and the night's beauty strikes him dumb. He falls to his knees. Sharp stones cut through his thin pajamas. The shock sends a shiver over him. He quivers. Tears mist his eyes. He writhes.

"God Almighty, dear God, dear Jesus, do not torture me with beauty. Take it away. Give me an ugly world. Ha, ugly. Stinking like unwashed niggers. Dear Jesus, do not chain me to myself and set these hills and valleys, heaving with folk-songs, so close to me that I cannot reach them. There is a radiant beauty in the night that touches and . . . tortures me. Ugh. Hell. Get up, you damn fool. Look around. Whats beautiful there? Hog pens and chicken yards. Dirty red mud. Stinking outhouse. Whats beauty anyway but ugliness if it hurts you? God, he doesnt exist, but nevertheless He is ugly. Hence, what comes from Him is ugly. Lynchers and business men, and that cockroach Hanby, especially. How come that he gets to be principal of a school? Of the school I'm driven to teach in? God's handiwork, doubtless. God and Hanby, they belong together. Two godam moral-spouters. Oh, no, I wont let that emotion come up in me. Stay down. Stay down, I tell you. O Jesus, Thou art beautiful . . . Come, Ralph, pull yourself together. Curses and adoration dont come from what is sane. This loneliness, dumbness, awful, intangible oppression is enough to drive a man insane. Miles from nowhere. A speck on a Georgia hillside. Jesus, can you imagine it—an atom of dust in agony on a hillside? Thats a spectacle for you. Come, Ralph, old man, pull yourself together."

Kabnis has stiffened. He is conscious now of the night wind, and of how it chills him. He rises. He totters as a man would who for the first time uses artificial limbs. As a completely artificial man would. The large frame house, squatting on brick pillars, where the principal of the school, his wife, and the boarding girls sleep, seems a curious shadow of his mind. He tries, but cannot convince himself of its reality. His gaze drifts down into the vale, across the swamp, up over the solid dusk bank of pines, and rests, bewildered-like, on the court-house tower. It is dull silver in the moonlight. White child that sleeps upon the top of pines. Kabnis' mind clears. He sees himself yanked beneath that tower. He sees white minds, with indolent assumption, juggle justice and a nigger . . . Somewhere, far off in the straight line of his sight, is Augusta. Christ, how cut off from everything he is. And hours, hours north, why not say a lifetime north? Washington sleeps. Its still, peaceful streets, how desirable they are. Its people whom he had always halfway despised. New York? Impossible. It was a fiction. He had dreamed it. An impotent nostalgia grips him. It becomes intolerable. He forces himself to narrow to a cabin silhouetted on a knoll about a mile away. Peace. Negroes within it are content. They farm. They sing. They love. They sleep. Kabnis wonders if perhaps they can feel him. If perhaps he gives them bad dreams. Things are so immediate in Georgia.

Thinking that now he can go to sleep, he re-enters his room. He builds a fire in the open hearth. The room dances to the tongues of flames, and sings to the crackling and spurting of the logs. Wind comes up between the floor boards, through the black cracks of the walls.

Kabnis: Cant sleep. Light a cigarette. If that old bastard comes over here and smells smoke, I'm done for. Hell of a note, cant even smoke. The stillness of it: where they burn and hang men, you cant smoke. Cant take a swig of licker. What do they think this is, anyway, some sort of temperance school? How did I ever land in such a hole? Ugh. One might just as well be in his grave. Still as a grave. Jesus, how still everything is. Does the world know how still it is? People make noise. They are afraid of silence. Of what lives, and God, of what dies in silence. There must be many dead things moving in silence. They come here to touch me. I swear I feel their fingers . . . Come, Ralph, pull yourself together. What in hell was that? Only the rustle of leaves, I guess. You know, Ralph, old man, it wouldnt surprise me at all to see a ghost. People dont think there are such things. They rationalize their fear, and call their cowardice science. Fine bunch, they are. Damit, that was a noise. And not the wind either. A chicken maybe. Hell, chickens dont wander around this time of night. What in hell is it?

A scraping sound, like a piece of wood dragging over the ground, is coming near.

"Ha, ha. The ghosts down this way havent got any chains to rattle, so they drag trees along with them. Thats a good one. But no joke, something is outside this house, as sure as hell. Whatever it is, it can get a good look at me and I cant see it. Jesus Christ!"

Kabnis pours water on the flames and blows his lamp out. He picks up a poker and stealthily approaches the outside door. Swings it open, and lurches into the night. A calf, carrying a yoke of wood, bolts away from him and scampers down the road.

"Well, I'm damned. This godam place is sure getting the best of me. Come, Ralph, old man, pull yourself together. Nights cant last forever. Thank God for that. Its Sunday already. First time in my life I've ever wanted Sunday to come. Hell of a day. And down here there's no such thing as ducking church. Well, I'll see Halsey and Layman, and get a good square meal. Thats something. And Halsey's a damn good feller. Cant talk to him, though. Who in Christ's world can I talk to? A hen. God. Myself . . . I'm going bats, no doubt of that. Come now, Ralph, go in and make yourself go to sleep. Come now . . . in the door . . . thats right. Put the poker down. There. All right. Slip under the sheets. Close your eyes. Think nothing . . . a long time . . . nothing, nothing. Dont even think nothing. Blank. Not even blank. Count. No, mustnt count. Nothing . . . blank . . . nothing . . . blank . . . space without stars in it. No, nothing . . . nothing . . .

Kabnis sleeps. The winds, like soft-voiced vagrant poets sing:

> White-man's land.
> Niggers, sing.
> Burn, bear black children
> Till poor rivers bring
> Rest, and sweet glory
> In Camp Ground.

kills him, feels remorse, cant sleep, forces himself to bed

2

The parlor of Fred Halsey's home. There is a seediness about it. It seems as though the fittings have given a frugal service to at least seven generations of middle-class shop-owners. An open grate burns cheerily in contrast to the gray cold changed autumn weather. An old-fashioned mantelpiece supports a family clock (not running), a figure or two in imitation bronze, and two small group pictures. Directly above it, in a heavy oak frame, the portrait of a bearded man. Black hair, thick and curly, intensifies the pallor of the high forehead. The eyes are daring. The nose, sharp and regular. The poise suggests a tendency to adventure checked by the necessities of absolute command. The portrait is that of an English gentleman who has retained much of his culture, in that money has enabled him to escape being drawn through a land-grubbing pioneer life. His nature and features, modified by marriage and circumstances, have been transmitted to his great-grandson, Fred. To the left of this picture, spaced on the wall, is a smaller portrait of the great-grandmother. That here there is a Negro strain, no one would doubt. But it is difficult to say in precisely what feature it lies. On close inspection, her mouth is seen to be wistfully twisted. The expression of her face seems to shift before one's gaze—now ugly, repulsive; now sad, and somehow beautiful in its pain. A tin wood-box rests on the floor below. To the right of the great-grandfather's portrait hangs a family group: the father, mother, two brothers, and one sister of Fred. It includes himself some thirty years ago when his face was an olive white, and his hair luxuriant and dark and wavy. The father is a rich brown. The mother, practically white. Of the children, the girl, quite young, is like Fred; the two brothers, darker. The walls of the room are plastered and painted green. An old upright piano is tucked into the corner near the window. The window looks out on a forlorn, box-like, whitewashed frame church. Negroes are gathering, on foot, driving questionable gray and brown mules, and in an occasional Ford, for afternoon service. Beyond, Georgia hills roll off into the distance, their dreary aspect heightened by the gray spots of unpainted one- and two-room shanties. Clumps of pine trees here and there are the dark points the whole landscape is approaching. The church bell tolls. Above its squat tower, a great spiral of buzzards reaches far into the heavens. An ironic comment upon the path that leads into the Christian land . . . Three rocking chairs are grouped around the grate. Sunday papers scattered on the floor indicate a recent usage. Halsey, a well-built, stocky fellow, hair cropped close, enters the room. His Sunday clothes smell of wood and glue, for it is his habit to potter around his wagon-shop even on the Lord's day. He is followed by Professor Layman, tall, heavy, loose-jointed Georgia Negro, by turns teacher and preacher, who has traveled in almost every nook and corner of the state and hence knows more than would be good for anyone other than a silent man. Kabnis, trying to force through a gathering heaviness, trails in behind them. They slip into chairs before the fire.

Layman: Sholy fine, Mr. Halsey, sholy fine. This town's right good at feedin folks, better'n most towns in th state, even for preachers, but I ken say this beats um all. Yassur. Now aint that right, Professor Kabnis?

Kabnis: Yes sir, this beats them all, all right—best I've had, and thats a fact, though my comparison doesnt carry far, y'know.

Layman: Hows that, Professor?

Kabnis: Well, this is my first time out—

Layman: For a fact. Aint seed you round so much. Whats th trouble? Dont like our folks down this away?

Halsey: Aint that, Layman. He aint like most northern niggers that way. Aint a thing stuck-up about him. He likes us, you an me, maybe all—its that red mud over yonder—gets stuck in it an cant get out. (Laughs.) An then he loves th fire so, warm as its been. Coldest Yankee I've ever seen. But I'm goin t get him out now in a jiffy, eh, Kabnis?

Kabnis: Sure, I should say so, sure. Dont think its because I dont like folks down this way. Just the opposite, in fact. Theres more hospitality and everything. Its diff—that is, theres lots of northern exaggeration about the South. Its not half the terror they picture it. Things are not half bad, as one could easily figure out for himself without ever crossing the Mason and Dixie line: all these people wouldnt stay down here, especially the rich, the ones that could easily leave, if conditions were so mighty bad. And then too, sometime back, my family were southerners y'know. From Georgia, in fact—

Layman: Nothin t feel proud about, Professor. Neither your folks nor mine.

Halsey (in a mock religious tone): Amen t that, brother Layman. Amen (turning to Kabnis, half playful, yet somehow dead in earnest). An Mr. Kabnis, kindly remember youre in th land of cotton—hell of a land. Th white folks get th boll; th niggers get th stalk. An dont you dare touch th boll, or even look at it. They'll swing y sho. (Laughs.)

Kabnis: But they wouldnt touch a gentleman—fellows, men like us three here—

Layman: Nigger's a nigger down this away, Professor. An only two dividins: good an bad. An even they aint permanent categories. They sometimes mixes um up when it comes t lynchin. I've seen um do it.

Halsey: Dont let th fear int y, though, Kabnis. This county's a good un. Aint been a stringin up I can remember. (Laughs.)

Layman: This is a good town an a good county. But theres some that makes up fer it.

Kabnis: Things are better now though since that stir about those peonage cases, arent they?

Layman: Ever hear tell of a single shot killin moren one rabbit, Professor?

Kabnis: No, of course not, that is, but then—

Halsey: Now I know you werent born yesterday, sprung up so rapid like you aint heard of th brick thrown in th hornets' nest. (Laughs.)

Kabnis: Hardly, hardly, I know—

Halsey: Course y do. (To Layman) See, northern niggers aint as dumb as they make out t be.

Kabnis (overlooking the remark): Just stirs them up to sting.

Halsey: T perfection. An put just like a professor should put it.

Kabnis: Thats what actually did happen?

Layman: Well, if it aint sos only because th stingers already movin jes as fast as they ken go. An been goin ever since I ken remember, an then some mo. Though I dont usually make mention of it.

Halsey: Damn sight better not. Say, Layman, you come from where theyre always swarmin, dont y?

Layman: Yassur. I do that, sho. Dont want t mention it, but its a fact. I've seed th time when there werent no use t even stretch out flat upon th ground. Seen um shoot an cut a man t pieces who had died th night befo. Yassur. An they didnt stop when they found out he was dead—jes went on ahackin at him anyway.

Kabnis: What did you do? What did you say to them, Professor?

Layman: Thems th things you neither does a thing or talks about if y want t stay around this away, Professor.

Halsey: Listen t what he's tellin y, Kabnis. May come in handy some day.

Kabnis: Cant something be done? But of course not. This preacher-ridden race. Pray and shout. Theyre in the preacher's hands. Thats what it is. And the preacher's hands are in the white man's pockets.

Halsey: Present company always excepted.

Kabnis: The Professor knows I wasnt referring to him.

Layman: Preacher's a preacher anywheres you turn. No use exceptin.

Kabnis: Well, of course, if you look at it that way. I didnt mean—But cant something be done?

Layman: Sho. Yassur. An done first rate an well. Jes like Sam Raymon done it.

Kabnis: Hows that? What did he do?

Layman: Th white folks (reckon I oughtnt tell it) had jes knocked two others like you kill a cow—brained um with an ax, when they caught Sam Raymon by a stream. They was about t do fer him when he up an says, "White folks, I gotter die, I knows that. But wont y let me die in my own way?" Some was fer gettin after him, but th boss held um back an says, "Jes so longs th nigger dies——" An Sam fell down ont his knees an prayed, "O Lord, Ise comin to y," and he up an jumps int th stream.

Singing from the church becomes audible. Above it, rising and falling in a plaintive moan, a woman's voice swells to shouting. Kabnis hears it. His face gives way to an expression of mingled fear, contempt, and pity. Layman takes no notice of it. Halsey grins at Kabnis. He feels like having a little sport with him.

Halsey: Lets go t church, eh, Kabnis?

Kabnis (seeking control): All right—no sir, not by a damn sight. Once a days enough for me. Christ, but that stuff gets to me. Meaning no reflection on you, Professor.

Halsey: Course not. Say, Kabnis, noticed y this morning. What'd y get up for an go out?

Kabnis: Couldnt stand the shouting, and thats a fact. We dont have that sort of thing up North. We do, but, that is, some one should see to it that they are stopped or put out when they get so bad the preacher has to stop his sermon for them.

Halsey: Is that th way youall sit on sisters up North?

Kabnis: In the church I used to go to no one ever shouted—

Halsey: Lungs weak?

Kabnis: Hardly, that is—

Halsey: Yankees are right up t th minute in tellin folk how t turn a trick. They always were good at talkin.

Kabnis: Well, anyway, they should be stopped.

Layman: Thats right. Thats true. An its th worst ones in th community that comes int th church t shout. I've sort a made a study of it. You take a man what drinks, th biggest licker-head around will come int th church an yell th loudest. An th sister whats done wrong, an is always doin wrong, will sit down in th

Amen corner an swing her arms an shout her head off. Seems as if they cant control themselves out in th world; they cant control themselves in church. Now dont that sound logical, Professor?

Halsey: Reckon its as good as any. But I heard that queer cuss over yonder—y know him, dont y, Kabnis? Well, y ought t. He had a run-in with your boss th other day—same as you'll have if you dont walk th chalk-line. An th quicker th better. I hate that Hanby. Ornery bastard. I'll mash his mouth in one of these days. Well, as I was sayin, that feller, Lewis's name, I heard him sayin somethin about a stream whats dammed has got t cut loose some-wheres. An that sounds good. I know th feelin myself. He strikes me as knowin a bucketful bout most things, that feller does. Seems like he doesnt want t talk, an does, sometimes, like Layman here. Damn queer feller, him.

Layman: Cant make heads or tails of him, an I've seen lots o queer possums in my day. Everybody's wonderin about him. White folks too. He'll have t leave here soon, thats sho. Always askin questions. An I aint seed his lips move once. Pokin round an notin somethin. Noted what I said th other day, an that werent fer notin down.

Kabnis: What was that?

Layman: Oh, a lynchin that took place bout a year ago. Th worst I know of round these parts.

Halsey: Bill Burnam?

Layman: Na. Mame Lamkins.

Halsey grunts, but says nothing.

The preacher's voice rolls from the church in an insistent chant-ing monotone. At regular intervals it rises to a crescendo note. The sister begins to shout. Her voice, high-pitched and hysterical, is almost perfectly attuned to the nervous key of Kabnis. Halsey notices his distress, and is amused by it. Layman's face is expressionless. Kabnis wants to hear the story of Mame Lamkins. He does not want to hear it. It can be no worse than the shouting.

Kabnis (his chair rocking faster): What about Mame Lamkins?

Halsey: Tell him, Layman.

The preacher momentarily stops. The choir, together with the entire congregation, sings an old spiritual. The music seems to quiet the shouter. Her heavy breathing has the sound of evening winds that blow through pinecones. Layman's voice is uniformly low and soothing. A canebrake, murmuring the tale to its neighbor-road would be more passionate.

Layman: White folks know that niggers talk, an they dont mind jes so long as nothing comes of it, so here goes. She was in th family-way, Mame Lamkins was. They killed her in th street, an some white man seein th risin in her stomach as she lay there soppy in her blood like any cow, took an ripped her belly open, an th kid fell out. It was living; but a nigger baby aint supposed t live. So he jabbed his knife in it an stuck it t a tree. An then they all went away.

Kabnis: Christ no! What had she done?

Layman: Tried t hide her husband when they was after him.

A shriek pierces the room. The bronze pieces on the mantel hum. The sister cries frantically: "Jesus, Jesus, I've found Jesus. O Lord, glory t God, one mo sinner is acomin home." At the height of this, a stone, wrapped round with paper, crashes through the window. Kabnis springs to his feet, terror-stricken. Layman is worried. Halsey picks up the stone. Takes off the wrapper, smooths it out, and reads: "You northern nigger, its time fer y t leave. Git along now." Kabnis knows that the command is meant for him. Fear squeezes him. Caves him in. As a violent external pressure would. Fear flows inside him. It fills him up. He bloats. He saves himself from bursting by dashing wildly from the room. Halsey and Layman stare stupidly at each other. The stone, the crumpled paper are things, huge things that weight them. Their thoughts are vaguely concerned with the texture of the stone, with the color of the paper. Then they remember the words, and begin to shift them about in sentences. Layman even construes them grammatically. Suddenly the sense of them comes back to Halsey. He grips Layman by the arm and they both follow after Kabnis.

A false dusk has come early. The countryside is ashen, chill. Cabins and roads and canebrakes whisper. The church choir, dipping into a long silence, sings:

> My Lord, what a mourning,
> My Lord, what a mourning,
> My Lord, what a mourning,
> When the stars begin to fall.

Softly luminous over the hills and valleys, the faint spray of a scattered star . . .

3

A splotchy figure drives forward along the cane- and corn-stalk hemmed-in road. A scarecrow replica of Kabnis, awkwardly animate. Fantastically plastered with red Georgia mud. It skirts the big house whose windows shine like mellow lanterns in the dusk. Its shoulder jogs against a sweet-gum tree. The figure caroms off against the cabin door, and lunges in. It slams the door as if to prevent some one entering after it.

"God Almighty, theyre here. After me. On me. All along the road I saw their eyes flaring from the cane. Hounds. Shouts. What in God's name did I run here for? A mud-hole trap. I stumbled on a rope. O God, a rope. Their clammy hands were like the love of death playing up and down my spine. Trying to trip my legs. To trip my spine. Up and down my spine. My spine . . . My legs . . . Why in hell didnt they catch me?"

Kabnis wheels around, half defiant, half numbed with a more immediate fear.

"Wanted to trap me here. Get out o there. I see you."

He grabs a broom from beside the chimney and violently pokes it under the bed. The broom strikes a tin wash-tub. The noise bewilders. He recovers.

"Not there. In the closet."

He throws the broom aside and grips the poker. Starts towards the closet door, towards somewhere in the perfect blackness behind the chimney.

"I'll brain you."

He stops short. The barks of hounds, evidently in pursuit, reach him. A voice, liquid in distance, yells, "Hi! Hi!"

"O God, theyre after me. Holy Father, Mother of Christ—hell, this aint no time for prayer—"

Voices, just outside the door:

"Reckon he's here."

"Dont see no light though."

The door is flung open.

Kabnis: Get back or I'll kill you.

He braces himself, brandishing the poker.

Halsey (coming in): Aint as bad as all that. Put that thing down.

Layman: Its only us, Professor. Nobody else after y.

Kabnis: Halsey. Layman. Close that door. Dont light that light. For godsake get away from there.

Halsey: Nobody's after y, Kabnis, I'm tellin y. Put that thing down an get yourself together.

Kabnis: I tell you they are. I saw them. I heard the hounds.

Halsey: These aint th days of hounds an Uncle Tom's Cabin, feller. White folks aint in fer all them theatrics these days. Theys more direct than that. If what they wanted was t get y, theyd have just marched right in an took y where y sat. Somebodys down by th branch chasin rabbits an atreein possums.

A shot is heard.

Halsey: Got him, I reckon. Saw Tom goin out with his gun. Tom's pretty lucky most times.

He goes to the bureau and lights the lamp. The circular fringe is patterned on the ceiling. The moving shadows of the men are huge against the bare wall boards. Halsey walks up to Kabnis, takes the poker from his grip, and without more ado pushes him into a chair before the dark hearth.

Halsey: Youre a mess. Here, Layman. Get some trash an start a fire.

Layman fumbles around, finds some newspapers and old bags, puts them in the hearth, arranges the wood, and kindles the fire. Halsey sets a black iron kettle where it soon will be boiling. Then takes from his hip-pocket a bottle of corn licker which he passes to Kabnis.

Halsey: Here. This'll straighten y out a bit.

Kabnis nervously draws the cork and gulps the licker down.

Kabnis: Ha. Good stuff. Thanks. Thank y, Halsey.

Halsey: Good stuff! Youre damn right. Hanby there dont think so. Wonder he doesnt come over t find out whos burnin his oil. Miserly bastard, him. Th boys what made this stuff—are y listenin t me, Kabnis? th boys what made this stuff have got th art down like I heard you say youd like t be with words. Eh? Have some, Layman?

Layman: Dont think I care for none, thank y jes th same, Mr. Halsey.

Halsey: Care hell. Course y care. Everybody cares around these parts. Preachers an school teachers an everybody. Here. Here, take it. Dont try that line on me.

Layman limbers up a little, but he cannot quite forget that he is on school ground.

Layman: Thats right. Thats true, sho. Shinin is th only business what pays in these hard times.

He takes a nip, and passes the bottle to Kabnis. Kabnis is in the middle of a long swig when a rap sounds on the door. He almost spills the bottle, but manages to pass it to Halsey just as the door swings open and Hanby enters. He is a well-dressed, smooth, rich, black-skinned Negro who thinks there is no one quite so suave and polished as himself. To members of his own race, he affects the manners of a wealthy white planter. Or, when he is up North, he lets it be known that his ideas are those of the best New England tradition. To white men he bows, without ever completely humbling himself. Tradesmen in the town tolerate him because he spends his money with them. He delivers his words with a full consciousness of his moral superiority.

Hanby: Hum. Erer, Professor Kabnis, to come straight to the point: the progress of the Negro race is jeopardized whenever the personal habits and examples set by its guides and mentors fall below the acknowledged and hard-won standard of its average member. This institution, of which I am the humble president, was founded, and has been maintained at a cost of great labor and untold sacrifice. Its purpose is to teach our youth to live better, cleaner, more noble lives. To prove to the world that the Negro race can be just like any other race. It hopes to attain this aim partly by the salutary examples set by its instructors. I cannot hinder the progress of a race simply to indulge a single member. I have thought the matter out beforehand, I can assure you.

Therefore, if I find your resignation on my desk by to-morrow morning, Mr. Kabnis, I shall not feel obliged to call in the sheriff. Otherwise . . ."

Kabnis: A fellow can take a drink in his own room if he wants to, in the privacy of his own room.

Hanby: His room, but not the institution's room, Mr. Kabnis.

Kabnis: This is my room while I'm in it.

Hanby: Mr. Clayborn (the sheriff) can inform you as to that.

Kabnis: Oh, well, what do I care—glad to get out of this mud-hole.

Hanby: I should think so from your looks.

Kabnis: You neednt get sarcastic about it.

Hanby: No, that is true. And I neednt wait for your resignation either, Mr. Kabnis.

Kabnis: Oh, you'll get that all right. Dont worry.

Hanby: And I should like to have the room thoroughly aired and cleaned and ready for your successor by to-morrow noon, Professor.

Kabnis (trying to rise): You can have your godam room right away. I dont want it.

Hanby: But I wont have your cursing.

Halsey pushes Kabnis back into his chair.

Halsey: Sit down, Kabnis, till I wash y.

Hanby (to Halsey): I would rather not have drinking men on the premises, Mr. Halsey. You will oblige me—

Halsey: I'll oblige you by stayin right on this spot, this spot, get me? till I get damned ready t leave.

He approaches Hanby. Hanby retreats, but manages to hold his dignity.

Halsey: Let me get you told right now, Mr. Samuel Hanby. Now listen t me. I aint no slick an span slave youve hired, an dont y think it for a minute. Youve bullied enough about this town. An besides, wheres that bill youve been owin me? Listen t me. If I dont get it paid in by tmorrer noon, Mr. Hanby (he mockingly assumes Hanby's tone and manner), I shall feel obliged t call th sheriff. An that sheriff'll be myself who'll catch y in th road an pull y out your buggy an lightly attend t y. You heard me. Now leave him alone. I'm takin him home with me. I got it fixed. Before you came in. He's goin t work with me. Shapin shafts and buildin wagons'll make a man of him what nobody, y get me? what nobody can take advantage of. Thats all . . .

Halsey burrs off into vague and incoherent comment.

Pause. Disagreeable.

Layman's eyes are glazed on the spurting fire.

Kabnis wants to rise and put both Halsey and Hanby in their places. He vaguely knows that he must do this, else the power of direction will completely slip from him to those outside. The conviction is just strong enough to torture him. To bring a feverish, quick-passing flare into his eyes. To mutter words soggy in hot saliva. To jerk his arms upward in futile protest. Halsey, noticing his gestures, thinks it is water that he desires. He brings a glass to him. Kabnis slings it to the floor. Heat of the conviction dies. His arms crumple. His upper lip, his mustache, quiver. Rap! rap, on the door. The sounds slap Kabnis. They bring a hectic color to his cheeks. Like huge cold finger tips they touch his skin and gooseflesh it. Hanby strikes a commanding pose. He moves toward Layman. Layman's face is innocently immobile.

Halsey: Whos there?

Voice: Lewis.

Halsey: Come in, Lewis. Come on in.

Lewis enters. He is the queer fellow who has been referred to. A tall wiry copper-colored man, thirty perhaps. His mouth and eyes suggest purpose guided by an adequate intelligence. He is what a stronger Kabnis might have been, and in an odd faint way resembles him. As he steps towards the others, he seems to be issuing sharply from a vivid dream. Lewis shakes hands with Halsey. Nods perfunctorily to Hanby, who has stiffened to meet him. Smiles rapidly at Layman, and settles with real interest on Kabnis.

Lewis: Kabnis passed me on the road. Had a piece of business of my own, and couldnt get here any sooner. Thought I might be able to help in some way or other.

Halsey: A good baths bout all he needs now. An somethin t put his mind t rest.

Lewis: I think I can give him that. That note was meant for me. Some Negroes have grown uncomfortable at my being here—

Kabnis: You mean, Mr. Lewis, some colored folks threw it? Christ Almighty!

Halsey: Thats what he means. An just as I told y. White folks more direct than that.

Kabnis: What are they after you for?

Lewis: Its a long story, Kabnis. Too long for now. And it might involve present company. (He laughs pleasantly and gestures vaguely in the direction of Hanby.) Tell you about it later on perhaps.

Kabnis: Youre not going?

Lewis: Not till my month's up.

Halsey: Hows that?

Lewis: I'm on a sort of contract with myself. (Is about to leave.) Well, glad its nothing serious—

Halsey: Come round t th shop sometime why dont y, Lewis? I've asked y enough. I'd like t have a talk with y. I aint as dumb as I look. Kabnis an me'll be in most any time. Not much work these

days. Wish t hell there was. This burg gets to me when there aint.
(In answer to Lewis' question.) He's goin t work with me. Ya.
Night air this side th branch aint good fer him. (Looks at Hanby.
Laughs.)

Lewis: I see . . .

His eyes turn to Kabnis. In the instant of their shifting, a vision
of the life they are to meet. Kabnis, a promise of a soil-soaked
beauty; uprooted, thinning out. Suspended a few feet above the
soil whose touch would resurrect him. Arm's length removed
from him whose will to help . . . There is a swift intuitive inter-
change of consciousness. Kabnis has a sudden need to rush into
the arms of this man. His eyes call, "Brother." And then a savage,
cynical twist-about within him mocks his impulse and strength-
ens him to repulse Lewis. His lips curl cruelly. His eyes laugh.
They are glittering needles, stitching. With a throbbing ache they
draw Lewis to. Lewis brusquely wheels on Hanby.

Lewis: I'd like to see you, sir, a moment, if you dont mind.

Hanby's tight collar and vest effectively preserve him.

Hanby: Yes, erer, Mr. Lewis. Right away.

Lewis: See you later, Halsey.

Halsey: So long—thanks—sho hope so, Lewis.

As he opens the door and Hanby passes out, a woman, miles
down the valley, begins to sing. Her song is a spark that travels
swiftly to the near-by cabins. Like purple tallow flames, songs jet
up. They spread a ruddy haze over the heavens. The haze swings
low. Now the whole countryside is a soft chorus. Lord. O Lord
. . . Lewis closes the door behind him. A flame jets out . . .

The kettle is boiling. Halsey notices it. He pulls the wash-tub
from beneath the bed. He arranges for the bath before the fire.

Halsey: Told y them theatrics didnt fit a white man. Th niggers, just like I told y. An after him. Aint surprisin though. He

aint bowed t none of them. Nassur. T nairy a one of them nairy an inch nairy a time. An only mixed when he was good an ready—

Kabnis: That song, Halsey, do you hear it?

Halsey: Thats a man. Hear me, Kabnis? A man—

Kabnis: Jesus, do you hear it.

Halsey: Hear it? Hear what? Course I hear it. Listen t what I'm tellin y. A man, get me? They'll get him yet if he dont watch out.

Kabnis is jolted into his fear.

Kabnis: Get him? What do you mean? How? Not lynch him?

Halsey: Na. Take a shotgun an shoot his eyes clear out. Well, anyway, it wasnt fer you, just like I told y. You'll stay over at th house an work with me, eh, boy? Good t get away from his nobs, eh? Damn big stiff though, him. An youre not th first an I can tell y. (Laughs.)

He bustles and fusses about Kabnis as if he were a child. Kabnis submits, wearily. He has no will to resist him.

Layman (his voice is like a deep hollow echo): Thats right. Thats true, sho. Everybody's been expectin that th bust up was comin. Surprised um all y held on as long as y did. Teachin in th South aint th thing fer y. Nassur. You ought t be way back up North where sometimes I wish I was. But I've hung on down this away so long—

Halsey: An there'll never be no leavin time fer y.

4

A month has passed.

Halsey's work-shop. It is an old building just off the main street of Sempter. The walls to within a few feet of the ground are of an age-worn cement mixture. On the outside they are considerably crumbled and peppered with what looks like musket-shot. Inside, the plaster has fallen away in great chunks, leaving the laths, grayed and cobwebbed, exposed. A sort of loft above the shop proper serves as a break-water for the rain and sunshine which otherwise would have free entry to the main floor. The shop is filled with old wheels and parts of wheels, broken shafts, and wooden litter. A double door, midway the street wall. To the left of this, a work-bench that holds a vise and a variety of wood-work tools. A window with as many panes broken as whole, throws light on the bench. Opposite, in the rear wall, a second window looks out upon the back yard. In the left wall, a rickety smoke-blackened chimney, and hearth with fire blazing. Smooth-worn chairs grouped about the hearth suggest the village meeting-place. Several large wooden blocks, chipped and cut and sawed on their upper surfaces are in the middle of the floor. They are the supports used in almost any sort of wagon-work. Their idleness means that Halsey has no worth-while job on foot. To the right of the central door is a junk heap, and directly behind this, stairs that lead down into the cellar. The cellar is known as "The Hole." Besides being the home of a very old man, it is used by Halsey on those occasions when he spices up the life of the small town.

Halsey, wonderfully himself in his work overalls, stands in the doorway and gazes up the street, expectantly. Then his eyes grow listless. He slouches against the smooth-rubbed frame. He lights a cigarette. Shifts his position. Braces an arm against the door. Kabnis passes the window and stoops to get in under Halsey's arm. He is awkward and ludicrous, like a schoolboy in his big brother's new overalls. He skirts the large blocks on the floor, and drops into a chair before the fire. Halsey saunters towards him.

Kabnis: Time f lunch.

Halsey: Ya.

He stands by the hearth, rocking backward and forward. He stretches his hands out to the fire. He washes them in the warm glow of the flames. They never get cold, but he warms them.

Kabnis: Saw Lewis up th street. Said he'd be down.

Halsey's eyes brighten. He looks at Kabnis. Turns away. Says nothing. Kabnis fidgets. Twists his thin blue cloth-covered limbs. Pulls closer to the fire till the heat stings his shins. Pushes back. Pokes the burned logs. Puts on several fresh ones. Fidgets. The town bell strikes twelve.

Kabnis: Fix it up f tnight?

Halsey: Leave it t me.

Kabnis: Get Lewis in?

Halsey: Tryin t.

The air is heavy with the smell of pine and resin. Green logs spurt and sizzle. Sap trickles from an old pine-knot into the flames. Layman enters. He carries a lunch-pail. Kabnis, for the moment, thinks that he is a day laborer.

Layman: Evenin, gen'lemun.

Both: Whats say, Layman.

Layman squares a chair to the fire and droops into it. Several town fellows, silent unfathomable men for the most part, saunter in. Overalls. Thick tan shoes. Felt hats marvelously shaped and twisted. One asks Halsey for a cigarette. He gets it. The blacksmith, a tremendous black man, comes in from the forge. Not even a nod from him. He picks up an axle and goes out. Lewis enters. The town men look curiously at him. Suspicion and an open liking contest for possession of their faces. They are uncomfortable. One by one they drift into the street.

Layman: Heard y was leavin, Mr. Lewis.

Kabnis: Months up, eh? Hell of a month I've got.

Halsey: Sorry y goin, Lewis. Just gettin acquainted like.

Lewis: Sorry myself, Halsey, in a way—

Layman: Gettin t like our town, Mr. Lewis?

Lewis: I'm afraid its on a different basis, Professor.

Halsey: An I've yet t hear about that basis. Been waitin long enough, God knows. Seems t me like youd take pity on a feller if nothin more.

Kabnis: Somethin that old black cockroach over yonder doesnt like, whatever it is.

Layman: Thats right. Thats right, sho.

Halsey: A feller dropped in here tother day an said he knew what you was about. Said you had queer opinions. Well, I could have told him you was a queer one, myself. But not th way he was driftin. Didnt mean anything by it, but just let drop he thought you was a little wrong up here—crazy; y'know. (Laughs.)

Kabnis: Y mean old Blodson? Hell, he's bats himself.

Lewis: I remember him. We had a talk. But what he found queer, I think, was not my opinions, but my lack of them. In half an hour he had settled everything: boll weevils, God, the World War. Weevils and wars are the pests that God sends against the sinful. People are too weak to correct themselves: the Redeemer is coming back. Get ready, ye sinners, for the advent of Our Lord. Interesting, eh, Kabnis? but not exactly what we want.

Halsey: Y could have come t me. I've sho been after y enough. Most every time I've seen y.

Kabnis (sarcastically): Hows it y never came t us professors?

Lewis: I did—to one.

Kabnis: Y mean t say y got somethin from that celluloid-collar-eraser-cleaned old codger over in th mud hole?

Halsey: Rough on th old boy, aint he? (Laughs.)

Lewis: Something, yes. Layman here could have given me

136

quite a deal, but the incentive to his keeping quiet is so much greater than anything I could have offered him to open up, that I crossed him off my mind. And you—

Kabnis: What about me?

Halsey: Tell him, Lewis, for godsake tell him. I've told him. But its somethin else he wants so bad I've heard him downstairs mumblin with th old man.

Lewis: The old man?

Kabnis: What about me? Come on now, you know so much.

Halsey: Tell him, Lewis. Tell it t him.

Lewis: Life has already told him more than he is capable of knowing. It has given him in excess of what he can receive. I have been offered. Stuff in his stomach curdled, and he vomited me.

Kabnis' face twitches. His body writhes.

Kabnis: You know a lot, you do. How about Halsey?

Lewis: Yes . . . Halsey? Fits here. Belongs here. An artist in your way, arent you, Halsey?

Halsey: Reckon I am, Lewis. Give me th work and fair pay an I aint askin nothin better. Went over-seas an saw France; an I come back. Been up North; an I come back. Went t school; but there aint no books whats got th feel t them of them there tools. Nassur. An I'm atellin y.

A shriveled, bony white man passes the window and enters the shop. He carries a broken hatchet-handle and the severed head. He speaks with a flat, drawn voice to Halsey, who comes forward to meet him.

Mr. Ramsay: Can y fix this fer me, Halsey?

Halsey (looking it over): Reckon so, Mr. Ramsay. Here, Kabnis. A little practice fer y.

Halsey directs Kabnis, showing him how to place the handle in the vise, and cut it down. The knife hangs. Kabnis thinks that it must be dull. He jerks it hard. The tool goes deep and shaves too much off. Mr. Ramsay smiles brokenly at him.

Mr. Ramsay (to Halsey): Still breakin in the new hand, eh, Halsey? Seems like a likely enough faller once he gets th hang of it.

He gives a tight laugh at his own good humor. Kabnis burns red. The back of his neck stings him beneath his collar. He feels stifled. Through Ramsay, the whole white South weighs down upon him. The pressure is terrific. He sweats under the arms. Chill beads run down his body. His brows concentrate upon the handle as though his own life was staked upon the perfect shaving of it. He begins to out and out botch the job. Halsey smiles.

Halsey: He'll make a good un some of these days, Mr. Ramsay.

Mr. Ramsay: Y ought t know. Yer daddy was a good un before y. Runs in th family, seems like t me.

Halsey: Thats right, Mr. Ramsay.

Kabnis is hopeless. Halsey takes the handle from him. With a few deft strokes he shaves it. Fits it. Gives it to Ramsay.

Mr. Ramsay: How much on this?

Halsey: No charge, Mr. Ramsay.

Mr. Ramsay (going out): All right, Halsey. Come down an take it out in trade. Shoe-strings or something.

Halsey: Yassur, Mr. Ramsay.

Halsey rejoins Lewis and Layman. Kabnis, hangdog-fashion, follows him.

Halsey: They like y if y work fer them.

Layman: Thats right, Mr. Halsey. Thats right, sho.

The group is about to resume its talk when Hanby enters. He is all energy, bustle, and business. He goes direct to Kabnis.

Hanby: An axle is out in the buggy which I would like to have shaped into a crow-bar. You will see that it is fixed for me.

Without waiting for an answer, and knowing that Kabnis will

follow, he passes out. Kabnis, scowling, silent, trudges after him.

Hanby (from the outside): Have that ready for me by three o'clock, young man. I shall call for it.

Kabnis (under his breath as he comes in): Th hell you say, you old black swamp-gut.

He slings the axle on the floor.

Halsey: Wheeee!

Layman, lunch finished long ago, rises, heavily. He shakes hands with Lewis.

Layman: Might not see y again befo y leave, Mr. Lewis. I enjoys t hear y talk. Y might have been a preacher. Maybe a bishop some day. Sho do hope t see y back this away again sometime, Mr. Lewis.

Lewis: Thanks, Professor. Hope I'll see you.

Layman waves a long arm loosely to the others, and leaves. Kabnis goes to the door. His eyes, sullen, gaze up the street.

Kabnis: Carrie K.'s comin with th lunch. Bout time.

She passes the window. Her red girl's-cap, catching the sun, flashes vividly. With a stiff, awkward little movement she crosses the doorsill and gives Kabnis one of the two baskets which she is carrying. There is a slight stoop to her shoulders. The curves of her body blend with this to a soft rounded charm. Her gestures are stiffly variant. Black bangs curl over the forehead of her oval-olive face. Her expression is dazed, but on provocation it can melt into a wistful smile. Adolescent. She is easily the sister of Fred Halsey.

Carrie K.: Mother says excuse her, brother Fred an Ralph, fer bein late.

Kabnis: Everythings all right an O.K., Carrie Kate. O.K. an all right.

The two men settle on their lunch. Carrie, with hardly a glance in the direction of the hearth, as is her habit, is about to take the second basket down to the old man, when Lewis rises. In doing so he draws her unwitting attention. Their meeting is a swift sun-burst. Lewis impulsively moves towards her. His mind flashes images of her life in the southern town. He sees the nascent woman, her flesh already stiffening to cartilage, drying to bone. Her spirit-bloom, even now touched sullen, bitter. Her rich beauty fading . . . He wants to—He stretches forth his hands to hers. He takes them. They feel like warm cheeks against his palms. The sun-burst from her eyes floods up and haloes him. Christ-eyes, his eyes look to her. Fearlessly she loves into them. And then something happens. Her face blanches. Awkwardly she draws away. The sin-bogies of respectable southern colored folks clamor at her: "Look out! Be a *good* girl. A *good* girl. Look out!" She gropes for her basket that has fallen to the floor. Finds it, and marches with a rigid gravity to her task of feeding the old man. Like the glowing white ash of burned paper, Lewis' eyelids, wavering, settle down. He stirs in the direction of the rear window. From the back yard, mules tethered to odd trees and posts blink dumbly at him. They too seem burdened with an impotent pain. Kabnis and Halsey are still busy with their lunch. They havent noticed him. After a while he turns to them.

Lewis: Your sister, Halsey, whats to become of her? What are you going to do for her?

Halsey: Who? What? What am I goin t do? . . .

Lewis: What I mean is, what does she do down there?

Halsey: Oh. Feeds th old man. Had lunch, Lewis?

Lewis: Thanks, yes. You have never felt her, have you, Halsey? Well, no, I guess not. I dont suppose you can. Nor can she . . . Old man? Halsey, some one lives down there? I've never heard of him. Tell me—

Kabnis takes time from his meal to answer with some emphasis:

Kabnis: Theres lots of things you aint heard of.

Lewis: Dare say. I'd like to see him.

Kabnis: You'll get all th chance you want tnight.

Halsey: Fixin a little somethin up fer tnight, Lewis. Th three of us an some girls. Come round bout ten-thirty.

Lewis: Glad to. But what under the sun does he do down there?

Halsey: Ask Kabnis. He blows off t him every chance he gets.

Kabnis gives a grunting laugh. His mouth twists. Carrie returns from the cellar. Avoiding Lewis, she speaks to her brother.

Carrie K.: Brother Fred, father hasnt eaten now goin on th second week, but mumbles an talks funny, or tries t talk when I put his hands ont th food. He frightens me, an I dunno what t do. An oh, I came near fergettin, brother, but Mr. Marmon—he was eatin lunch when I saw him—told me t tell y that th lumber wagon busted down an he wanted y t fix it fer him. Said he reckoned he could get it t y after he ate.

Halsey chucks a half-eaten sandwich in the fire. Gets up. Arranges his blocks. Goes to the door and looks anxiously up the street. The wind whirls a small spiral in the gray dust road.

Halsey: Why didnt y tell me sooner, little sister?

Carrie K.: I fergot t, an just remembered it now, brother.

Her soft rolled words are fresh pain to Lewis. He wants to take her North with him What for? He wonders what Kabnis could do for her. What she could do for him. Mother him. Carrie gathers the lunch things, silently, and in her pinched manner, curtsies, and departs. Kabnis lights his after-lunch cigarette. Lewis, who has sensed a change, becomes aware that he is not included in it. He starts to ask again about the old man. Decides not to. Rises to go.

Lewis: Think I'll run along, Halsey.

Halsey: Sure. Glad t see y any time.

Kabnis: Dont forget tnight.

Lewis: Dont worry. I wont. So long.

Kabnis: So long. We'll be expectin y.

Lewis passes Halsey at the door. Halsey's cheeks form a vacant smile. His eyes are wide awake, watching for the wagon to turn from Broad Street into his road.

Halsey: So long.

His words reach Lewis halfway to the corner.

5

Night, soft belly of a pregnant Negress, throbs evenly against the torso of the South. Night throbs a womb-song to the South. Cane- and cotton-fields, pine forests, cypress swamps, sawmills, and factories are fecund at her touch. Night's womb-song sets them singing. Night winds are the breathing of the unborn child whose calm throbbing in the belly of a Negress sets them somnolently singing. Hear their song.

> White-man's land.
> Niggers, sing.
> Burn, bear black children
> Till poor rivers bring
> Rest, and sweet glory
> In Camp Ground.

Sempter's streets are vacant and still. White paint on the wealthier houses has the chill blue glitter of distant stars. Negro cabins are a purple blur. Broad Street is deserted. Winds stir

beneath the corrugated iron canopies and dangle odd bits of rope
tied to horse- and mule-gnawed hitching-posts. One store window has a light in it. Chesterfield cigarette and Chero-Cola cardboard advertisements are stacked in it. From a side door two men
come out. Pause, for a last word and then say good night. Soon
they melt in shadows thicker than they. Way off down the street
four figures sway beneath iron awnings which form a sort of cor-
ridor that imperfectly echoes and jumbles what they say. A fifth
form joins them. They turn into the road that leads to Halsey's
workshop. The old building is phosphorescent above deep shade.
The figures pass through the double door. Night winds whisper in
the eaves. Sing weirdly in the ceiling cracks. Stir curls of shavings
on the floor. Halsey lights a candle. A good-sized lumber wagon,
wheels off, rests upon the blocks. Kabnis makes a face at it. An
unearthly hush is upon the place. No one seems to want to talk.
To move, lest the scraping of their feet . . .

Halsey: Come on down this way, folks.

He leads the way. Stella follows. And close after her, Cora,
Lewis, and Kabnis. They descend into the Hole. It seems huge,
limitless in the candle light. The walls are of stone, wonderfully
fitted. They have no openings save a small iron-barred window
toward the top of each. They are dry and warm. The ground
slopes away to the rear of the building and thus leaves the south
wall exposed to the sun. The blacksmith's shop is plumb against
the right wall. The floor is clay. Shavings have at odd times been
matted into it. In the right-hand corner, under the stairs, two
good-sized pine mattresses, resting on cardboard, are on either
side of a wooden table. On this are several half-burned candles
and an oil lamp. Behind the table, an irregular piece of mirror
hangs on the wall. A loose something that looks to be a gaudy
ball costume dangles from a near-by hook. To the front, a second

table holds a lamp and several whiskey glasses. Six rickety chairs are near this table. Two old wagon wheels rest on the floor. To the left, sitting in a high-backed chair which stands upon a low platform, the old man. He is like a bust in black walnut. Gray-bearded. Gray-haired. Prophetic. Immobile. Lewis' eyes are sunk in him. The others, unconcerned, are about to pass on to the front table when Lewis grips Halsey and so turns him that the candle flame shines obliquely on the old man's features.

Lewis: And he rules over—

Kabnis: Th smoke an fire of th forge.

Lewis: Black Vulcan? I wouldnt say so. That forehead. Great woolly beard. Those eyes. A mute John the Baptist of a new religion —or a tongue-tied shadow of an old.

Kabnis: His tongue is tied all right, an I can vouch f that.

Lewis: Has he never talked to you?

Halsey: Kabnis wont give him a chance.

He laughs. The girls laugh. Kabnis winces.

Lewis: What do you call him?

Halsey: Father.

Lewis: Good. Father what?

Kabnis: Father of hell.

Halsey: Father's th only name we have fer him. Come on. Lets sit down an get t th pleasure of the evenin.

Lewis: Father John it is from now on . . .

Slave boy whom some Christian mistress taught to read the Bible. Black man who saw Jesus in the ricefields, and began preaching to his people. Moses- and Christ-words used for songs. Dead blind father of a muted folk who feel their way upward to a life that crushes or absorbs them. (Speak, Father!) Suppose your eyes could see, old man. (The years hold hands. O Sing!) Suppose your lips . . .

Halsey, does he never talk?

Halsey: Na. But sometimes. Only seldom. Mumbles. Sis says he talks—

Kabnis: I've heard him talk.

Halsey: First I've ever heard of it. You dont give him a chance. Sis says she's made out several words, mostly one—an like as not cause it was "sin."

Cora laughs in a loose sort of way. She is a tall, thin, mulatto woman. Her eyes are deep-set behind a pointed nose. Her hair is coarse and bushy. Seeing that Stella also is restless, she takes her arm and the two women move towards the table. They slip into chairs. Halsey follows and lights the lamp. He lays out a pack of cards. Stella sorts them as if telling fortunes. She is a beautifully proportioned, large-eyed, brown-skin girl. Except for the twisted line of her mouth when she smiles or laughs, there is about her no suggestion of the life she's been through. Kabnis, with great mock-solemnity, goes to the corner, takes down the robe, and dons it. He is a curious spectacle, acting a part, yet very real. He joins the others at the table. They are used to him. Lewis is surprised. He laughs. Kabnis shrinks and then glares at him with a furtive hatred. Halsey, bringing out a bottle of corn licker, pours drinks.

Halsey: Come on, Lewis. Come on, you fellers. Heres lookin at y.

Then, as if suddenly recalling something, he jerks away from the table and starts towards the steps.

Kabnis: Where y goin, Halsey?

Halsey: Where? Where y think? That oak beam in th wagon—

Kabnis: Come ere. Come ere. Sit down. What in hell's wrong with you fellers? You with your wagon. Lewis with his Father John. This aint th time fer foolin with wagons. Daytime's bad enough f that. Ere, sit down. Ere, Lewis, you too sit down. Have a drink. Thats right. Drink corn licker, love th girls, an listen t th old man mumblin sin.

There seems to be no good-time spirit to the party. Something in the air is too tense and deep for that. Lewis, seated now so that his eyes rest upon the old man, merges with his source and lets the pain and beauty of the South meet him there. White faces, pain-pollen, settle downward through a cane-sweet mist and touch the ovaries of yellow flowers. Cotton-bolls bloom, droop. Black roots twist in a parched red soil beneath a blazing sky. Magnolias, fragrant, a trifle futile, lovely, far off . . . His eyelids close. A force begins to heave and rise . . . Stella is serious, reminiscent.

Stella: Usall is brought up t hate sin worse than death—

Kabnis: An then before you have y eyes half open, youre made t love it if y want t live.

Stella: Us never—

Kabnis: Oh, I know your story: that old prim bastard over yonder, an then old Calvert's office—

Stella: It wasnt them—

Kabnis: I know. They put y out of church, an then I guess th preacher came around an asked f some. But thats your body. Now me—

Halsey (passing him the bottle): All right, kid, we believe y. Here, take another. Wheres Clover, Stel?

Stella: You know how Jim is when he's just out th swamp. Done up in shine an wouldnt let her come. Said he'd bust her head open if she went out.

Kabnis: Dont see why he doesnt stay over with Laura, where he belongs.

Stella: Ask him, an I reckon he'll tell y. More than you want.

Halsey: Th nigger hates th sight of a black woman worse than death. Sorry t mix y up this way, Lewis. But y see how tis.

Lewis' skin is tight and glowing over the fine bones of his face. His lips tremble. His nostrils quiver. The others notice this and smile knowingly at each other. Drinks and smokes are passed around. They pay no neverminds to him. A real party is being worked up. Then Lewis opens his eyes and looks at them. Their smiles disperse in hot-cold tremors. Kabnis chokes his laugh. It sputters, gurgles. His eyes flicker and turn away. He tries to pass the thing off by taking a long drink which he makes considerable fuss over. He is drawn back to Lewis. Seeing Lewis' gaze still upon him, he scowls.

Kabnis: Whatsha lookin at me for? Y want t know who I am? Well, I'm Ralph Kabnis—lot of good its goin t do y. Well? Whatsha keep lookin for? I'm Ralph Kabnis. Aint that enough f y? Want th whole family history? Its none of your godam business, anyway. Keep off me. Do y hear? Keep off me. Look at Cora. Aint she pretty enough t look at? Look at Halsey, or Stella. Clover ought t be here an you could look at her. An love her. Thats what you need. I know—

Lewis: Ralph Kabnis gets satisfied that way?

Kabnis: Satisfied? Say, quit your kiddin. Here, look at that old man there. See him? He's satisfied. Do I look like him? When I'm dead I dont expect t be satisfied. Is that enough f y, with your godam nosin, or do you want more? Well, y wont get it, understand?

Lewis: The old man as symbol, flesh, and spirit of the past, what do you think he would say if he could see you? You look at him, Kabnis.

Kabnis: Just like any done-up preacher is what he looks t me. Jam some false teeth in his mouth and crank him, an youd have God Almighty spit in torrents all around th floor. Oh, hell, an he reminds me of that black cockroach over yonder. An besides, he aint my past. My ancestors were Southern blue-bloods—

Lewis: And black.

Kabnis: Aint much difference between blue an black.

Lewis: Enough to draw a denial from you. Cant hold them, can you? Master; slave. Soil; and the overarching heavens. Dusk; dawn. They fight and bastardize you. The sun tint of your cheeks, flame of the great season's multi-colored leaves, tarnished, burned. Split, shredded: easily burned. No use . . .

His gaze shifts to Stella. Stella's face draws back, her breasts come towards him.

Stella: I aint got nothin f y, mister. Taint no use t look at me.

Halsey: Youre a queer feller, Lewis, I swear y are. Told y so, didnt I, girls? Just take him easy though, an he'll be ridin just th same as any Georgia mule, eh, Lewis? (Laughs.)

Stella: I'm goin t tell y somethin, mister. It aint t you, t th Mister Lewis what noses about. Its t somethin different, I dunno what. That old man there—maybe its him—is like m father used t look. He used t sing. An when he could sing no mo, they'd allus come f him an carry him t church an there he'd sit, befo th pulpit, aswayin an aleadin every song. A white man took m mother an it broke th old man's heart. He died; an then I didnt care what become of me, an I dont now. I dont care now. Dont get it in y head I'm some sentimental Susie askin for yo sop. Nassur. But theres somethin t yo th others aint got. Boars an kids an fools—thats all I've known. Boars when their fever's up. When their fever's up they come t me. Halsey asks me over when he's off th job. Kabnis—it ud be a sin t play with him. He takes it out in talk.

Halsey knows that he has trifled with her. At odd things he has been inwardly penitent before her tasking him. But now he wants to hurt her. He turns to Lewis.

Halsey: Lewis, I got a little licker in me, an thats true. True's what I said. True. But th stuff just seems t wake me up an make my mind a man of me. Listen. You know a lot, queer as hell as y are, an I want t ask y some questions. Theyre too high fer them, Stella an Cora an Kabnis, so we'll just excuse em. A chat between ourselves. (Turns to the others.) You-all cant listen in on this. Twont interest y. So just leave th table t this gen'lemun an myself. Go long now.

Kabnis gets up, pompous in his robe, grotesquely so, and makes as if to go through a grand march with Stella. She shoves him off, roughly, and in a mood swings her body to the steps. Kabnis grabs Cora and parades around, passing the old man, to whom he bows in mock-curtsy. He sweeps by the table, snatches the licker bottle, and then he and Cora sprawl on the mattresses. She meets his weak approaches after the manner she thinks Stella would use.

Halsey contemptuously watches them until he is sure that they are settled.

Halsey: This aint th sort o thing f me, Lewis, when I got work upstairs. Nassur. You an me has got things t do. Wastin time on common low-down women—say, Lewis, look at her now— Stella—aint she a picture? Common wench—na she aint, Lewis. You know she aint. I'm only tryin t fool y. I used t love that girl. Yassur. An sometimes when th moon is thick an I hear dogs up th valley barkin an some old woman fetches out her song, an th winds seem like th Lord made them fer t fetch an carry th smell o pine an cane, an there aint no big job on foot, I sometimes get t thinkin that I still do. But I want t talk t y, Lewis, queer as y are. Y know, Lewis, I went t school once. Ya. In Augusta. But it wasnt a regular school. Na. It was a pussy Sunday-school masqueradin under a regular name. Some goody-goody teachers from th North had come down t teach th niggers. If you was nearly white, they liked y. If you was black, they didnt. But it wasnt that—I was all right, y see. I couldnt stand em messin an pawin over m business like I was a child. So I cussed em out an left. Kabnis there ought t have cussed out th old duck over yonder an left. He'd a been a better man tday. But as I was sayin, I couldnt stand their ways. So I left an came here an worked with my father. An been here ever since. He died. I set in f myself. An its always been; give me a good job an sure pay an I aint far from being satisfied, so far as satisfaction goes. Prejudice is everywheres about this country. An a nigger aint in much standin anywheres. But when it comes t pottin round in doin nothin, with nothin bigger'n an ax-handle t hold a feller down, like it was a while back befo I got this job— that beam ought t be—but tmorrow mornin early's time enough f that. As I was sayin, I gets t thinkin. Play dumb naturally t white folks. I gets t thinkin. I used to subscribe t th *Literary Digest* an that helped along a bit. But there werent nothing I could sink m teeth int. Theres lots I want t ask y, Lewis. Been askin y t come around. Couldnt get y. Cant get in much tnight. (He glances at the others. His mind fastens on Kabnis.) Say, tell me this, whats on your mind t say on that feller there? Kabnis' name. One queer bird ought t know another, seems like t me.

Licker has released conflicts in Kabnis and set them flowing. He pricks his ears, intuitively feels that the talk is about him, leaves Cora, and approaches the table. His eyes are watery, heavy with passion. He stoops. He is a ridiculous pathetic figure in his showy robe.

Kabnis: Talkin bout me. I know. I'm th topic of conversation everywhere theres talk about this town. Girls an fellers. White folks as well. An if its me youre talkin bout, guess I got a right t listen in. Whats sayin? Whats sayin bout his royal guts, the Duke? Whats sayin, eh?

Halsey (to Lewis): We'll take it up another time.

Kabnis: No nother time bout it. Now. I'm here now an talkin's just begun. I was born an bred in a family of orators, thats what I was.

Halsey: Preachers.

Kabnis: Na. Preachers hell. I didnt say wind-busters. Y misapprehended me. Y understand what that means, dont y? All right then, y misapprehended me. I didnt say preachers. I said orators. O R A T O R S. Born one an I'll die one. You understand me, Lewis. (He turns to Halsey and begins shaking his finger in his face.) An as f you, youre all right f choppin things from blocks of wood. I was good at that th day I ducked th cradle. An since then, I've been shapin words after a design that branded here. Know whats here? M soul. Ever heard o that? Th hell y have. Been shapin words t fit m soul. Never told y that before, did I? Thought I couldnt talk. I'll tell y. I've been shapin words; ah, but sometimes theyre beautiful an golden an have a taste that makes them fine t roll over with y tongue. Your tongue aint fit f nothin but t roll an lick hog-meat.

Stella and Cora come up to the table.

Halsey: Give him a shove there, will y, Stel?

Stella jams Kabnis in a chair. Kabnis springs up.

Kabnis: Cant keep a good man down. Those words I was tellin y about, they wont fit int th mold thats branded on m soul. Rhyme, y see? Poet, too. Bad rhyme. Bad poet. Somethin else youve learned tnight. Lewis dont know it all, an I'm atellin y. Ugh. Th form thats burned int my soul is some twisted awful thing that crept in from a dream, a godam nightmare, an wont stay still unless I feed it. An it lives on words. Not beautiful words. God Almighty no. Misshapen, split-gut, tortured, twisted words. Layman was feedin it back there that day you thought I ran out fearin things. White folks feed it cause their looks are words. Niggers, black niggers feed it cause theyre evil an their looks are words. Yallar niggers feed it. This whole damn bloated purple country feeds it cause its goin down t hell in a holy avalanche of words. I want t feed th soul—I know what that is; th preachers dont—but I've got t feed it. I wish t God some lynchin white man ud stick his knife through it an pin it to a tree. An pin it to a tree. You hear me? Thats a wish f y, you little snot-nosed pups who've been makin fun of me, an fakin that I'm weak. Me, Ralph Kabnis weak. Ha.

Halsey: Thats right, old man. There, there. Here, so much exertion merits a fittin reward. Help him t be seated, Cora.

Halsey gives him a swig of shine. Cora glides up, seats him, and then plumps herself down on his lap, squeezing his head into her breasts. Kabnis mutters. Tries to break loose. Curses. Cora almost stifles him. He goes limp and gives up. Cora toys with him. Ruffles his hair. Braids it. Parts it in the middle. Stella smiles contemptuously. And then a sudden anger sweeps her. She would like to lash Cora from the place. She'd like to take Kabnis to some distant pine grove and nurse and mother him. Her eyes flash. A quick tensioning throws her breasts and neck into a poised strain. She starts towards them. Halsey grabs her arm and pulls her to him. She struggles. Halsey pins her arms and kisses her. She settles, spurting like a pine-knot afire.

Lewis finds himself completely cut out. The glowing within him subsides. It is followed by a dead chill. Kabnis, Carrie, Stella, Halsey, Cora, the old man, the cellar, and the work-shop, the southern town descend upon him. Their pain is too intense. He cannot stand it. He bolts from the table. Leaps up the stairs. Plunges through the work-shop and out into the night.

6

The cellar swims in a pale phosphorescence. The table, the chairs, the figure of the old man are amœba-like shadows which move about and float in it. In the corner under the steps, close to the floor, a solid blackness. A sound comes from it. A forcible yawn. Part of the blackness detaches itself so that it may be seen against the grayness of the wall. It moves forward and then seems to be clothing itself in odd dangling bits of shadow. The voice of Halsey, vibrant and deepened, calls.

Halsey: Kabnis. Cora. Stella.

He gets no response. He wants to get them up, to get on the job. He is intolerant of their sleepiness.

Halsey: Kabnis! Stella! Cora!

Gutturals, jerky and impeded, tell that he is shaking them.

Halsey: Come now, up with you.

Kabnis (sleepily and still more or less intoxicated): Whats th big idea? What in hell—

Halsey: Work. But never you mind about that. Up with you.

Cora: Oooooo! Look here, mister, I aint used t bein thrown int th street befo day.

Stella: Any bunk whats worked is worth in wages moren this. But come on. Taint no use t arger.

Kabnis: I'll arger. Its preposterous—

The girls interrupt him with none too pleasant laughs.

Kabnis: Thats what I said. Know what it means, dont y? All right, then. I said its preposterous t root an artist out o bed at this ungodly hour, when there aint no use t it. You can start your damned old work. Nobody's stoppin y. But what we got t get up for? Fraid somebody'll see th girls leavin? Some sport, you are. I hand it t y.

Halsey: Up you get, all th same.

Kabnis: Oh, th hell you say.

Halsey: Well, son, seeing that I'm th kindhearted father, I'll give y chance t open your eyes. But up y get when I come down.

He mounts the steps to the work-shop and starts a fire in the hearth. In the yard he finds some chunks of coal which he brings in and throws on the fire. He puts a kettle on to boil. The wagon draws him. He lifts an oak-beam, fingers it, and becomes abstracted. Then comes to himself and places the beam upon the work-bench. He looks over some newly cut wooden spokes. He goes to the fire and pokes it. The coals are red-hot. With a pair of long prongs he picks them up and places them in a thick iron bucket. This he carries downstairs. Outside, darkness has given way to the impalpable grayness of dawn. This early morning light, seeping through the four barred cellar windows, is the color of the stony walls. It seems to be an emanation from them. Halsey's coals throw out a rich warm glow. He sets them on the floor, a safe distance from the beds.

Halsey: No foolin now. Come. Up with you.

Other than a soft rustling, there is no sound as the girls slip into their clothes. Kabnis still lies in bed.

Stella (to Halsey): Reckon y could spare us a light?

Halsey strikes a match, lights a cigarette, and then bends over and touches flame to the two candles on the table between the beds. Kabnis asks for a cigarette. Halsey hands him his and takes a fresh one for himself. The girls, before the mirror, are doing up their hair. It is bushy hair that has gone through some straightening process. Character, however, has not all been ironed out. As they kneel there, heavy-eyed and dusky, and throwing grotesque moving shadows on the wall, they are two princesses in Africa going through the early-morning ablutions of their pagan prayers. Finished, they come forward to stretch their hands and warm them over the glowing coals. Red dusk of a Georgia sunset, their heavy, coal-lit faces . . . Kabnis suddenly recalls something.

Kabnis: Th old man talked last night.

Stella: And so did you.

Halsey: In your dreams.

Kabnis: I tell y, he did. I know what I'm talkin about. I'll tell y what he said. Wait now, lemme see.

Halsey: Look out, brother, th old man'll be getting int you by way o dreams. Come, Stel, ready? Cora? Coffee an eggs f both of you.

Halsey goes upstairs.

Stella: Gettin generous, aint he?

She blows the candles out. Says nothing to Kabnis. Then she and Cora follow after Halsey. Kabnis, left to himself, tries to rise. He has slept in his robe. His robe trips him. Finally, he manages to stand up. He starts across the floor. Half-way to the old man, he falls and lies quite still. Perhaps an hour passes. Light of a new sun is about to filter through the windows. Kabnis slowly rises to support upon his elbows. He looks hard, and internally gathers himself together. The side face of Father John is in the direct line of his eyes. He scowls at him. No one is around. Words gush from Kabnis.

Kabnis: You sit there like a black hound spiked to an ivory pedestal. An all night long I heard you murmurin that devilish word. They thought I didnt hear y, but I did. Mumblin, feedin that ornery thing thats livin on my insides. Father John. Father of Satan, more likely. What does it mean t you? Youre dead already. Death. What does it mean t you? To you who died way back there in th 'sixties. What are y throwin it in my throat for? Whats it goin t get y? A good smashin in th mouth, thats what. My fist'll sink int y black mush face clear t y guts—if y got any. Dont believe y have. Never seen signs of none. Death. Death. Sin an Death. All night long y mumbled death. (He forgets the old man as his mind begins to play with the word and its associations.) Death . . . these clammy floors . . . just like th place they used t stow away th worn-out, no-count niggers in th days of slavery . . . that was long ago; not so long ago . . . no windows (he rises higher on his elbows to verify this assertion. He looks around, and, seeing no one but the old man, calls.) Halsey! Halsey! Gone an left me. Just like a nigger. I thought he was a nigger all th time. Now I know it. Ditch y when it comes right down t it. Damn him anyway. Godam him. (He looks and re-sees the old man.) Eh, you? T hell with you too. What do I care whether you can see or hear? You know what hell is cause youve been there. Its a feelin an its ragin in my soul in a way that'll pop out of me an run you through, an scorch y, an burn an rip your soul. Your soul. Ha. Nigger soul. A gin soul that gets drunk on a preacher's words. An screams. An shouts. God Almighty, how I hate that shoutin. Where's th beauty in that? Gives a buzzard a windpipe an I'll bet a dollar t a dime th buzzard ud beat y to it. Aint surprisin th white folks hate y so. When you had eyes, did you ever see th beauty of th world? Tell me that. Th hell y did. Now dont tell me. I know y didnt. You couldnt have. Oh, I'm drunk an just as good as dead, but no eyes that have seen beauty ever lose their sight. You aint got no sight. If you had, drunk as I am, I hope Christ will kill me if I couldnt see it. Your eyes are dull and watery, like fish eyes. Fish eyes are dead eyes. Youre an old man, a dead fish man, an black at that. Theyve put y here t die, damn fool y are not t know it. Do y know how many feet youre under ground? I'll tell y. Twenty. An do y think you'll ever see th light of day again, even if you wasnt blind? Do y think youre out of slavery? Huh? Youre where they used t throw th worked-out, no-count slaves. On a damp clammy floor of a dark scum-hole. An they called that an infirmary. Th sons-a. . . . Why I can already see you toppled off that stool an stretched out on th floor beside me—not beside me, damn you, by yourself, with th flies buzzin an lickin God knows what they'd find on a dirty, black, foul-breathed mouth like yours . . .

Some one is coming down the stairs. Carrie, bringing food for the old man. She is lovely in her fresh energy of the morning, in the calm untested confidence and nascent maternity which rise from the purpose of her present mission. She walks to within a few paces of Kabnis.

Carrie K.: Brother says come up now, brother Ralph.

Kabnis: Brother doesnt know what he's talkin bout.

Carrie K.: Yes he does, Ralph. He needs you on th wagon.

Kabnis: He wants me on th wagon, eh? Does he think some wooden thing can lift me up? Ask him that.

Carrie K.: He told me t help y.

Kabnis: An how would you help me, child, dear sweet little sister?

She moves forward as if to aid him.

Carrie K.: I'm not a child, as I've more than once told you, brother Ralph, an as I'll show you now.

Kabnis: Wait, Carrie. No, thats right. Youre not a child. But twont do t lift me bodily. You dont understand. But its th soul of me that needs th risin.

Carrie K.: Youre a bad brother an just wont listen t me when I'm tellin y t go t church.

Kabnis doesnt hear her. He breaks down and talks to himself.

Kabnis: Great God Almighty, a soul like mine cant pin itself onto a wagon wheel an satisfy itself in spinnin round. Iron prongs an hickory sticks, an God knows what all . . . all right for Halsey . . . use him. Me? I get my life down in this scum-hole. Th old man an me——

Carrie K.: Has he been talkin?

Kabnis: Huh? Who? Him? No. Dont need to. I talk. An when I really talk, it pays th best of them t listen. Th old man is a good listener. He's deaf; but he's a good listener. An I can talk t him. Tell him anything.

Carrie K.: He's deaf an blind, but I reckon he hears, an sees too, from th things I've heard.

Kabnis: No. Cant. Cant I tell you. How's he do it?

Carrie K.: Dunno, except I've heard that th souls of old folks have a way of seein things.

Kabnis: An I've heard them call that superstition.

The old man begins to shake his head slowly. Carrie and Kabnis watch him, anxiously. He mumbles. With a grave motion his head nods up and down. And then, on one of the down-swings——

Father John (remarkably clear and with great conviction): Sin.

He repeats this word several times, always on the downward nodding. Surprised, indignant, Kabnis forgets that Carrie is with him.

Kabnis: Sin! Shut up. What do you know about sin, you old black bastard. Shut up, an stop that swayin an noddin your head.

Father John: Sin.

Kabnis tries to get up.

Kabnis: Didnt I tell y t shut up?

Carrie steps forward to help him. Kabnis is violently shocked at her touch. He springs back.

Kabnis: Carrie! What . . . how . . . Baby, you shouldnt be down here. Ralph says things. Doesnt mean to. But Carrie, he doesnt know what he's talkin about. Couldnt know. It was only a preacher's sin they knew in those old days, an that wasnt sin at all. Mind me, th only sin is whats done against th soul. Th whole world is a conspiracy t sin, especially in America, an against me. I'm th victim of their sin. I'm what sin is. Does he look like me? Have you ever heard him say th things youve heard me say? He couldnt if he had th Holy Ghost t help him. Dont look shocked, little sweetheart, you hurt me.

Father John: Sin.

Kabnis: Aw, shut up, old man.

Carrie K.: Leave him be. He wants t say somethin. (She turns to the old man.) What is it, Father?

Kabnis: Whatsha talkin t that old deaf man for? Come away from him.

Carrie K.: What is it, Father?

The old man's lips begin to work. Words are formed incoherently. Finally, he manages to articulate—

Father John: Th sin whats fixed . . . (Hesitates.)

Carrie K. (restraining a comment from Kabnis): Go on, Father.

Father John: . . . upon th white folks—

Kabnis: Suppose youre talkin about that bastard race thats roamin round th country. It looks like sin, if thats what y mean. Give us somethin new an up t date.

Father John:—f tellin Jesus—lies. O th sin th white folks 'mitted when they made th Bible lie.

Boom. Boom. BOOM! Thuds on the floor above. The old man sinks back into his stony silence. Carrie is wet-eyed. Kabnis, contemptuous.

Kabnis: So thats your sin. All these years t tell us that th white folks made th Bible lie. Well, I'll be damned. Lewis ought t have been here. You old black fakir—

rie K.: Brother Ralph, is that your best Amen?

___ turns him to her and takes his hot cheeks in her firm cool hands. Her palms draw the fever out. With its passing, Kabnis crumples. He sinks to his knees before her, ashamed, exhausted. His eyes squeeze tight. Carrie presses his face tenderly against her. The suffocation of her fresh starched dress feels good to him. Carrie is about to lift her hands in prayer, when Halsey, at the head of the stairs, calls down.

Halsey: Well, well. Whats up? Aint you ever comin? Come on. Whats up down there? Take you all mornin t sleep off a pint? Youre weakenin, man, youre weakenin. Th axle an th beam's all ready waitin f y. Come on.

Kabnis rises and is going doggedly towards the steps. Carrie notices his robe. She catches up to him, points to it, and helps him take it off. He hangs it, with an exaggerated ceremony, on its nail in the corner. He looks down on the tousled beds. His lips curl bitterly. Turning, he stumbles over the bucket of dead coals. He savagely jerks it from the floor. And then, seeing Carrie's eyes upon him, he swings the pail carelessly and with eyes downcast and swollen, trudges upstairs to the work-shop. Carrie's gaze follows him till he is gone. Then she goes to the old man and slips to her knees before him. Her lips murmur, "Jesus, come."

Light streaks through the iron-barred cellar window. Within its soft circle, the figures of Carrie and Father John.

Outside, the sun arises from its cradle in the tree-tops of the forest. Shadows of pines are dreams the sun shakes from its eyes. The sun arises. Gold-glowing child, it steps into the sky and sends a birth-song slanting down gray dust streets and sleepy windows of the southern town.

THE END

AFTERWORD

"Song of the Son":
The Emergence and Passing of Jean Toomer

by Rudolph P. Byrd and Henry Louis Gates, Jr.

In memoriam

*To Charles T. Davis, beloved teacher, mentor, and pioneering scholar
in African American Studies who set the highest standards for us and
who generously prepared a way for us in the academy.*

and

*To Ingrid Saunders Jones, teacher, bibliophile, race woman, and leader
in global commerce who nurtures and actualizes the dreams of so many.*

Toomer

I did not wish to "rise above"
or "move beyond" my race. I wished

to contemplate who I was beyond
my body, this container of flesh.

I made up a language in which to exist.
I wondered what God breathed into me.

I wondered who I was beyond
this complicated, milk-skinned, genital-ed body.

I exercised it, watched it change and grow.
I spun like a dervish to see what would happen. Oh,

to be a Negro is—is?—
to be a Negro, is. To be.

(Jean Toomer)

—*Elizabeth Alexander*

"THE SETTING WAS crude in a way," Jean Toomer would recall of the rural Georgia landscape that inspired him to write *Cane*, "but strangely rich and beautiful. I began feeling its effects despite my state, or, perhaps, just because of it. There was a valley, the valley of 'Cane,' with smoke-wreaths during the day and mist at night." And in that valley, Toomer encountered, perhaps for the first time, the spirituals, the traditional music of the African American sacred vernacular: "A family of back-country Negroes had only recently moved into a shack not too far away. They sang. And this was the first time I'd ever heard the folk-songs and spirituals. They were very rich and sad and joyous and beautiful."[1] In this lyrical remembrance of things all-too-soon to pass, Toomer suggests something of the beauty and poignancy of a landscape, a people, and an art form in transition in the first quarter of the twentieth century, a moment he would render in a loving yet searching experimental form, in the single work that would define his career and his legacy as a writer. *Cane*, a compelling, haunting amalgam of fiction, poetry, and drama unified formally and thematically and replete with leitmotifs, would elevate Toomer, virtually overnight, to the status of a canonical writer in two branches of American modernism: the writers and critics who

---

1. Jean Toomer, "The Cane Years," in *The Wayward and The Seeking: A Collection of Writings by Jean Toomer*, ed. Darwin T. Turner (Washington, D.C.: Howard University Press, 1980), 123.

compose the New Critics and the "Lost Generation," and those who compose the New Negro movement or the Harlem Renaissance. Toomer was an important, admired, influential figure in both of these articulations of high American modernism, which reached their zenith in the 1920s and which unfolded downtown and uptown, respectively, in New York City.

The man who would startle his small but enthusiastic readership with the originality of *Cane* entered the cultural world of the Lost Generation downtown in Greenwich Village primarily through his close friend, the writer and critic, Waldo Frank. Uptown, simultaneously, Toomer was emerging as one of the New Negro writers of the Harlem Renaissance, chiefly through the stewardship of its erstwhile "dean," Alain Locke, who edited the movement's signature manifesto, *The New Negro,* in 1925. In the two or three years preceding the publication of *Cane* in 1923, Toomer—perhaps more than any other black writer—moved seemingly effortlessly between these two cultural worlds. Both movements were shaped by their own vibrant and defiant theories of language, art, culture, and history, some of which they shared, some of which they did not. But both, in their ways, challenged, to an unprecedented degree, conventional American definitions of race and social strictures defined by the so-called color line. In so very many ways, these two movements were mutually constitutive, Janus faces of a larger, unfolding concept of American modernism, although they have been frequently and mistakenly cast as discrete, isolated formations in American literature and culture.[2]

---

2. Perhaps the earliest scholar to query Toomer's relationship to the writers of the "Lost Generation" and the New Negro movement or Harlem Renaissance was Robert A. Bone in *The Negro Novel in America* (1958). Since then Toomer's relationship to the communities of writers who collectively constitute the various forms of American modernism has been examined by Rudolph P. Byrd, Charles T. Davis, Ann Douglas, Richard Eldridge, Genevieve Fabre, Maria Farland, Michel Feith, Alice P. Fisher, Karen S. Ford, S. P. Fullwinder, Henry Louis

Jean Toomer, circa 1932. Jean Toomer Papers, Yale Collection of American Literature, Beinecke and Rare Book Manuscript Library.

Gates, Jr., Jane Goldman, Nathan Grant, Leonard Harris, Mark Helbling, George Hutchinson, Robert B. Jones, Cynthia R. Kerman, Catherine G. Kodat, Victor Kramer, Vera Kutzinski, Charles R. Larson, Nellie Y. McKay, Charles Molesworth, Arnold Rampersad, Frederick L. Rusch, Mark A. Sanders, Charles Scruggs, Robert B. Stepto, Alan Trachtenberg, Darwin T. Turner, Mark Whalan, and Jon Woodson, among other scholars.

Raised as an African American but, to most observers, racially indeterminate, Toomer embodied in his person, in his disposition, and in his art many of the signal elements—hybridity, alienation, fragmentation, dislocation, migration, fluidity, experimentation—that define American modernism, and that he would so imaginatively address in *Cane*. Throughout his life, Toomer displayed a marked ambivalence toward his Negro ancestry, addressing it—or erasing it—again and again in his posthumously published autobiographical writings. The relation of this deep and abiding ambivalence to the various forms of fragmentation that wind their way through *Cane* has intrigued critics virtually since *Cane* was published in 1923. Indeed, one could say that the great theme of *Cane* is fragmentation itself, rendered through close and careful encounters between blacks and blacks, and blacks and whites, in an almost mythic, transitional, pre-Jazz Age, Jim Crow rural South. Toomer tells us that the impact of the southern agrarian setting upon his northern, urbane sensibility was dramatic, referring to the psychological and emotional "state" created by his first encounters with southern black culture in the town of Sparta, Georgia. Put another way, Toomer is describing the particular structures of feeling and thought generated when he encountered a region of the country that fundamentally shaped his parents and grandparents, a region about which he would grow increasingly ambivalent almost as soon as, if not before, he published *Cane*.

Jean Toomer was born Nathan Pinchback Toomer on December 26, 1894, in Washington, D.C., the first and only child of Nina Pinchback and Nathan Toomer, both African Americans. Toomer's name at birth was the source of some controversy in a family that, from the start, seems to have been totally devoted to him. This controversy is, in its way, emblematic of what would become

Toomer's own preoccupation with naming and self-definition, with determining what to call himself and how to define himself ethnically, and with exercising control over his public image in a society that favored the shorthand of labels, especially when defining a person's color or race.

Toomer's middle name, Pinchback, linked him directly to his grandfather, Pinckney Benton Stewart Pinchback (1837–1921), the husband of Nina Emily Hethorn, with whom he had four children. P. B. S. Pinchback (as he was known) was the son of Major William Pinchback, a white Virginia planter, and Eliza Stewart, a mulatto slave, and the brother of an undetermined number of siblings, some of whom disappeared into the white world. Born a free Negro in Macon, Georgia, in 1837, Pinchback was a captain in the second regiment of Louisiana's Native Guard, the black soldiers in the white army who fought on the side of the Union during the Civil War, from October 1862 to September 1863. As the only "cullid officer" at Fort Pike, he served as the spokesman for his fellow black officers who were unrelenting in their protest of the discrimination experienced by the black enlisted men under their command in the Union Army.[3] Pinchback would become, during Reconstruction, the first black lieutenant governor of Louisiana. For thirty-five days in December 1872 to January 1873, he even served as the Acting Governor.[4] Pinchback's "brief tenure as acting governor was the political high-water mark for Louisiana blacks during the nineteenth century."[5] A colorful and imperial

3. James G. Hollandsworth, Jr., *The Louisiana Native Guards: The Black Military Experience During the Civil War* (Baton Rouge: Louisiana State University Press, 1995), 73.

4. Ibid., 111.

5. Ibid., 111. As a lawmaker, Pinchback sponsored civil rights legislation that granted blacks equal access in public transportation, business, and places of entertainment. He also introduced legislation in Louisiana's 1879 constitutional convention that would establish a "university for the education of persons of color." This legislation would lead to the establishment of Southern University in 1880. From 1883 to 1885, Pinchback served on the board of trustees of Southern University. See pp. 108 and 115 in Hollandsworth's *The Louisiana Native Guards.*

figure who was sometimes mistaken for Andrew Carnegie, Pinchback derived his wealth from lucrative investments and political
appointments, and derived his influence and standing within the
deeply stratified society of Washington, D.C., to which he moved
after his political career ended in Louisiana, from his historic
achievements in office, and his light-skin privilege, often a visible
marker of class.

The grandson would recount with some pride the grandfather's improbable, dramatic rise to power in the corrupting,
byzantine, and multicultural world of the Pelican State, specu-
lating that his motives for becoming a public servant were perhaps not entirely altruistic, even suggesting, incredulously, that
Pinchback may have been a white man who only passed for black
to facilitate his chances of being elected in Reconstruction Louisiana: "Then, the war ended and the black men freed and enfran-
chised, came Pinchback's opportunity in the political arena. He
claimed he had Negro blood, linked himself with the cause of
the Negro, and rose to power. How much he was an opportunist, how much he was in sincere sympathy with the freedmen,
is a matter which need not concern us here . . . it would be
interesting if we knew what Pinchback himself believed about
his racial heredity. Did he believe he had some Negro blood?
Did he not? I do not know. What I do know is this—his belief or
disbelief would have had no necessary relation to the facts—and
this holds true as regards his Scotch-Welsh-German and other
bloods also."[6]

Nowhere, to our knowledge, was Pinchback ever ambivalent
about being a Negro, even if, as W. E. B. Du Bois once wrote
of him, to "all intents and purposes . . . [he] was an educated

6. *The Wayward and the Seeking*, 23–24.

well-to-do congenial white man with but a few drops of Negro blood," as fair as, say, the novelist Charles W. Chesnutt or the civil rights leader Walter White.[7] In fact, elsewhere in his writings, when discussing why he attended an all-black elementary school, Henry Highland Garnet, in Washington, Toomer contradicts himself about Pinchback's racial identity: "For Pinckney Benston Stewart Pinchback to send his grandson to a white school, no, that will not do. It might look as if he were going back on his race and wanting me to be white."[8] Toomer is being disingenuous here, however; schools in Washington, D.C., were rigorously segregated; Pinchback would have had no choice, even if, as does not appear to be the case, he had sought to educate his grandson across the color line. Clearly the issue of his grandfather's ethnic ancestry was a vexed one for Toomer, one crucial for him to position and reposition as he sought to redefine his own racial identity.

And a large part of his strategy of strongly implying that his grandfather most probably was "passing for black" was rooted in Toomer's desire to paint the roots of this branch of his family tree white; to do so, he had to stress that Pinchback was the political opportunist par excellence: "I say he [Pinchback] was an adventurer. I think he was. I doubt that he saw himself bearing a mission to secure and maintain the rights of the freedmen."[9] His grandfather, moreover, Toomer reasoned, saw in the Louisiana of Reconstruction a certain fluidity of identity that allowed for an unprecedented amount of social mobility: "More than anything else Pinchback saw himself as a winner

7. Barbara Foley, "Jean Toomer's Washington and the Politics of Class: From 'Blue Veins' to Seventh-street Rebels," *Modern Fiction Studies* 42.2 (1996): 298.

8. Ibid., 313.

9. *The Wayward and the Seeking,* 24.

of a dangerous game. He liked to play the game. He liked to win. This—the reconstruction situation in Louisiana—was the chance his personal ambition had been waiting for. He was not a reformer. He was not primarily a fighter for a general human cause. He was, or was soon to become, a politician—but far more picturesque, courageous, and able than the majority of the men who bear that name."[10] If his grandfather had been a white man who passed for black, perhaps his grandson could be a black man who could pass for white.

Despite Toomer's highly dubious claim about his grandfather's racial identity, his assessment of his grandfather's career in politics is all the more compelling for being critical and unsentimental. Clearly, P. B. S. Pinchback was a man who inspired a great degree of awe, in Toomer and in just about everyone else: "For myself— I was fascinated by him. His goings and comings were the big events in the house . . . No one could speak to me and make me laugh and get me excited the way he could. He made me feel I was having a part in everything he did. Sometimes he would take me downtown with him and I might even have lunch with 'the men,' who made much to-do over me, giving me the feeling that I was the scion of a great family."[11] "This was my grandfather as I knew him," Toomer writes with fond admiration. "I saw him as a dashing commanding figure, the centre of an unknown but exciting world. He created an atmosphere which thrilled me; and there is no doubt that his image, and the picture and sense of his life, were deeply impressed upon me, later to function as an unconscious ideal for myself, for how I wished to look and be; and also to serve as standards by means of which I measured men and life."[12]

10. Ibid., 25.
11. Ibid., 35–36.
12. Ibid., 30.

Toomer's loving portrait of his grandfather as a bold and quest-
ing Victorian patriarch, however, is complicated by the fact that
as he grew into adulthood, he was often at war with Pinchback,
who grew increasingly bewildered and disappointed by his scion's
seeming lack of purpose and direction. "Not till I was seven could
I rule my mother and grandmother," Toomer tells us; but "Not
till I was twenty-seven did I finally conquer my grandfather."[13]
While his relationship with Pinchback would become increasingly
fraught, Toomer, nevertheless, dutifully and lovingly cared for his
grandfather in the final weeks of his life, immediately following
his pivotal sojourn in Georgia. "Once again in Washington I had
my grandfather brought back from the hospital. His condition
there was too pitiable for me to bear. He touched my heart so
strongly that I resolved to care for him till the very end. And this I
did."[14] Precisely as Pinchback's health declined, Toomer found his
voice as an artist: "He sank very rapidly. All during December I
nursed him; and, at the same time, I wrote the materials of *Cane*.
In these last days he seemed to know just what I meant to him. I
knew and realized all he had done for me."[15]

In the small apartment he also shared with his resilient, long-
suffering grandmother, Toomer and Pinchback reconciled in the
days before his death, precisely as he was completing the powerful, final, haunting section of his first book: "Our almost life-long
struggle and contest was finished, and all my love and gratitude
for the once so forceful and dominant but now so broken and
tragic man came to the fore. He died the day after I had finished
the first draft of 'Kabnis,' the long semi-dramatic closing-piece

13. Ibid., 17.
14. Ibid., 124.
15. Ibid., 124.

of *Cane*."[16] Toomer would write to Waldo Frank that "Kabnis is *Me*," one of his last admissions of his awareness of the primacy of his own Negro ancestry in the shaping of his cultural and ethnic identity. But it is altogether reasonable to speculate that the powerful, quasi-mythic encounter at *Kabnis*'s conclusion—between the northern, mulatto would-be intellectual and old, black Father John, the haunting figure of the slave past—was informed by this final, intense encounter and reconciliation between Toomer and Pinchback himself.

Toomer's Christian name and surname tie him to his father, Nathan Toomer. Born in 1839 in Chatham County, North Carolina, Nathan was the slave of Richard Pilkinson, who subsequently sold him to John Toomer.[17] When John Toomer died in 1859, his brother Henry Toomer purchased Nathan, his mother, Kit, and seven of her children from the estate. Nathan became the body servant of Henry Toomer, and adopted the surname of the family who had purchased him and most of his family. In the 1860s, Nathan Toomer married Harriet, a mulatta with whom he had four daughters. After Harriet's death in 1890, Toomer married Amanda America Dickson, regarded as "the richest colored woman alive."[18] Dickson, born in 1849, was the daughter of David Dickson, a prosperous planter of Hancock County, Georgia, and Julia Frances Lewis Dickson, a mulatta. Amanda was reared in the Dickson household by Elizabeth Dickson, her paternal grandmother. When David Dickson died in 1885 he left much of his estate, valued at approximately $400,000, including 15,000 acres of land, to Amanda America Dickson. Nathan

---

16. Ibid., 124.

17. Kent Anderson Leslie and Willard B. Gatewood, Jr., " 'This Father of Mine . . . a Sort of Mystery': Jean Toomer's Georgia Heritage," *The Georgia Historical Quarterly* LXXVII. 4 (Winter 1993): 793.

18. Ibid., 790.

Toomer and Amanda Dickson married on August 7, 1891, and
took up residence in her well-appointed mansion located on Tel-
fair Street among the wealthy white elite in Augusta, Georgia.
Almost two years later, on June 11, 1893, Amanda would die,
from "complications of disease."[19] Since Amanda left no will,
Nathan found himself in a protracted court battle over the
disposition of the estate with his two stepchildren, Julian and
Charles, whom Amanda bore in her first marriage to Charles
Eubanks, a white Civil War veteran. Adhering to the terms of
David Dickson's will, the court awarded the bulk of Amanda's
estate to her children.[20]

Nathan Toomer was a handsome widower in search of new
sources of income as well as a third wife. Both of these needs
were met in the person of Nina Pinchback, whom he met in
December 1893. They met at her Bacon Street home during a
"housewarming reception" hosted by her parents.[21] Soon after,
Nathan began courting Nina. Three months later on March 24,
1894, they were married by none other than the Reverend Francis J. Grimké, the nephew of the South Carolina abolitionists
and suffragettes Angelina Weld and Sarah Moore Grimké, a
graduate of Lincoln, Howard, and Princeton universities, co-
founder of the American Negro Academy, and the very able and
famous pastor of Washington's 15th Street Presbyterian Church.
Grimké was a celebrity himself, as grand and as well known as
Pinchback.

Pinchback objected to the marriage volcanically, disapproving
of Nathan Toomer for several reasons. First of all, Nathan was
twenty-seven years older than Nina (Pinchback himself was only

19. Ibid., 798.
20. Ibid., 794.
21. Ibid., 789.

two years older than his son-in-law). Second, he had been previously married. Third, Nathan impressed Pinchback as being
"unreliable,"[22] perhaps because Nathan engendered a certain dis-
turbing sense of self-recognition of his own adventurous past and
temperament. But the Governor was accurate, indeed, prophetic
in his identification of this defect in his future son-in-law's character. Nathan deserted Nina within a year of their marriage. Nevertheless, their only child refused to cast the failed union in a
disreputable light: "I have been told and have reason to believe
it was a love marriage. This was the one clear affirmation of her
[Nina's] life."[23] Without an income, she was unable to support herself in the home located on Twelfth Street, which her husband had
irresponsibly purchased with $12,000 in cash for his bride and
infant son. Converting the bridal nest into rental property, Nina
was forced to return, most reluctantly, to the Bacon Street home
of her parents.

Predictably, the Governor "set conditions for readmitting his
wayward daughter and her infant son. The biggest stumbling
block was the boy's name."[24] Intent upon nothing short of patro-
nymic erasure of the errant Nathan Toomer, Pinchback insisted
that "if he was to support the baby," the surname had to be "legally
changed to Pinchback and the first name changed to anything
else."[25] According to Cynthia Earl Kerman and Richard Eldridge,
"Nina rejected that proposed legal action but accepted the family's
informal adaptation. The first name was soon replaced by Eugene,
after Eugene Laval, [Toomer's] godfather . . ."[26] Throughout his

---

22. *The Lives of Jean Toomer: A Hunger for Wholeness* (Baton Rouge: Louisiana State University Press, 1987), 26.

23. *The Wayward and the Seeking*, 33.

24. *The Lives of Jean Toomer*, 28.

25. Ibid., 28.

26. Ibid., 28.

Jean Toomer as a young boy. Undated. Jean Toomer Papers, Yale Collection of American Literature, Beinecke and Rare Book Manuscript Library.

life, Toomer's grandparents addressed him as Eugene Pinchback, while his mother stubbornly addressed him as Eugene Toomer, though she herself had reverted to her family name, Pinchback. Toomer's playmates on Bacon Street, he writes, called him "Pinchy—short for Pinchback. To them I was a Pinchback. They knew nothing of Toomer."[27] "In my own home there were still other names," he confides. "Mother called me Booty [after beauty]. Uncle Bis called me Kid. Uncle Walter—Snootz. And grandfather—the little whippersnapper. I was, then, well-supplied."[28]

When he made the commitment to become a writer, Toomer gave himself the androgynous name of Jean, which stemmed from his admiration of Romain Rolland's novel *Jean-Christophe*.[29] During the 1930s and the 1940s, Toomer published under the name of N. J. Toomer, initials for Nathan Jean, for two reasons: first, to distance himself from *Cane* and the racial identity of its author, since *Cane* was the work by which he had come to be known as a Negro writer; and second, to mark a rebirth in his life, following his conversion to Quakerism, a rebirth that marked a certain return. By taking the name Nathan Jean, Toomer himself had come full circle, finally rendering futile his family's efforts to banish the memory of his father, Nathan.

The memory of the father kindled the imagination of the son. For years, Toomer kept a photograph of his father, from which he constructed a rather fanciful portrait of Nathan as a "handsome stirring," wealthy planter from Georgia.[30] And Toomer, in the drafts of an autobiography that he never published, wistfully re-creates the first and only meeting between the two. It

---

27. Ibid., 35.
28. Ibid., 35.
29. Ibid., 101.
30. For Toomer's portrait of his father Nathan Toomer see *The Wayward and the Seeking*, 32–33.

is clear that through this anecdote, Toomer sought to recuperate his father from grandfather Pinchback's relentless traducing. Nathan Toomer returned to Washington in 1900, six years after Toomer's birth, and during this visit, according to Jean, he materialized before the Bacon Street house, presumably to see his son. Because he refused to pay alimony of $60 per month and the court costs of his divorce from Nina, the Supreme Court of the District of Columbia on January 20, 1899, declared Nathan in contempt. Nathan's return to Washington, accordingly, carried with it considerable risk; he could have been arrested and jailed.

One afternoon while playing in his front yard, Toomer tells us that he found himself in the arms of a stranger he intuitively recognized as his father: "I do not know how I knew him. But, soon, I was running up the way a bit towards a large man who was holding out his arms to me. He took me in them, raised me and kissed me, and I liked him very much. He said things to me which I didn't understand, but I knew he was my father and that he was showing how much he loved me and what a fine little man I had grown to be. He raised me high in the air, and then he saw mother come out. He lowered me, pressed a bright silver half-dollar in my hand, kissed me again, and told me to run back to her. He went off."[31] It was their first and only meeting, and it is clear that Toomer carefully nurtured this memory of his father, which uncannily recalls the first encounter between the mixed-race protagonist and his white father in James Weldon Johnson's novel, *The Autobiography of an Ex-Coloured Man* (1912), a novel about passing, itself "passing" as autobiography.[32]

31. *The Wayward and the Seeking*, 34.
32. See *Jean Toomer's Racial Self-Identification*, lxvi.

Though he knew nothing of his father's marriage to Amanda America Dickson, over time Toomer's memory of his father acquired a certain luster through his inheritance of artifacts that once belonged to him: "The only worldly possessions that came to me from him were some beautiful large silk handkerchiefs, a set of small diamond shirt studs, and a slender ebony cane with a gold head."[33] While Nathan Toomer never saw his son again, in correspondence between the elder Toomer and an acquaintance, Whitefield McKinlay, of Washington, D.C., between 1898 and 1905, there is evidence of his father's continued, genuine interest in a son whom he called in his letters to McKinlay the "Little Colonel."[34] Some years later, in the very Sparta, Georgia, that inspired *Cane,* the "Little Colonel" would encounter someone who had actually known his father—a barber who claimed to have some knowledge of Nathan Toomer. According to Kerman and Eldridge, Toomer asked the barber "whether his father had been regarded by the community as white or 'colored,'" and the barber "replied that Nathan stayed at the white hotel, did business with white men, and courted a black woman."[35] Like his grandfather and his father, Jean Toomer would live in both the black and the white worlds over the course of his life, and in both worlds the act of naming and self-definition would remain an obsession with him. There is new evidence that, like the nameless protagonist of James Weldon Johnson's novel, Toomer did in fact pass for white, as many of his black literary contemporaries assumed or believed he did.

Toomer's uncle, Bismarck Pinchback, also played a profoundly important role in his development. Bismarck was the second of

---

33. *The Lives of Jean Toomer,* 27.

34. "'This Father of Mine . . . a Sort of Mystery': Jean Toomer's Georgia Heritage," 802–809.

35. *The Lives of Jean Toomer,* 85.

his grandfather's three sons, along with Pinckney and Walter. It was Uncle Bis who introduced the "Kid," as he called him, to the world of literature, science, and the life of the mind, gradually inculcating in him a desire to become a writer. Toomer lovingly acknowledged Bismarck's role in his larger education, recalling how his relationship with his uncle transformed itself into that of master and apprentice: "Then something happened which swiftly transferred my interests from the world of things to the world of ideas and imagination. Uncle Bis and I suddenly discovered each other. He had been there all along, and his sensitivity and affection had drawn me to him. . . . All at once the veils of familiarity dropped from our eyes and each in his own way beheld the wonder of the other."[36]

Bismarck Pinchback, a civil servant, was an avid reader and possessed some literary ambitions of his own. According to Toomer, his uncle was his Virgil, his first nurturing guide to the far shores of the imagination. Toomer vividly recounts his uncle's evening ritual of reading and writing in bed: "There he would get in bed with a book, cigarettes, and a saucer of sliced peaches prepared with sugar in a special way, and read far into the night. Sometimes he would write, trying his hand at fiction. . . . This position—my uncle in bed surrounded by the materials of a literary man—was impressed upon me as one of the desirable positions in life."[37] Bismarck was the father figure that neither Nathan nor his grandfather could ever be, and to him Toomer gives all the credit for the life of thought and feeling that he would pursue: "By nature he was far more the artist and thinker than a man of action; and, as far as possible, he evoked

36. *The Wayward and the Seeking*, 41–42.
37. Ibid., 42.

the thinker in me."[38] Bismarck Toomer would be the last black man whom Toomer would acknowledge as a shaping influence on the man of letters he would become.

Bismarck introduced Toomer not only to literature but also to physics and to astronomy, especially the earth's relation to other planets in the universe. "It was all wonderful," Toomer so fondly remembers. "And, young though I was, I was growing a sense of and forming an attitude towards my and our position on earth and in the universe. I had a new way of seeing things. This was the beginning of my world view. And for this alone I will be forever grateful to my uncle for having taken such interest in me." Bismarck would read historical works to his nephew, as well as "myths and fables, folk tales, romances and adventures. Often he would phrase the tale in his own words and himself tell it. He liked to do this. . . . For myself—I eagerly absorbed them. My imagination took flight and I was thrilled to follow it into those worlds of wonder."[39] Bismarck's gas-light tutorials in the Bacon Street house constituted Toomer's first meaningful introduction to the wonders of learning. At a time when he perhaps most needed it, Uncle Bismarck functioned as both teacher and mentor to his nephew, and thus provided him with a means by which to apprehend his potential as an intellectual, and more especially as thinker and writer: "He was, in truth, my real teacher. In comparison with him and with what I learned from him, my formal teachers and schooling were as nothing. . . . I truly learned with and from Bismarck. . . . Our evenings together were periods of genuine education. . . . My mind was born and nurtured during those times with him."[40]

38. Ibid., 42.
39. Ibid., 44.
40. Ibid., 45, 48.

As we have seen, Toomer attended the all-black Henry Highland Garnet School (named in honor of the pioneering nineteenth-century black nationalist) for his elementary education, and then the famous Paul Laurence Dunbar High School, previously known as M Street High School, the District's first public high school for African Americans, named after the famous black poet, from which he graduated in 1914. Dunbar High School was more like a black private school, an Exeter or Andover for African Americans, than a normal public school. Its teachers and students, incredibly, included several members of the Negro intellectual elite, the group that W. E. B. Du Bois would call "the talented tenth," the "college-bred Negro." Among its stellar alumni were the poet Sterling A. Brown, the feminist Nannie Helen Burroughs, the physician Charles R. Drew, and the lawyer and civil rights advocate Charles Hamilton Houston. (Both Brown and Houston would take advanced degrees from Harvard.) Dunbar High School's distinguished faculty included many Ph.D.'s, such as the sociologist Kelly Miller and the Harvard-trained historian, Carter G. Woodson, along with the woman's rights activist Mary Church Terrell, poet Angelina Weld Grimké (the niece of Reverend Francis J. Grimké, who had married Toomer's parents), and Anna Julia Cooper, Toomer's Latin teacher, the first African American to earn a Ph.D. at the Sorbonne. Scholars who should have been professors in the Ivy League found their best job opportunities at this public high school.

Despite these extraordinarily well-trained teachers, however, Toomer's education at school was apparently not nearly as fulfilling as those evenings spent with his beloved Uncle Bismarck, when he was the center of attention and Bismarck's mesmerizing pedagogical methods opened his nephew's mind to facts and mysteries at a pace that suited him best. Toomer found in Bismarck a badly needed father figure, of course; but he also had learning difficulties that even a school as sophisticated as Dunbar would have been ill-prepared to meet: "I had difficulty in learning to read. For some reason or other, try as hard as I would I couldn't get on the inside of the thing: the letters and characters obstinately withheld their sense from me, and the lines of words behind which meaning lurked were like closed doors which stubbornly refused me entrance. I gazed with hopeless amazement at the older children, the teacher, the grownup members of my family who read so easily and seemed to think nothing of it."[41] Whether Toomer was dyslexic or merely a slow reader it is difficult to know, but in due course he overcame this frustration with deciphering the written word: "In time, however, reading had become just an ordinary thing which I was compelled to continue. I found but little to attract me in the various school readers. Some of the stories I liked, but they were not half as wonderful as those told me by Bismarck, and moreover, whatever pleasure or interest they may have had for me was spoiled when they were put through the mill of classroom recitations."[42]

Toomer, like many people with learning disabilities embarrassed by their inability to learn at a pace with other students, created diversions in school: "I was the class-room cut up," he recalls, "and the teacher's problem."[43] Kerman and Eldridge speculate that Toomer's disruptive classroom behavior may have had its roots in his resentment at being separated from his white friends on Bacon Street and the shock of attending a black

41. Ibid., 45.
42. Ibid., 46.
43. Ibid., 45.

school: "Surely resentment at being arbitrarily shut out of his group, as well as the inevitable lack of resources at a black school in Washington at the height of the Jim Crow era, would have affected what was offered to him and how Jean would accept it."[44] Though highly unlikely, as we shall see, these factors could possibly explain why the "little whippersnapper," as his grandfather called him, was uncomfortable at the Garnet School, and necessarily at odds with its pedagogy: "I resented and resisted it. I had an almost constant feeling that I was being maltreated."[45] Nonetheless, as something of a self-consciously privileged child—a child with an almost mythic grandfather and an absent father whom he would seek to transform into a myth—living in a community in which light skin color could signify upper-class status, Toomer was able to use his class status to his advantage in the classroom: "At the same time, I had a lot of fun in school. Some of this fun was natural to the gay spirit of childhood. Some sprang from an instinctive resistance to authority. . . . I felt somewhat privileged and immune owing to grandfather's position and influence . . ."[46]

Toomer's matriculation at Garnet Elementary School and Dunbar High School afforded him the opportunity to acquire a very special education in what James Weldon Johnson, describing his years at Atlanta University (both the preparatory school and the university), termed the "arcana of race."[47] For Johnson, who would later correspond with Toomer regarding the possibility of the inclusion of some of his poems in a revised edition of his *The Book of American Negro Poetry* (1922, 1931), "the initiation into the

44. *The Lives of Jean Toomer*, 36.
45. *The Wayward and the Seeking*, 47.
46. Ibid., 47.
47. James Weldon Johnson, *Along This Way* (New York: Penguin Books, 1933; 1990), 66.

arcana of race" meant "preparation to meet the tasks and exigen-
cies of life as a Negro, a realization of the peculiar responsibilities
due to my own racial group, and a comprehension of the applica-
tion of American democracy to Negro citizens."[48] Toomer's initiation into the arcana of race would mean something quite different
altogether. As he claims in his autobiography, he "formed and formulated" his racial position in the summer of 1914 just before he
left Washington to matriculate at the University of Wisconsin.[49]
He took this important step toward self-definition because he was
keenly aware of his hybrid racial background, the racial ambiguity
of his physical appearance, the questions and stares it elicited, the
fact that he had lived in both the white and black worlds, and that
he could, if he chose, continue to do so, or even choose one over
the other.

When Toomer attended the Garnet School, he was living in
the home of his grandparents, which was located on Bacon Street
in a neighborhood that at the time was composed of wealthy
whites. During these years between 1894 and 1906, Toomer's
neighbors and playmates were white, but his classmates at Garnet School were all black. In 1906, Toomer's mother, Nina
Pinchback, remarried and moved to New York with her son and
second husband, Archibald Combes, a traveling salesman for the
Metropolitan Life Insurance Company. During this second and
relatively brief marriage, Toomer lived and attended schools for
three years in the white neighborhoods in Brooklyn and also in

---

48. Ibid., 66.

49. Darwin Turner, *The Wayward and the Seeking* (Washington, D.C.: Howard University Press, 1980), 91.
Toomer "formed and formulated" his racial position in the summer of 1914. This racial position is set forth in
"Outline of an Autobiography," which Toomer wrote, according to Darwin Turner, between 1931 and 1932.
Toomer claims that as a student at the University of Wisconsin that he "had no use" for his racial position because
the "question [of race] was never raised." He contradicts himself here for in a later section of his autobiography
he recounts the experience of having to contend with the campus rumor that he was a "Hindu" and an "Indian,"
as well as the racism of a white male classmate. See pp. 95–96 of *The Wayward and the Seeking.*

New Rochelle. After his mother's tragic, apparently avoidable death by appendicitis in the summer of 1909, Toomer returned to Washington, D.C.

Here, he lived with his Uncle Bismarck and his family on Florida Avenue in a black neighborhood. A year later in 1910 he enrolled at Dunbar High School. Now, for the second time in his life, Toomer found himself attending school in what he described as "the colored world."[50] But in fact, all of Toomer's primary and secondary education, except for the three years in New York, took place in "the colored world," under black teachers, surrounded by all-black classmates, in an all-black cultural environment. For Toomer, however, "the initiation into the arcana of race" did not mean preparation for "life as a Negro" and leadership among the race as it would be for Johnson and other members of Du Bois's talented tenth. Rather, Toomer would have us believe that this initiation would be a means of acquiring an understanding of social relations and the operations of power as a member of what he termed "an aristocracy—such as never existed before and perhaps never will exist again in America—midway between the white and Negro worlds."[51]

But Toomer and his family did not live "midway" between these two worlds; rather, they lived, to a greater or lesser degree, as light-skinned black people who, for a time, managed to defy the color line and live in white residential neighborhoods. The Pinchbacks were undoubtedly aristocrats within the black world, but more likely were visitors or voyeurs or interlopers within the white world. The fact that Toomer attended the Garnet School even when his family lived in a white neighborhood

50. *The Wayward and the Seeking*, 84.
51. Ibid., 84.

underscores how rigid racial boundaries, in fact, were in Washington. By no stretch of the imagination, despite Toomer's claims to the contrary, did this class of Negroes enjoy equal status with their white class peers, especially in racially stratified Washington, D.C., at the beginning of the twentieth century. Toomer, clearly, is asserting this claim—just as he had done about his grandfather passing as a Negro—to lay the autobiographical and sociological groundwork for his self-fashioning as a pioneering member of a new elite, an upper class of mixed-race individuals who would be points of mediation between white Americans and black Americans.

From 1909 to 1914, Toomer once again was a member of Washington's fabled colored aristocracy, a world he would analyze and critique to great effect. Toomer is at pains to assure us that the transition into this world involved no hardship for him: "It was not difficult to do so. I accepted this as readily as I had accepted living in Brooklyn and New Rochelle."[52] Writing in an elegiac mode, Toomer reconstructs the character of the world he entered when he took up residence with his Uncle Bismarck after returning from New York, along the way arguing implausibly that this class of Negroes just "happened" arbitrarily to be defined as Negroes, as if the history of their families' racial identification and the history of their participation in Negro culture had had no relevance on the shaping of their identities: "In the Washington of those days—and those days have gone now—there was a flowering of a natural but transient aristocracy, thrown up by the, for them, creative conditions of the post-war period. These people, whose racial strains were mixed and for the most part unknown, happened to find themselves in the colored group.

---

52. Ibid., 84.

They had a personal refinement, a certain inward culture and beauty, a warmth of feeling such as I have seldom encountered elsewhere and again. . . . All were comfortably fixed financially, and they had a social life that satisfied them. . . . The children of these families became my friends."[53]

Because of the similarities in class, the transition from the white world into the colored world was, Toomer is arguing, a seamless one, in spite of the fact that, he would have us believe, he had effectively been "white" in New York and now was "black" in Washington. It is important to emphasize that Toomer is postulating an almost mythic class and racial formation, a "people, whose racial strains were mixed and for the most part unknown, and who happened to find themselves in the colored group," who have, alas, disappeared ("those days are gone now"). He writes here of a racially and culturally distinct group *within* the "colored group," "an aristocracy . . . midway between the white and Negro worlds,"[54] which enjoyed considerable economic privilege, a class of which he and his family were always a part. Toomer's depiction of this class-within-a-class, as it were, a point of mediation between black and white, is another component in his rhetorical strategy of declaring racial independence as a member of the vanguard of a raceless *tertium quid*.

In Washington, Toomer most certainly lived among the Negro elite, but it was disingenuous of him to suggest that its members were racially or culturally indeterminate; they were legally defined as Negroes, whether they liked it or not. And this would have been especially the case at the turn of the century following the *Plessy v. Ferguson* Supreme Court ruling of 1896, which

53. Ibid., 85.
54. Ibid., 84.

declared "separate but equal" as the law of the land, the ruling itself a desperate attempt to police the boundaries that interracial sexual liaisons had hopelessly blurred. Toomer never tells us, if we but pause to think about it, why his family, living effortlessly as "white" in New York, found itself sending its child to an all-black school in Washington. Surely, no white family would have done that out of choice. But Toomer does this to establish the experiential justification for his subsequent decision to define himself as an "American."

Toomer assures us that he identified implicitly with this new way of life, and certainly his earlier life on Bacon Street had prepared him for it: "They were my kind, as much as children of my early Washington years had been."[55] Toomer emphasizes their social, racial, and cultural uniqueness: "These youths had their round of activity, parties, interests—and were self-sufficient. In their world they were not called colored by each other. They seldom or never came in contact with members of the white group in any way that would make them racially self-conscious."[56] Occupying this liminal world of a mulatto elite, Toomer is arguing, it is not difficult to understand how he could define himself as "neither white nor black."[57]

And yet it is also difficult to understand how Toomer could even suggest that within this period of American racial history that any white American at the time would label him as anything other than black. Anticipating the curiosity, confusion, and misunderstanding that his body, speech, and appearance would engender, and no doubt seeking to escape the boundaries imposed upon persons of African descent, Toomer tells us he formed his

55. Ibid., 85.
56. Ibid., 86.
57. Ibid., 93.

own "racial position" before leaving what he would have us believe was a "special" race world of Washington, D.C., to attend college in 1914. If so, he became one of the earliest proponents of the theory that "race" was socially constructed, even if his motives for doing so were quite mixed. Moreover, he would spend the rest of his life, following the publication of *Cane*, socially constructing his racial indeterminacy, and simultaneously deconstructing his Negro ancestry.

"By hearsay," writes Toomer, echoing W. E. B. Du Bois's famous description, in *The Souls of Black Folk,* of his own ancestry, "there were in my heredity the following strains: Scotch, Welsh, German, English, French, Dutch, Spanish, with some dark blood. [Let us] assume the dark blood was Negro—or let's be generous and assume that it was both Negro and Indian. I personally can readily assume this because I cannot feel with certain of my countrymen that all of the others are all right but that Negro is not. Blood is blood. . . . My body is my body, with an already given and definite racial composition."[58] After identifying the various racial "strains" in his ethnic heredity, Toomer raises the vital question of genetic ancestry, of race: "Of what race am I? To this question there can be but one true answer—I am of the human race. . . ." Rejecting the one-drop rule (one drop of Negro blood doth forever a Negro make) as well as the reigning preoccupation with racial purity that governed conceptions of race in the United States at the beginning of the twentieth century, Toomer claimed a social identity that would inevitably place him at odds with the American mainstream and, in retrospect, make him a pioneering theorist of hybridity, perhaps the first in the African American tradition. Nevertheless,

58. Ibid., 92.

he remained indifferent to the consequences of this position, and quite determined to maintain and justify it, returning to the subject seemingly endlessly in his autobiographical writings. Adopting an unorthodox, progressive, and certainly idealistic position on race that would be the source of some suffering even now in the twenty-first century, he defined himself as an "American, neither black nor white, rejecting these divisions, accepting all people as people."[59]

Toomer's "racial position" anticipates by *eleven* years a complementary theory of race conceptualized by the Mexican writer and political leader Jose Vasconcelos in *La raza cosmica* (*The Cosmic Race*), published in 1925. In this treatise, Vasconcelos defines the Mexican people as a new race composed of *all* the races of the world. The central claim of *La raza cosmica* is that "the various races of the earth tend to intermix at a gradually increasing pace, and eventually will give rise to a new human type, composed of selections from each of the races already in existence."[60] According to Vasconcelos, the "new human type" or alternately "the fifth universal race," the "synthetic race," "the definitive race," or the "cosmic race" has its origins in the pre-Mayan legendary civilization of Atlantis.[61]

In prose that is marked by a mixture of philosophy, poetry, and mysticism, Vasconcelos asserts that this new cosmic race will be "made up of the genius and the blood of all peoples and, for that reason, more capable of true brotherhood and of a truly universal vision."[62] It will emerge from the continent of South America,

59. Ibid., 93.

60. Jose Vasconcelos, *The Cosmic Race: A Bilingual Edition* (Baltimore: The Johns Hopkins University Press, 1997), 3.

61. Ibid., for Vasconcelos the terms "the fifth race," "synthetic race," "definitive race," and "cosmic race" are fungible. *The Cosmic Race* 3, 7, 9, 18–19, 40.

62. Ibid., 20.

thus fulfilling, according to Vasconcelos, the historic destiny of Latin American people or the "Hispanic race" to bring the races of the world to an advanced state of spiritual development.[63] Based in the "Amazon region," Vasconcelos calls the capital of this new empire of the spirit "Universopolis," which will rise on the banks of the Amazon River.[64] One of the "fundamental dogmas of the fifth race" is love as it is expressed within the framework of Christianity which, according to Vasconcelos, "frees and engenders life, because it contains universal, not national, revelation."[65] Writing as an idealist and a visionary, Vasconcelos argues that we "have all the races and all the aptitudes. The only thing lacking is for true love to organize and set in march the law of History."[66] Love, then, is the expanding floor upon which will rise "a new race fashioned out of the treasures of all the previous ones: The final race, the cosmic race."[67]

While there is no concrete evidence that Toomer was familiar with the writings of Vasconcelos, there are many affinities between their respective views on race.[68] But it is quite possible that Toomer knew Vasconcelos's work, given its wide popularity and given Toomer's sojourns in New Mexico. Toomer and Vasconcelos emerge as prophets of a new order in which the mixed-race person is a pivotal figure, a metaphor or harbinger of a hybrid culture and a fusion of many ethnic and genetic strands. The claims of both are based upon an appeal to the universal, the posi-

63. Ibid., 38.
64. Ibid., 35.
65. Ibid., 35.
66. Ibid., 39.
67. Ibid., 40.

68. In her article " 'A Small Man in Big Spaces': The New Negro, the Mestizo, and Jean Toomer's Southwestern Writing," Emily Lutenski asserts "there is no clear evidence that Toomer used Vasconcelos as a source when studying the Southwest. Regardless, there are clear parallels between Toomer's and Vasconcelos' writings." *MELUS* 33. 1 (Spring 2008) See this volume, p. 417.

tive values associated with hybridity and thus a rejection of racial purity, and the belief that racial mixture or *mestizaje* possesses the potential to unify humankind. For Toomer and Vasconcelos, the mixed-race person or the mulatto emerges as a symbol of "cosmic" possibility, and the spiritual resolution of all human conflict rather than as a symbol of human conflict and degeneracy. Gilberto Freye would develop a related theory of "racial democracy" as a hallmark of Brazilian culture in his classic work, *Casa-Grande e Senzaca,*[69] published in 1933. Ferdinand Ortiz would elaborate a similar theory for Cuban culture a few years later in his book, Contrapunteo cubano del tabaco y el azúcar, published in 1940.[70] Vasconcelos's theory (either directly, or through Toomer) influenced Zora Neale Hurston as well. In "How It Feels to Be Colored Me," Hurston writes, "At certain times, I am no race, I am *me.* . . . The cosmic Zora emerges."[71]

Toomer arrived at his definition of his own race when most Americans implicitly accepted a "scientific" or biological definition of race, and believed that the world was composed of several distinct racial groups, each with its own history, each with its own place in a racial hierarchy, each with its own special contribution to make to world civilization. W. E. B. Du Bois's essay, "The Conservation of Races" (1896), theorizes race as a biological or natural concept, but rejects a racial hierarchy, assigning to the Negro a positive value and function among the world's races: "We are that people whose subtle sense of song has given America its only American music, its only American fairy tales, its only touch of pathos and humor amid its mad money-

---

69. This was translated as *The Masters and the Slaves* in 1946.

70. This was translated as *Cuban Counterpoint? Tobacco and Sugar* in 1947.

71. Zora Neale Hurston, "How It Feels to Be Colored Me," in *I love myself when I am laughing . . . and then again when I am looking mean and impressive: A Zora Neale Hurston Reader*, edited by Alice Walker, with an introduction by Mary Helen Washington (Old Westbury, NY: Feminist Press, 1979), 154.

getting plutocracy."[72] He would later dismiss "The Conservation of Races" as an instance of "youthful effusion."[73] In *Dusk of Dawn* (1940), Du Bois revisited the question of race, abandoning the biological or scientific concept of race: "Perhaps it is wrong to speak of it at all as 'a concept' rather than as a group of contradictory forces, facts and tendencies."[74] In this final definition, Du Bois theorized race as a social construct. In doing so, he prepared the ground for a subsequent generation of scholars— Kwame Anthony Appiah, Jacqueline Nassy Brown, Henry Louis Gates, Jr., Paul Gilroy, Stuart Hall, Patricia Williams—who would build upon Du Bois's insight, and theorize race as a social construction or floating signifier. In Du Bois's writing, we witness the evolution of race from a biological concept to a discursive concept. But unlike Toomer, Du Bois heartily embraced a Negro social and cultural identity, never using its constructed nature as an excuse to "transcend" it; rather to de-biologize or de-essentialize it.

Toomer observed that "it is even more difficult to determine the nature of a man; so most of us are even more content to have a label for him."[75] In an era when the views of such white supremacists as Lothrop Stoddard and Earnest Cox were in the ascendancy and referenced even in such fictional works as F. Scott Fitzgerald's *The Great Gatsby,* Toomer proclaimed that in "my body were many bloods, some dark blood, all blended in the fire of six or more generations. I was, then, either a new type of man or the very oldest. In any case I was inescapably myself. . . .

72. W. E. B. Du Bois, "The Conservation of Races," in *W. E. B. Du Bois: Writings*, ed. Nathan Huggins (New York: Library of America, 1986), 822.

73. David Levering Lewis, *W. E. B. Du Bois: Biography of a Race* (New York: Henry Holt & Company, 1993), 174.

74. *W. E. B. Du Bois: Writings*, 651.

75. *The Wayward and the Seeking*, 91.

As for myself, I would live my life as far as possible on the basis of what was true for me."[76] While Toomer's metaphor of "bloods" recalls a biological conception of race, the direction of his thinking is toward a discursive concept of race. Toomer developed the following plan for its use in the protean, contested world of social relations: "To my real friends of both groups, I would, at the right time, voluntarily define my position. As for people at large, naturally I would go my way and say nothing unless the question was raised. If raised, I would meet it squarely, going into as much detail as seemed desirable for the occasion. Or again, if it was not the person's business I would either tell him nothing or the first nonsense that came into my head."[77] It would be left to him, not to others, to define and to determine his location in the social world, or so he imagined. Toomer would soon come to realize the limitations of his own power to shape the manner in which he would be perceived and defined by others, notwithstanding the appeal of his person and personality, and his great confidence in his ability to explain and to rationalize himself.

After graduating from Dunbar High School in January 1914, Toomer matriculated at six colleges and universities between 1914 and 1918, but failed to earn a degree. He attended the University of Wisconsin at Madison, and the Massachusetts College of Agriculture to pursue his interests in scientific agriculture. No longer interested in becoming a farmer, he pursued his new passion for exercise and bodybuilding at the American College of Physical Training in Chicago in January 1916. Toomer remained in Chicago through the fall and enrolled in courses that introduced him to atheism and socialism at the University of Chicago. In the spring

76. Ibid., 93.
77. Ibid., 93.

of 1917 he decided to travel to New York, and there enrolled in summer school at New York University and the City College of New York where, respectively, he took a course in sociology and history. "Opposed to war but attracted to soldiering," wrote Kerman and Eldridge, Toomer volunteered for the army, but he was "classified as physically unfit 'because of bad eyes and a hernia gotten in a basketball game.' "[78] As we reveal in "Jean Toomer's Racial Self-Identification," Toomer registered as a Negro.

In 1918, Toomer returned to the Midwest, where he held a series of odd jobs, including becoming a car salesman at a Ford dealership in Chicago. During this second period in Chicago, he wrote "Bona and Paul," his first short story, in which he explored questions of passing and mixed-race identity, a powerful work that would eventually find its way into the second section of *Cane*. In February 1918, Toomer accepted an appointment in Milwaukee as a substitute physical education director, and continued his readings in literature, especially the works of George Bernard Shaw.[79]

Returning briefly to Washington, D.C., Toomer set out again for New York where he worked as a clerk with the grocery firm Acker, Merrall, and Condit Company. While in New York, his reading expanded to include Ibsen, Santayana, and Goethe; he attended meetings of radicals and the literati at the Rand School, as well as lectures by Alfred Kreymborg, who, a decade later, would describe Toomer as "one of the finest artists among the dark race, if not the finest."[80] In the spring of 1919, he left Manhattan to vacation in the resort town of Ellenville, New York. Indigent though somewhat rested, he then returned to Washing-

78. *The Lives of Jean Toomer*, 69.
79. Ibid., 69.
80. Alfred Kreymborg, *Our Singing Strength* (New York: Coward-McCann, 1929), 575.

*College photograph of Jean Toomer, bare-chested with arms folded, 1916.
Jean Toomer Papers, Yale Collection of American Literature, Beinecke and
Rare Book Manuscript Library.*

Group portrait with Toomer at center (four men in front blindfolded), from the Lunkentus Class of 1917 yearbook (American College of Physical Education). Jean Toomer Papers, Yale Collection of American Literature, Beinecke and Rare Book Manuscript Library.

ton in the fall, where he was confronted by the condemnations of his grandfather who was far from pleased with his grandson's vagabond existence.

Unable to endure any longer the aging but vigorous Governor's harangues on personal responsibility, in December 1919, his twenty-fifth birthday only days away, Toomer was on the road again. With only ten dollars to his name, he walked from Washington, D.C., to Baltimore. Winter had arrived, and as Toomer recalled, it was "cold as the mischief."[81] After an overnight stay in Baltimore, he then walked to Wilmington, Delaware, and from there hitchhiked to Rahway, New Jersey, where he worked for a time as a fitter in the New Jersey shipyards for $22 per week.[82] This practical experience with the working class disabused him of his romantic notions about socialism. Toomer's destination was New York, and when he arrived there he once again took a job at Acker, Merrall and Condit. As he made his way from Washington to New York on Walt Whitman's open road, as it were, Toomer was alone; his only company was the ambitious, yet unrealized desire to become a writer.

In 1920, Pinchback sold the Washington home that Nathan Toomer had purchased as a wedding present for Nina Pinchback. In spite of his disappointment with his grandson, Pinchback sent Toomer $600, the small profit derived from the sale of the rental property after the payment of the mortgage and taxes. With this windfall, Toomer decided to remain in New York to continue what turned out to be the beginning of his apprenticeship as a writer: "I decided that I was at one of the turning points of my life, and that I needed all my time, and that the money would be well spent. I

81. *The Wayward and the Seeking*, 111.
82. *The Lives of Jean Toomer*, 71.

quit Acker Merrall. I devoted myself to music and literature."[83] And then, through yet another unexpected turn of events, he once again gained entrée into the rather closed world of New York's literati. In August 1920 he was invited by Helena DeKay, whose lectures on Romain Rolland and Jean-Christophe he had attended at the Rand School, to a party hosted by Lola Ridge, editor of the new literary magazine *Broom*. "This was my first literary party," according to Toomer.[84] Actually, it would be more accurate for Toomer to claim that Ridge's soirée was his first "literary party" in New York, for he had attended the literary salons hosted by the black poet Georgia Douglas Johnson in Washington, D.C., as early as 1919.[85] Known among the cognoscenti of the nation's capital as Saturday Nighters, these gatherings attracted such luminaries of the Harlem Renaissance as Zora Neale Hurston, Richard Bruce Nugent, Sterling A. Brown, Countee Cullen, Langston Hughes, and Alain Locke.

Leonard Harris and Charles Molesworth suggest that it was within the charmed circle of the Saturday Nighters that Toomer came to know Locke, with whom he had a cordial relationship in the years preceding the publication of *Cane*. In search of a community of writers in his native Washington he found, to a certain extent, such a community among those black writers and artists who attended the Saturday Nighters. According to Kerman and Eldridge, Toomer shared some of his early writing with Johnson.[86]

---

83. *The Wayward and the Seeking*, 112.

84. Ibid., 113.

85. Leonard Harris and Charles Molesworth, *Alain L. Locke: The Biography of a Philosopher* (Chicago: The University of Chicago Press, 2008), 171. Toomer's correspondence with Georgia Douglas Johnson and Alain Locke reveals a level of familiarity absent in his autobiographical writings. For Toomer's correspondence with Douglas Johnson and Locke, see *The Letters of Jean Toomer, 1919–1924* (Knoxville: The University of Tennessee Press, 2006), edited by Mark Whalan. See also George Hutchinson's "Jean Toomer and the 'New Negroes of Washington,'" in *American Literature* 63 (December 1991).

86. *The Lives of Jean Toomer*, 94.

"Toomer was almost certainly the only writer in America," as Harris and Molesworth assert, with the possible exception of the Jamaican immigrant Claude McKay, who flowed easily between Harlem and socialist literary circles downtown, "who visited literary groups as diverse as Johnson's Saturday Nighters and the *Seven Arts* circle around Lewis Mumford, Sherwood Anderson, and Waldo Frank."[87] They are also correct in asserting that Toomer never conceived of himself as a bridge between these two discrete literary communities, both of which were committed to the project of American modernism.[88] Rather, he took what was useful from each in his efforts to create a work that expressed his own particular artistic and philosophical vision. Keenly aware of what he regarded as the differences and limitations of both artistic communities, Toomer, however, felt a much greater degree of affinity for those writers and artists whom he came to know through Ridge, chief among them Waldo Frank.

Toomer's attendance at Johnson's Saturday Nighters provided him with some preparation for the unmixable mix of banter, bravado, earnestness, narcissism, and posturing he would encounter at Ridge's "literary party" in Greenwich Village. In the main, he was not impressed by his first encounter with the literati of the Lost Generation which, on this particular occasion, was represented by Edwin Arlington Robinson, Witter Bynner, and Scofield Thayer, among others. Hungry to learn about this new world, Toomer felt "that there was far too much buzz about publishers, magazines, reviews, personalities; not enough talk of life and experience."[89] However, one "man stood out. . . . He had a fine animated face and a pair of lively active eyes. . . . I didn't

---

87. *Alain L. Locke: The Biography of a Philosopher*, 175.
88. Ibid., 175.
89. *The Wayward and the Seeking*, 114.

know his name, but I marked him."[90] The man in question was none other than Waldo Frank, the celebrated author of *Our America,* a meditation on race, ethnicity, and spirituality in American culture. A few days after the party, Toomer encountered Frank while walking through Central Park. Both men stopped and introduced themselves, and thus began a friendship in letters that for Toomer would be instrumental in the publication of *Cane.* At this stage in his apprenticeship as a writer, Toomer had written the poem "The First Americans," the forerunner of his epic, "The Blue Meridian," and the short stories "Withered Skin of Berries" and "Bona and Paul." He shared his work with Frank, and was heartened by the encouragement he received from the older, established writer.

Shortly after this propitious meeting with Frank, Toomer returned to Washington, having spent his inheritance of $600. This was the end of the summer of 1920. Needless to say, Pinchback raged against Toomer's return. "Grandfather put up a fight but I beat him," Toomer remembers rather defiantly.[91] Possessing a sense of purpose and direction for the first time in five years, Toomer wrote, "I was wholly convinced that I had found my true direction in life, and no one was going to stop me. On the contrary, everyone, including grandfather, was going to help me. . . . I had matured considerably. And, I was filled with a purpose that was to keep me working for the next three years. But what terrible years they were!"[92]

And why would Toomer characterize the three years preceding the publication of *Cane* as "terrible"? The answer lies in part in the fact that during this period of his apprenticeship he lived in greatly

90. Ibid., 114.
91. *The Wayward and the Seeking*, 114.
92. Ibid., 114–15.

reduced circumstances with his aging grandparents. "I was in the house with two old people whom," as Toomer wrote in his auto- biography, "despite the continual struggle with grandfather— he never gave up completely; he was a game fighting cock to the end—I loved. And they were dying. No, they weren't dying. Grandfather gradually declined—a tragic sight—and, one day he broke. . . . I had to take over whatever of his affairs needed attention. And I ran the house, even cooking meals and sweep- ing and cleaning. In a way, it was a good thing for them that I had returned."[93] Of his grandmother, Nina Emily Hethorn Pinch- back, Toomer remembered her as strong, vivid, and humorous even as she declined amid circumstances of near poverty: "Yet she bore up. Not a whimper from her. She was glad to have me there . . . She would say every now and again that she only lived for me. But this was the miracle—as her body failed her, her spirit began taking on a more and more vivid life. Her mind became sharper—and also her tongue. She showed a vein of humor and satire that was the delight and amazement of all who came in."[94]

This was not the first time in his life when Toomer had respon- sibility for the care of his grandmother. In 1909 when Pinchback held an appointment in New York at the Department of Inter- nal Revenue, Toomer and his grandmother lived with his Uncle Walter and his family. Owing to Pinchback's absence and the indifference of his uncle and wife, his grandmother, as he wrote, "becomes my responsibility. I look after her, and often, instead of going out at nights to play . . . I have to stay indoors and keep her company."[95] While he admired and loved his grandfather, Toomer

93. Ibid., 116.
94. Ibid., 116.
95. Ibid., 89.

also loved his grandmother. He understood her function and value in the household through its rise and decline: "She stood without flinching at Pinchback's side all through his stormy and danger-ous political career. She saw the rise of the family and, outliv-ing her husband and all but one of her children, she endured its rather tragic fall." Toomer also acknowledged the important fact of his grandmother's support, when everyone else, in particu-lar his grandfather, had dismissed him as a ne'er-do-well: "She was the one person in my home who sustained her faith in me after I turned black sheep, who supported me through thick and thin. . . ."[96] Nina Emily Hethorn Pinchback lived to see the pub-lication of *Cane*, which bears the dedication: "To my grandmother . . ." She died five years later.

Along with accepting the multiplying responsibilities of car-ing for his aging grandparents, Toomer also became the caretaker of his beloved Uncle Bismarck: "Bismarck got very sick. I took over the running of his house also, and each day I went over and massaged him. He was over a month recovering. This took it out of me."[97] Plainly, the responsibility of caring for aging relatives sapped Toomer's energy and strength, yet it also, paradoxically, introduced a certain discipline and structure that advanced his goal of becoming a writer. "My days were divided between atten-tion to the house and my grandparents," as Toomer wrote of this period, "and my own work. At all possible times I was either writ-ing or reading."[98]

Toomer inevitably came face to face with his own limitations and deficiencies as a writer. There was the dream, and there was the reality. To realize the potentialities of the one clear affirma-

96. Ibid., 23.
97. Ibid., 118.
98. Ibid., 117.

tion of his life at this juncture, he had to confront and overcome the division between his own aspirations and his abilities: "But what difficulties I had! I had in me so much experience so twisted up that not a thing would come out until by sheer force I had dragged it forth. Only now and again did I experience spontaneous writing. Most of it was will and sweat. And nothing satisfied me. . . . I wrote and wrote and put each thing aside, regarding it as simply one of the exercises of my apprenticeship. Often I would be depressed and almost despaired over the written thing."[99] These periods of despair were balanced by successes, few and far between though they were at the time. And these successes bolstered his confidence and renewed his faith in his capacity to become a writer: "But, on the other hand, I became more and more convinced that I had the real stuff in me. And slowly but surely I began getting the 'feeling' of my medium, a sense of form, of words, of sentences, rhythms, cadences, and rhythmic patterns. And then, after several years work, suddenly, it was as if a door opened and I knew without doubt that I was *inside, I knew literature*. And what was my joy! But many things happened before that time came!"[100]

Before he found his way "inside" literature, Toomer would have to endure another period when the accumulating responsibilities of being the sole caretaker of his aging grandparents would again drain him of his energy and focus. He had arrived at this state in the spring of 1922. "It was during this spring that I began feeling dangerously drained of energy," Toomer wrote. "I had used so much in my own work. So much had been used on my grandparents and uncles. I seldom went out. . . . Sometimes

99. Ibid., 117.
100. Ibid., 117.

for weeks my grandmother would be laid up in bed, and by now my grandfather was almost helpless. The apartment seemed to suck my very life."[101] As the summer approached, Toomer's situation became even more desperate: "I felt I would die or murder someone if I stayed in that house another day."[102] Almost out of thin air, he managed to piece together enough funds for a week at Harpers Ferry, West Virginia, where he had often traveled to vacation. He made arrangements for the care of his grandparents during his absence. The time at Harpers Ferry was restorative, but all too short: "I returned with a small store of force which was soon spent . . . ," remembered Toomer. "The situation was slowly but steadily getting worse. . . . It was as if life were a huge snake that had coiled about me—and now it had me at almost my last breath."[103]

The much needed relief from this suffocating regimen would eventually come in the form of an invitation from Linton Stephens Ingraham, founder and principal of the Sparta Agricultural and Industrial Institute located in Sparta, Georgia. Ingraham was eager to hire an acting principal while he traveled to Boston to raise funds for his school. Toomer regarded this opportunity as a "God-send." He accepted Ingraham's offer to serve as acting principal. Toomer again made arrangements for the care of his grandparents, and prepared for his fateful trip by train to Georgia. Girding himself for what he would encounter on "the southern road," as his contemporary, Sterling A. Brown, put it, Toomer recalled that "I had always wanted to see the heart of the South. Here was my chance."[104]

101. Ibid., 122.
102. Ibid., 122.
103. Ibid., 123.
104. Ibid., 123.

As acting principal of the Sparta Agricultural and Industrial Institute located in Hancock County, Georgia, Toomer provided continuity at an institution with an important history and mission. Ingraham was the institute's founder and principal. He was born a slave in Hancock County, Georgia, on August 24, 1855, the property of Judge Linton Stephens. He was taught to read and write by Alexander Stephens, the brother of Judge Stephens, and then matriculated at Atlanta University. He established the institute on October 10, 1910, on three acres of land on his former master's plantation. The institute was located one mile and a half west of Sparta, approximately eighty miles southwest of Atlanta, Georgia, in the county contiguous to Putnam County, Georgia, the birthplace of the writers Flannery O'Connor and Alice Walker.

At the time of Toomer's arrival in September 1921, the trustees of the institute had secured funding from the Julius Rosenwald Fund to erect a second building. By 1923 the institute was composed of two buildings perched on fifty-three acres with 210 students. A co-educational institution whose curriculum was a mix of industrial education and grade school instruction in reading, writing, and arithmetic, the institute prepared students for vocations in agriculture and industry. It served the African American community of Sparta, and the communities beyond it.[105] Toomer lived, like the teachers, in a residence provided by the institute. "As the [acting] principal, [he] was required to visit homes, businesses, and churches."[106]

---

105. The history of the Sparta Agricultural and Industrial Institute and its founder, Linton Stephens Ingraham, is derived from online sources composed of articles from the *Atlanta Constitution* and the *Augusta Chronicle* assembled by Eileen B. McAdams (2005). Ingraham died on September 20, 1935, after which his wife, Anna Turner Ingraham, became principal. The institute eventually became L. H. Ingraham High School. In addition to these sources, we recommend the overview of Sparta, Georgia, that appears in Charles Scruggs and Lee Van-Demarr's *Jean Toomer and the Terror of American History* (Philadelphia: The University of Pennsylvania Press, 1998), 8–32. We also recommend Barbara Foley's "Jean Toomer's Sparta" in *American Literature* 67.4 (December 1995).

106. *The Lives of Jean Toomer*, 81.

Toomer was acting principal at the Institute from September to November 1921. This seminal, three-month sojourn in the South provided him with the materials, inspiration, and much of the setting for what became the first and third sections of *Cane*. Prior to his first visit to the South, Toomer's writing lacked a specific sense of place that could serve as the setting and foundation for his art. The landscape of Sparta, Georgia, with its history of slavery and an ancestral past that connected Toomer to his father, was precisely what the emerging writer needed at this vital juncture in his apprenticeship. Under the spell of an alien and yet somehow familiar landscape, Toomer eagerly embraced this new body of impressions and sensations and thoughts, immersing himself in a set of experiences that he would interpret with impressive originality, without being nostalgic in any way. He saw it as a world in transition, and a world of transition for himself. In Sparta, as we have noted, he heard for the first time, he claimed, the traditional Negro "folk-songs and spirituals." Because he was baptized as a Roman Catholic and reared in an upper-middle-class home in Washington, it is feasible that Toomer could have remained ignorant of the secular and sacred traditions in African American music whose origins were in slavery and that reached their maturity in the post-Reconstruction Jim Crow Deep South.

To be sure, these were not traditions often or openly embraced by the black men and women of Toomer's class or color background, even at the two all-black schools he attended in Washington. As the eponymous hero of his first play, *Natalie Mann*, written in 1922 following his stay in Georgia, would assert in almost self-righteous fashion: "What has become of the almost obligatory heritage of folk-songs? Jazz on the one hand, and on the other, a respectability which is never so vigorous as when it denounces and rejects the true art of the race's past. They are ashamed of the past made permanent by the spirituals."[107] Potentially, Toomer could have come to know the traditions emerging from the "race's past" in the person of Old Willis, a former slave who "did odd jobs" for the Pinchback family.[108] He writes that "I was very fond of [Old Willis]." But Toomer's encounters with him apparently did not introduce him to the black cultural past that was now unfolding all around him in Sparta. Toomer discovered the slave and folk traditions of which Old Willis was doubtless a vessel as a young adult, precisely when he was struggling to find his voice as an artist, drawing upon these forms and traditions to illuminate his sense of his own identity and the historical experiences that had shaped that identity. As he went about his duties as acting principal in Sparta, he moved daily through a past that was also present, a past that helped him to understand the physical and cultural landscapes out of which he would shape the most original and seminal work of literature published in the entire Harlem Renaissance.

Like his contemporaries in the broad current of American modernism, Toomer was searching for—and ironically would discover in Sparta, Georgia, of all places—a "useable past," to summon a phrase much in circulation at the time and attributed to the critic Van Wyck Brooks (a classmate of Alain Locke at Harvard), which would give shape and heft to his art, but also allow him further to define his racial identity. As he observed in a letter to Sherwood Anderson, whose novel *Winesburg, Ohio* left its imprint upon *Cane*: "My seed was planted in the cane—and cotton-fields, and in the souls of the black and white people in the small southern

107. Jean Toomer, *Natalie Mann*, in *The Wayward and the Seeking*, 290.
108. Ibid., 57.

town. My seed was planted in *myself* down there."[109] The image of the "seed" that Toomer uses to dramatic effect in his letter to Anderson would function as one of the unifying, fecund conceits in his poem "Song of the Son," in which he celebrates the ancestral past and cultural landscape of Sparta, the fictional community of Sempter in *Cane*.

In the same letter to Anderson, who asked Toomer's permission to write the introduction to *Cane*, Toomer elaborated upon the deep impact that the land, people, and music of Sparta had upon his sensibility and identity: "Here were cabins. Here Negroes and their singing. I had never heard the spirituals and work songs. They were like a part of me. At times, I identified with my whole sense so intensely that I lost my own identity."[110] Or, perhaps, we might say that here Toomer found his identity, if not his racial or cultural identity, then most certainly his identity as a creative writer, as the first American modernist writer to represent the complex culture of race in America in such a richly resonant and intricate manner. And because of this, Toomer's book stands as one of the truly great works of American modernism.

Toomer arrived in the South during a period of profound transformation. He witnessed firsthand the ebb and flow of the Great Migration. Beginning in the 1890s and then picking up the pace in 1915, African Americans were leaving rural communities like Sparta for the urban centers of the South, first, and then the North, in search of expanding industrial economic opportunities, and a less repressive racial climate. As they left the southern agrarian way of life for modernity in the cities, some also sought

109. *The Lives of Jean Toomer*, 84.
110. Ibid., 84.

to distance themselves from their slave past and its cultural traditions, which they regarded with a mixture of contempt, shame,
and obsolescence. Regarding the "folk-songs and spirituals,"
Toomer lamented, "I learned that the Negroes of the town [Sparta]
objected to them. They called them 'shouting.' They had victrolas
and player-pianos. So, I realized with deep regret, that the spirituals, meeting ridicule, would be certain to die out. With Negroes
also the trend was towards the small town and then towards the
city—and industry and commerce and machines. The folk-spirit
was walking in to die on the modern desert. That spirit was so
beautiful. Its death so tragic."[111]

The poignancy of the passing of an era and the folk culture that
defined it is a central theme of *Cane*. The speaker of "Song of the
Son" exquisitely expresses this fateful sense of timing: "O land and
soil, red soil and sweet-gum tree, / So scant of grass, so profligate
of pines, / Now just before an epoch's sun declines / Thy son,
in time, I have returned to thee. . . ."[112] In a subsequent line, the
speaker explains why he has returned to the land of his ancestors:
"To catch thy plaintive soul, leaving, soon gone. . . ."[113] This was
Toomer's own purpose, too, in writing *Cane,* to bear witness to
the passing of an epoch: "And this was the feeling I put into *Cane.*
Cane was a swan-song. It was a song of an end. And why no one
has seen and felt that, why people have expected me to write a
second and a third and a fourth book like *Cane,* is one of the queer
misunderstandings of my life."[114] It is difficult to imagine that
Toomer could be unaware that this urging that he write "a second
and a third and a fourth book like *Cane*" stemmed both from that

111. *The Wayward and the Seeking*, 123.
112. Jean Toomer, *Cane, A Norton Critical Edition*, ed. Darwin T. Turner (New York: Norton, 1988), 14.
113. Ibid., 14.
114. *The Wayward and the Seeking*, 123.

book's majesty and power and from his repeated failure to create anything that remotely approached it in sophistication throughout the remainder of his life, as he fruitlessly sought to find a language to express what being "neither white nor black" actually meant, without the soul-base of region that the deep black South had provided him in *Cane*.

At the end of his appointment in Sparta, Toomer wrote that on "the train coming north I began to write the things that later appeared in that book [*Cane*]."[115] As we have mentioned, he completed the first draft of "Kabnis," the dramatic piece that composes the third section of *Cane,* in December 1921 in the last weeks of Pinchback's life. Toomer then wrote "Fern," which according to Kerman and Eldridge, would be published "almost without revision."[116] By April 1922 he had composed the parts of *Cane* in which Georgia is predominant. Having written so much, Toomer realized he had much more to write: "But I had not enough for a book. I had at most a hundred typed pages. These were about Georgia. It seemed that I had said all I had to say about it. So what, then? I'd fill out. The middle section of *Cane* was thus manufactured."[117]

The middle section of *Cane* began with "Bona and Paul," the story Toomer wrote in 1918 during his second stay in Chicago. He wrote many of the other stories and poems in this section throughout the summer of 1922. In July 1922, Toomer wrote to Waldo Frank and John McClure, editor of the New Orleans–based journal *Double Dealer*, to share with them his vision of the content and organization of *Cane*. Even at this early date, he imagined a book with a three-part structure. Toomer wrote that

---

115. Ibid., 124.
116. *The Lives of Jean Toomer*, 86.
117. *The Wayward and the Seeking*, 125.

Part 1 would consist of all of the prose works in which Georgia is the setting; this first section he called "Cane Stalks and Choruses." Part 2 would consist of his poems, and at the time was entitled "Leaves and Syrup Songs." The third and final section would be prose works that now form the second section of *Cane,* and this section he entitled "Leaf Traceries in Washington."[118] Toomer was eager to assemble the various parts of his book into a unified whole for, as he declared to Frank and McClure, the "concentrated volume will do a good deal more than isolated pieces possibly could."[119]

Toomer's outline constituted a change of strategy. In the spring of 1922, he had sought help with publication of his work from two black writers: Alain Locke, professor of philosophy at Howard, and Claude McKay, the Jamaican immigrant poet who would be cast by Locke as a rising star, along with Toomer, among the younger generation of writers of the Harlem Renaissance. Locke had enormous influence within the black cultural world, and McKay was the associate editor of the white, socialist periodical, the *Liberator.*[120] Toomer wrote to them seeking their assistance in publishing the stories and poems that would eventually be published in *Cane.* As a result, Toomer's first and second appearances in print were in a black publication; with Locke's aid, "Song of the Son" was published in April 1922, in *Crisis,* the national monthly magazine of the National Association for the Advancement of Colored People, edited by Du Bois. This was followed by the publication of the poem "Banking Coal" in the June issue of *Crisis.*

The outcome of Toomer's efforts to promote his work with

118. *The Lives of Jean Toomer,* 88.
119. Ibid., 88.
120. Ibid., 92.

McKay yielded slightly more in the way of results. McKay accepted "Carma," "Reapers," and "Becky" and published these in the September and October issues of the *Liberator*. Toomer enjoyed similar good fortune with other magazines. By the end of 1922, his growing list of publications included "Storm Ending," "Calling Jesus," and "Harvest Song" in *Double Dealer*; "Face," "Portrait in Georgia," and "Conversion" in *Modern Review*; and "Seventh Street" in *Broom*. In addition to appealing to Locke for guidance in publishing his writings, Toomer also solicited his assistance in securing a patron to support him as he continued to write *Cane*. Although a patron never materialized, Locke, who functioned as the midwife to so many young black writers, did exert himself on Toomer's behalf.[121]

As his poems and short stories began to appear, Toomer traveled with Frank back to the South, this time to Spartanburg, South Carolina. Toomer suggested the weeklong visit to Frank, in the fall of 1922, as a means of helping him to solidify his vision of the black world so central to *Holiday*, his novel-in-progress. Traveling as "blood brothers," the trip strengthened the friendship between the two writers as well as their shared belief that out of the materials of the black folk experience they were creating a new art that would transform American literature.[122] At a crucial point in their developing friendship, Toomer expressed just this view to Frank: "I cannot think of myself as being separated from you in the dual task of creating an American literature, and of developing a public, however large or small, capable of responding to our creations. Those who read and know me, should read and know you."[123]

When Toomer returned from Spartanburg, he worked for two

---

121. *Alain L. Locke: The Biography of a Philosopher*, 173.
122. *The Lives of Jean Toomer*, 89.
123. Ibid., 89.

weeks as an assistant to the manager of Washington's all-black
Howard Theater. Out of this experience he wrote "Theater"
and "Box Seat,"[124] and these beautifully written but nevertheless searching critiques of black middle-class Washington would
appear in the middle section of *Cane*. Toomer sent these stories
to Frank for his comments. Encouraged by his response, he sent
Frank the complete manuscript of *Cane* in December 1922. He
enclosed the now famous, widely quoted letter that reveals the
latent design and theme of *Cane*: "My brother! CANE is on its
way to you! For two weeks I have worked steadily at it. The book
is done. From three angles, CANE's design is a circle. Aestheti-
cally, from simple forms to complex ones, and back to simple
forms. Regionally, from the South up into the North, and back
into the South again. Or, from the North down into the South,
and then a return North. From the point of view of the spiritual entity behind the work, the curve really starts with Bona and
Paul (awakening), plunges into Kabnis, emerges in Karintha etc.
swings upward into Theatre and Boxseat, and ends (pauses) in
Harvest Song. Whew!"[125] Elated and expectant that the book he
had carried so long in his head would soon be in the world because
of the support of his best friend, Toomer provided Frank with
clues as to the structure of a work that would generate debates
among scholars about its formal identity for decades: "You will
understand the inscriptions, brother mine: the book to grandma;
Kabnis, the spirit and the soil, to you. . . . Between each of the
three sections, a curve. These, to vaguely indicate the design. I'm
wide open to you for criticism and suggestion. Just these few lines
now. . . . love Jean."[126]

124. Ibid., 91.
125. Jean Toomer to Waldo Frank, December 12, 1922.
126. Jean Toomer to Waldo Frank, December 12, 1922, Norton Critical Edition of *Cane* (1988), 152.

At the height of their friendship and doubtless appreciative of Toomer's dedication of "Kabnis" to him, Frank shepherded the manuscript to Horace Liveright, the co-founder of Boni and Liveright Publishers along with Albert Boni. On January 2, 1923, Frank sent Toomer a telegram informing him that Liveright had accepted *Cane* for publication. With Liveright as his publisher, Toomer would make his literary debut in splendid modernist company: just a year before, Liveright had published T. S. Eliot's *The Waste Land*. In years to come, they would publish the first books of Ernest Hemingway, William Faulkner, Hart Crane, Dorothy Parker, and other bright stars in the firmament of American modernism.

In the months following Frank's excellent news, Toomer made preparations for his departure from Washington to New York: "I saw that it was very important for me to be in New York." He would never again live in his native Washington. For the last time, Toomer dutifully made arrangements for the care of his beloved grandmother, who spent her last years with her son Walter and his family. He then boarded a train to New York, and "thus ended the three-year period of death and birth in Washington."[127] Having left New York in the summer of 1920 as an aspiring, unpublished writer, Toomer returned to the nation's literary capital in the summer of 1923 as a published, respected, and admired author through the sheer force of "will and sweat," and through the support of McKay and especially Locke, though chiefly through the influence, counsel, and friendship of Frank.

In his recollection of this crucial period in his development as an artist, Toomer conveyed the excitement of his encounters with the major figures of white American modernism that summer:

127. *The Wayward and the Seeking*, 126.

"In New York, I stepped into the literary world. Frank, Gorham Munson, Kenneth Burke, Hart Crane, Matthew Josephson, Malcom Cowley, Paul Rosenfield, Van Wyck Brooks, Robert Littell—*Broom,* the *Dial,* the *New Republic* and many more. I lived on Gay Street and entered into the swing of it. It was an extraordinary summer. . . . I met and talked with Alfred Stieglitz and saw his photographs. I was invited here and there."[128] In this recollection, Toomer is describing his pleasure at being introduced into a world populated by the key writers of the Lost Generation and the small, but influential magazines through which they shaped the mainstream of American modernism.

The sometimes overlapping, sometimes separate, other world of writers who contributed to the shape and direction of Afro-American modernism included most influentially Langston Hughes, Zora Neale Hurston, Claude McKay, Countee Cullen, and Sterling A. Brown, among two dozen others, coalescing around the slight, though formidable figure of Locke in his *pied-à-terre* in Harlem. But Toomer is largely silent about his encounters with them. These writers published in two magazines primarily: *Opportunity,* the monthly magazine of the Urban League, edited by the enterprising sociologist, Charles S. Johnson, who along with Locke, was one of the two midwives of the Harlem Renaissance; and in Du Bois's *Crisis.* Locke's *The New Negro* anthology, as we have seen, gave the nascent movement a form and a manifesto. A few other periodicals, such as *Fire,* the short-lived magazine founded by Hughes, Hurston, and Wallace Thurman, also played a role in shaping the course of the Renaissance, but none had the canonical presence of *Crisis* and *Opportunity.*

128. Ibid., 126.

Perhaps a sign of Toomer's evolving thoughts about how he would identify himself racially, when he arrived in New York in that heady summer of 1923, is the fact that he did not seek lodging in Harlem but rather in Greenwich Village, sharing an apartment on Grove Street with Gorham Munson after the departure of his roommate Hart Crane. Munson's hospitality prepared the ground for a lifelong friendship with Toomer. Sometime later, he moved to the black section of the Village, renting a "small row-house apartment on Gay Street . . . distinctive then as being a predominantly black settlement in an otherwise white part of town." According to his biographers, "Toomer spent his days in the backyard reading or in the apartment writing. During that summer he was trying to establish himself as a free-lance writer for various New York journals and little magazines."[129] At the end of that summer, Toomer's long-cherished dream of publishing a book—"I wanted a published book as I wanted nothing else"—became a reality. Liveright brought out *Cane* in September 1923.[130] Much to Toomer's delight, the reviews were uniformly positive. High praise came from the members of the two literary worlds who regarded him as a member. Comparing Toomer's debut work with the Frank's fiction, Robert Littell offered this assessment of *Cane* in the *New Republic*: "Toomer's view is unfamiliar and bafflingly subterranean, the vision of a poet far more than the account of things seen by a novelist—lyric, symbolic, oblique, seldom actual."[131] Allen Tate, a member of the Fugitive Poets, also praised *Cane* in the pages of Nashville's *Tennessean*. Countee Cullen sent Toomer a congratulatory note in which he

---

129. *The Lives of Jean Toomer*, 105.
130. *The Wayward and the Seeking*, 124.
131. Robert Littell, *"Cane," New Republic* 37 (December 26, 1923): 126.

described *Cane* as a "classical portrayal of things as they are."[132] A month after the publication of *Cane,* the critic Edward O'Brien wrote from England requesting permission to reprint "Blood-Burning Moon" in the anthology *The Best Short Stories of 1923.*[133] Du Bois and Locke expressed their admiration for Toomer's achievement in an essay entitled "The Younger Literary Movement" in 1924 in *Crisis.* The influential African American critic William Stanley Braithwaite offered high praise of *Cane* in the pages of *The New Negro*: "*Cane* is a book of gold and bronze, of dusk and flame, of ecstasy and pain, and Jean Toomer is a bright morning star of a new day of the race in literature."[134] Two years later in the summer of 1927, Langston Hughes and Zora Neale Hurston paid homage to Toomer's artistic achievement by visiting Sparta, the inspiration for *Cane,* on their return North from a road trip through the South.[135]

Reflecting upon *Cane's* reception and impact almost forty years after its publication, Arna Bontemps, a member of the younger generation of writers of the Harlem Renaissance, said this of Toomer's shaping influence on the forms his black contemporaries and literary heirs would craft: "*Cane's* influence was by no means limited to the joyous band that included Langston Hughes, Countee Cullen, Eric Walrond, Zora Neale Hurston, Wallace Thurman, Rudolph Fisher and their contemporaries of the Twenties. Subsequent writing by Negroes in the United States, as well as in the West Indies and Africa, has continued to reflect its mood and

132. *The Lives of Jean Toomer*, 108.

133. Ibid., 108–09.

134. William Stanley Braithwaite, "The Negro in American Literature," *The New Negro*, ed. Alain Locke. (New York: Simon & Schuster, 1925; 1992), 44.

135. Arnold Rampersad, *The Life of Langston Hughes Volume I: 1902–1941; I, Too, Sing America* (New York: Oxford University Press), 152–53; Valerie Boyd, *Wrapped in Rainbows: The Life of Zora Neale Hurston* (New York: Scribner Books, 2003), 151; *The Lives of Jean Toomer*, 182.

often its method and, one feels, it has also influenced the writing about Negroes by others. Certainly, no earlier volume of poetry or fiction or both had come close to expressing the ethos of the Negro in the Southern setting as *Cane* did."[136] While acknowledging his broad influence, Darwin T. Turner maintained that Toomer's signal contribution to American letters was to reverse years of stereotypical portrayals of rural, southern black language and life: "No matter how he influenced others, it cannot be denied that Jean Toomer was the first writer of the twenties to delineate southern black peasant life perceptively."[137]

Toomer's deft portrayal of southern black peasantry, his sensitive portrayal of black women, his power as a lyric poet, the manner in which he combined philosophy with fiction, and his exploration of the relationship between region and race directly influenced the shape of Zora Neale Hurston's *Their Eyes Were Watching God*, and through her, the theme of Ralph Ellison's *Invisible Man*. What's more, *Cane* has profoundly influenced both the fictions and the poetry of key African American writers who came of age since its republication in the late 1960s, including Alice Walker, Michael S. Harper, Rita Dove, Charles Johnson, Gloria Naylor, Elizabeth Alexander, and Natasha Trethewey. Though Ernest J. Gaines discovered *Cane* after he had developed his particular style of writing, he regards Toomer as a fellow artist with whom he shares a commitment to portray realistically the experiences of southern black farmers. Despite his desire to flee it, Toomer's literary legacy survives primarily because of *Cane*'s canonization in the black literary tradition.

While *Cane* was clearly an artistic success, sales were disap-

---

136. Arna Bontemps, "Introduction," *Cane* (New York: Harper & Row, 1923; 1969).

137. Darwin T. Turner, "Introduction," *Cane* (New York: Boni & Liveright, 1975); Norton Critical Edition of *Cane* (1988), 133.

pointing. It sold only one thousand copies, but it was printed in a second edition. As Toomer himself remarked: "The reviews were splendid. It didn't sell well, but it made its literary mark—that was all I asked."[138] The strength of the reviews was doubtless a factor in Liveright's decision to reissue the second, smaller edition in 1927. While scholars would continue to praise *Cane*, it would remain out of print until the appearance of the third edition in 1967, followed by editions in 1969 and 1975. Doubtless, the renewed interest in the Harlem Renaissance by the writers of the Black Arts movement of the 1960s, the institutionalization of the field of African American Studies in 1969, and the dramatic growth of African American literary studies through the 1980s led to the first Norton Critical Edition in 1988, splendidly edited by Darwin T. Turner.

Though *Cane* had "made its literary mark," Toomer's relationship to the book he so much desired to be published began to shift as early as the fall of 1923. This shift, which would eventually result in his rejection of the book he once regarded as the "passport" that "would lead [him] from the cramped conditions of Washington which [he] had outgrown, into the world of writers and literature," would be catalyzed by his friend Waldo Frank and his publisher, George Liveright,[139] involving the launch of *Cane* itself and the efforts by Liveright to promote it. Frank had written, by all accounts, a beautiful foreword to *Cane*. He lavished praise upon his friend and protégé's debut book: "A poet has arisen among our American youth who has known how to turn the essences and materials of his Southland into the essences and materials of literature."[140] Quite perceptively, the ever-supportive

---

138. *The Wayward and the Seeking*, 127.

139. Ibid., 124.

140. Waldo Frank, "Foreword," *Cane* (New York: Boni and Liveright, 1923) as reprinted in the Norton Critical Edition of *Cane* (1988), 138 and 140.

Frank described *Cane* as "an aesthetic equivalent of the land." So far, so good.

However, the language that disturbed Toomer, was this: "A poet has arisen in that land who writes, not as a Southerner, not as a rebel against Southerners, not as a Negro, not apologist or priest or critic: who writes as a *poet*."[141] Moreover Frank's references to Toomer as "the gifted Negro" and "an American Negro" inadvertently only made matters worse so far as Toomer was concerned, undermining his desire to position himself publicly as a writer "neither white nor black." Frank's straightforward description of Toomer as a Negro, notwithstanding Toomer's belabored efforts to explain his racial sense of himself to his friend privately, felt first like disappointment, and then betrayal: "One day in the mail his [Frank's] preface [*sic*] to my book came. I read it and had as many mixed feelings as I have ever had. On the one hand, it was a tribute and a send-off as only Waldo Frank could have written it, and my gratitude for his having gotten the book accepted rose to the surface and increased my gratitude for the present piece of work in so far as it affirmed me as a literary artist of great promise. On the other hand, in so far as the racial thing went, it was evasive, or, in any case, indefinite."[142]

For reasons that are not clear to us, Toomer obsessed and fretted about Frank's references to his race in the foreword, as if Frank had either invented his black ancestry or publicly unmasked him as a Negro writer, leading him inevitably to question Frank's motives: "Well, I asked myself, why should the reader know? Why should any such thing be incorporated in a foreword to *this* book? Why should Waldo Frank or any other be my spokesman in this

141. Ibid., 138–39.
142. *The Wayward and the Seeking*, 125.

matter? All of this was true enough, and I was more or less reconciled to let the preface [sic] stand as it was, inasmuch as it was so
splendid that I could not take issue with it on this, after all, minor
point, inasmuch as my need to have the book published was so
great, but my suspicions as to Waldo Frank's lack of understanding of, or failure to accept, my actuality became active again."[143]
Toomer would also claim that he learned from mutual friends that
it was Frank who had constructed a portrait of him as a Negro in
the literary circles of New York, a portrait that, he felt, misrep-
resented the "actuality" of his race, or his racelessness. Toomer,
no doubt unfairly given his extensive contacts with other black
writers in Washington and New York and his grandfather's historical status as the highest ranking black elected official in the
whole of Reconstruction, claimed to believe that it was "through
Frank's agency that an erroneous picture of me was put in the
minds of certain people in New York before my book came out.
Thus was started a misunderstanding in the very world, namely
the literary art world, in which I expected to be really understood. I knew none of this at the time. . . ."[144] While Kerman
and Eldridge write that Toomer and Margaret Naumburg, Frank's
wife, "were entranced with each other from the first time they
met," the unhappy poet of Cane may have ended his friendship
with Frank by seeking his revenge, in part, by seducing his mentor's wife.[145]

While Toomer was still reeling from Frank's "betrayal," Liveright requested that Toomer capitalize upon his African American ancestry in the publicity for Cane, and this, as it turned out,
would further complicate his relationship to his publisher and

143. Ibid., 125–26.
144. Ibid., 126.
145. The Lives of Jean Toomer, 112.

his first book. It is clear that Toomer wanted to write about the Negro, but not be regarded as a Negro. In fact, it is also clear that Toomer wanted to break out of the race itself through art, transcending the Negro world in a manner, say, that never would have occurred to Irish writers such as William Butler Yeats or James Joyce. Toomer objected to the oversimplification of what he seems, at times, genuinely to have believed was a truly complex, new racial identity, one too subtle, hybrid, or nuanced to be classified by those gross signifiers "black" and "white," especially to be exploited for the commercial purpose of selling the very book that he hoped would be his transport out of blackness. Accordingly, he refused to cooperate with Liveright, notwithstanding the risk that his refusal might jeopardize his book's publication. Toomer defiantly declared his position on race and marketing in a well-known letter to Liveright, dated September 23, 1923: "First, I want to make a general statement from which detailed statements will follow. My racial composition and my position in the world are realities which I alone may determine. . . . As a unit in the social milieu, I expect and demand acceptance of myself on their basis. I do not expect to be told what I should consider myself to be."[146] But Toomer did not stop there: "As a Boni and Liveright author, I make the distinction between my fundamental position, and the position which your publicity department may wish to establish for me in order that *Cane* reach as large a public as possible. In this connection I have told you . . . to make use of whatever racial factors you wish. Feature Negro if you wish, but do not expect me to feature it in advertisements for you. I have sufficiently featured Negro in

---

146. Jean Toomer to Horace Liveright, September 23, 1923, Norton Critical Edition of *Cane* (1988), 156–57.

Cane."[147] Toomer's dispute with Liveright over his book's marketing, following close upon his reaction to Frank's foreword, only added insult to injury, further alienating him from *Cane.*

It should not surprise us, then, that Alain Locke's decision to reprint excerpts from *Cane* in *The New Negro* without Toomer's permission just about drove Toomer to distraction: "But when Locke's book, *The New Negro,* came out, there was the [Winold] Reiss portrait, and there was a story from *Cane* [Locke reprinted the stories "Carma" and "Fern," as well as the poems "Georgia Dusk" and "Song of the Son"], and there in the introduction, were words about me which have caused as much or more misunderstanding than Waldo Frank's."[148] Toomer felt betrayed by the two major figures at the center of the literary worlds that claimed him, and by both he felt completely misunderstood. But between the two, Toomer reserved his greater scorn for Locke: "However, there was and is, among others, this great difference between Frank and Locke. Frank helped me at a time when I most needed help. I will never forget it. Locke tricked and misused me."[149] Toomer seriously considered contesting Locke's representation of him as a black writer, ultimately deciding against doing so because he was convinced that he probably could never correct the record, and fearing that his efforts at any sort of clarification would only contribute to the confusion. So Jean Toomer—despite his vehement objections— came to be known as a black writer through *Cane,* the book that ironically brought him the fame and acceptance in the literary world he had been seeking for so long.

Toomer's decision, just a few months after *Cane*'s publication, to become a student of Georges I. Gurdjieff, the Russian mystic and psychologist, and originator of the Gurdjieff system or method, also contributed to his estrangement from the book. Throughout much of his adult life, Toomer had been in search of what he called an "intelligible scheme, a sort of whole into which everything fit," and toward the end of 1923 he believed he had at last found this grand and unifying pattern in Gurdjieff's teachings. Toomer's introduction to Gurdjieff's philosphy came through P. D. Ouspensky's *Tertium Organum*, which he read in December 1923. Ouspensky's writings were the object of some fascination among the members of his literary community in Greenwich Village, particularly to Hart Crane, Gorham Munson, and Waldo Frank. After reading Ouspensky, Toomer acquired a pamphlet describing the history and mission of Gurdjieff's Institute for the Harmonious Development of Man in Fontainebleau, France. "In it I found expressed," he wrote, "more completely and with more authority than with anything possible from me, just the conditions of man which I myself realized. Moreover, a method, a means of *doing something about it* was promised. It was no wonder that I went heart and soul into the Gurdjieff work."[150]

It should be emphasized that in *Cane* we find ample evidence of an orientation toward spiritual and philosophical concerns that would assume a larger, more marked significance in Toomer's later writings. These concerns help to explain why he went "heart and soul into the Gurdjieff work." Even in his 1923 letter to Frank, Toomer had written of what he called the "spiritual entity behind the work." A few years before his introduction to Gurdjieff's theories, Toomer, an autodidact who early on saw himself as a philosopher-poet, found as his great theme moder-

150. Ibid., 131.

nity's attendant fragmentation and alienation. *Cane* is his most successful treatment of this theme, as it juxtaposes fragmentation with intense spirituality. Kerman and Eldridge describe the "spiritual entity" in the writing and in the writer thusly: "While others may have read *Cane* to see how a man could fit his human view into his blackness, Jean was trying to fit the blackness that was a part of him into a more comprehensive human view. Nor was he trying to 'pass' in a racial sense; rather, he was passing from preoccupations with external, visible reality to concentration on internal, invisible reality."[151] Perhaps. But Toomer did find a most original and compelling way to render the relation among fragmentation, alienation, and spirituality in the tripartite, lyrical form of *Cane.*

In fact, the grand achievement of Toomer is this: *Cane* is, perhaps, the first work of fiction by a black writer to take the historical experiences and social conditions of the Negro, and make them the metaphor for the human condition, in this case, the metaphor for modernity itself. Du Bois had, famously and brilliantly, redefined the concept of "double consciousness" as a metaphor for the Negro's duality, a duality created by racial segregation. For Du Bois, double consciousness was a malady, a malady that could be cured only by the end of segregation. For Toomer, however, fragmentation, or duality, is the very condition of modernity. It cannot be "cured," any more than the gap between the conscious mind and the unconscious can be obliterated. *Cane* is a book about nothing if not fragmentation; it is a book about dualities, unreconciled dualities, and this theme is repeated in each of its sections, whether in the South or the North, whether in the country or the city, whether in the book's black characters or its white characters.

151. *The Lives of Jean Toomer,* 115.

Everybody and everything is hopelessly, inescapably fragmented. And nowhere is this better expressed than in the "Kabnis" section of *Cane,* in this exchange between Lewis and Kabnis, each other's alter egos, through Lewis's list of binaries:

> Kabnis: . . . My ancestors were Southern blue-bloods.
> Lewis: And black.
> Kabnis: Aint much difference between blue and black.
> Lewis: Enough to draw a denial from you. Cant hold them, can you? Master; slave. Soil; and the overarching heavens. Dusk; dawn. They fight and bastardize you. The sun tint of your cheeks, flame of the great season's multi-colored leaves, tarnished, burned. Split, shredded; easily burned. No use . . .

The use of binary oppositions has a long history in African American literature, going back at least to Frederick Douglass's *Narrative of the Life of Frederick Douglass* (1845). Du Bois transformed these in *The Souls of Black Folk* into the duality of the Negro citizen, a necessary and problematic by-product of anti-black racism and segregation. Toomer, however, takes Du Bois's concept of double consciousness, and boldly declares that this fragmentation is, ultimately, the sign of the Negro's modernity, first, and that the Negro, therefore, is America's harbinger of and metaphor for modernity itself. It is a stunningly brilliant claim, this rendering by Toomer of the American Negro as the First Modern Person. There is no end to the manifestations of fragmentation in *Cane* and no false gestures to the unity of opposites at the text's end. No, in *Cane,* fragmentation is here to stay, for such is the stuff of modern life. When Kabnis ascends the stairs from his encounter with Father John in the basement at the end of the text, he carries a bucket of dead coals, undermining what would be the false nod to hope through reconciliation possibly suggested by the text's image of a rising sun. Zora Neale Hurston revises this very scene at the end of *Their Eyes Were Watching God,* having depicted her protagonist's coming to voice not as the result of reconciling binaries, but of developing the capacity to negotiate back and forth between them, acutely mindful of the fragmentation that Toomer defined as the necessary precondition for finding one's identity, an identity always split, or doubled, or divided. In *Cane,* Jean Toomer became a lyrical prophet of modernism. And then, abruptly, he decided to pursue other passages.

In January 1924, Toomer marked his passing from "external, visible reality" to "internal, invisible reality" by attending lectures by Gurdjieff and demonstrations of his method at Manhattan's Leslie Hall and the Neighborhood Playhouse. He writes about how deeply moved he was by his first encounter with Gurdjieff's teachings. Gurdjieff claimed that human beings are mechanical beings, and that they lack unity, and thus true consciousness. In the Gurdjieff system there are four levels of consciousness: the sleeping state, waking consciousness, self-consciousness, and objective or cosmic consciousness. Advanced levels of consciousness can only be attained through the practice of such exercises as self-remembering or self-observation as well as non-identification. Practiced in one's daily life, these exercises possessed the potential to liberate one from mechanical modes of thought and behavior, and to move one toward the attainment of higher levels of consciousness.

Toomer, to say the least, was captivated by the promise of Gurdjieff's teachings. By the summer of 1924 he had left New York to study at Gurdjieff's institute in France. Put another way, in less than a year after the publication of *Cane* and when the

Harlem Renaissance and other expressions of high cultural modernism were approaching their apex, Toomer had passed into a vastly different cultural orbit. When he returned to New York in early 1925, he set about in almost priestly fashion to promote the Gurdjieff method through public lectures. It was as a Gurdjieff lecturer that Hughes and Hurston first met Toomer in Harlem in 1925.

Neither as a writer nor as a lecturer did Toomer earn an income substantial enough to support himself. Like his father Nathan Toomer, he was fortunate that he married well. In 1931, Toomer married the writer Margery Latimer, who died in 1932 after giving birth to their daughter, Margery Toomer. Two years later, Toomer married Marjorie Content, the daughter of a wealthy stockbroker, and the former wife of Harold Loeb, the founder of the magazine *Broom*. Marjorie Content and Toomer came close to meeting one another in 1923 at her East Ninth Street townhouse, in the basement of which were the offices of *Broom*. Lola Ridge attempted to introduce Content to Toomer, whose work she admired, but she shyly demurred. Toomer married her in Taos, New Mexico, on September 1, 1934, with his former lover Georgia O'Keeffe in attendance as witness. He would be her fourth and last husband.

Prior to his marriage to Content, however, Toomer had developed a reputation as the inamorato of two of the women who played central roles in the cultural world of American modernism. Its center of gravity shifted between *Seven Arts*, presided over to a very large degree by Waldo Frank, and the Photo-Secession Group, perhaps an even more exalted stratum of the arts, whose headquarters was Manhattan's 291 Gallery, of which the photographer Alfred Stieglitz was the imperious head. Shortly after the publication of *Cane* in the fall of 1923, Toomer had an affair with Margaret Naumburg, an educator who also happened to be Waldo Frank's wife, which not surprisingly led to the dissolution of their friendship.[152] Sometime later in 1933, Toomer also had an affair with the artist Georgia O'Keeffe during one of his visits to The Hill, Stieglitz and O'Keeffe's retreat on Lake George, New York.[153] Toomer was extraordinarily handsome and beguiling, and no doubt cut a striking figure, often finding himself one of the very few swarthy men in the inner sanctums of white American modernism.

As a result of his marriage to Marjorie Content, Toomer could continue with his work as a Gurdjieff lecturer without fear of impoverishment. He would lecture on the Gurdjieff method most intensely for the next two decades, not only in New York but in Chicago; Portage, Wisconsin; Taos, New Mexico; and Doylestown, Pennsylvania, his final home. Toomer continued to write novels, short stories, plays, aphorisms, and poems, but most of these bear the unmistakable imprint of Gurdjieff's philosophy and teachings, stimuli not nearly as fecund as the rural Georgian landscape. Except for autobiographical excerpts edited by Darwin T. Turner, including the poem "The Blue Meridian," and *Essentials*, edited by Rudolph P. Byrd, a collection of aphorisms, Toomer's post-*Cane* writings remain largely unpublished. Lacking *Cane*'s lyrical originality, Toomer's philosophical and psychological writings often read like sophomoric, prosaic, bloodless translations of Gurdjieff's philosophy and method.

As Toomer passed into Gurdjieff's world, he passed into literary obscurity. While his search for enlightenment or the "intelligible scheme" took him to India, through Jungian analysis, and to

---

152. Ibid., 112.
153. Laurie Lisle, *Portrait of an Artist: A Biography of Georgia O'Keeffe* (New York: Seaview Books, 1981), 260–65.

his conversion to the Society of Friends, Toomer's commitment to Gurdjieff, while fluctuating in its intensity, nevertheless remained the organizing principle of his life. He recommitted himself to this work in 1953, and remained a disciple until he passed away on March 30, 1967—the year in which the third edition of *Cane* was published.

Jean Toomer's Racial Self-Identification: A Note on the Newly Found Documents

Of course, we are still confronted with the vital question that has arisen in various ways throughout this introduction: Was Jean Toomer a Negro who passed for white?

Thanks to pioneering research conducted at the editors' request by the genealogist Megan Smolenyak Smolenyak, we can now understand more fully than ever before Jean Toomer's conflicted thinking about his racial identification, as he expressed them in public documents, including the federal census, two draft registrations, and on his marriage license to Margery Latimer. In addition, we also now know how Toomer's grandfather and grandmother, Pinckney Benton Stewart Pinchback and Nina Emily Hethorn, his mother, Nina Pinchback, and his father, Nathan Toomer, are all identified in federal census records.

In every census taken between 1850 and 1920, P. B. S. Pinchback and Nina Emily Hethorn are identified either as black or as mulattos. Between 1870 and her death in 1909, Nina Pinchback is identified as a mulatto or black. Likewise, Nathan Toomer is identified between 1870 and 1900 as either mulatto or black. (Nathan's previous wife, Amanda America Dixon, is also identified as a mulatto in the 1870 and 1880 censuses and as black on her marriage license with Nathan. Amanda's mother, Julia Frances

Lewis Dixon, is also identified in the censuses taken between 1870 and 1910 as a mulatto or black.) In other words, Jean Toomer's mother, father, grandfather, and grandmother all self-identified as Negroes.

In the 1900 federal census, Eugene Toomer is listed as black. In the 1910 federal census he is listed as mulatto. In June 1917, Eugene Pinchback Toomer registered for the draft in Washington, D.C. He is recorded to be an unemployed student, single, as having an unspecified disability, and as being a "Negro." According to Kernan and Eldridge, the "unspecified disability" was actually "bad eyes and a hernia gotten in a basketball game."[154]

The 1920 United States Federal Census shows Toomer boarding with other lodgers in the home of an Italian couple on East Ninth Street in Manhattan. He is assigned New York as a birthplace, suggesting that someone else responded on his behalf, in his absence. His race is listed as "white."

In the 1930 United States Federal Census, Toomer is listed as a resident, with many others, at 11 Fifth Avenue, in Manhattan. Because of the accuracy of the other data contained in this document—including his birthplace, his parents' states of birth, and his occupation as a freelance writer—it is likely that he furnished these details himself. His race is listed as white.

A year later Toomer married "Marjery" or Margery Latimer on October 30, 1931, in Portage, Wisconsin. Both the bride and the groom are identified as "white" on the marriage license. According to Kerman and Eldridge, Margery Latimer was aware of what she terms "the racial thing," that is, that Toomer was black.[155] Though this is true and though she shared Toomer's vision of a

---

154. *The Lives of Jean Toomer*, 69.
155. Ibid., 199.

new race in America, she was nevertheless unprepared for headlines such as this one published in the national press regarding her
marriage to Toomer: "Negro Who Wed White Writer Sees New
Race."[156] While Toomer proclaimed that his marriage to Margery
Latimer was evidence of a "new race in America, . . . neither
white nor black nor in-between," and that their marriage was simply one between "two Americans," the white press chose to focus
upon only the most sensational aspects of their nuptials.[157]

In 1942, Toomer registered once again for the draft, as part
of the World War II Draft Registration. He identified himself as
Nathan Jean Toomer, and he was living with his second wife, Marjorie C. Toomer, in Doylestown, Pennsylvania. He is described as
5'10" tall, weighing 178 pounds, with black hair and eyes, and a
"dark brown complexion." He identified himself as a "Negro."

These documents reveal that Jean Toomer self-identified as
Negro in 1917, when he first registered for the draft. Then either
he or a roommate decided to identify him as "white" in the federal census of 1920. Similarly, Toomer self-identified as "white"
in the 1930 census and a year later on his marriage license with
Margery Latimer. He then self-identified again as a Negro in 1942
on his second draft registration. Given the fact that draft boards
at the time were local, Toomer's decision to identify himself as a
black man is quite surprising. Since the draft board would have
been unaware of Toomer's previous identification of himself as a
Negro in 1917, we are left wondering why he did this after he had
decided to pass as a white man.

In the course of the twenty-five years between his 1917 and
1942 army registrations, Toomer was endlessly deconstructing his

156. Ibid., 202.

157. Frederick L. Rusch, *A Jean Toomer Reader: Selected and Unpublished Writings* (New York: Oxford University Press, 1993), 105.

Negro ancestry. We recall that during his childhood and adolescence in Washington, D.C., and New York, Toomer lived in both the white and the black worlds, and here we must emphasize the fact that during his adolescence he was educated and lived in the world occupied by Washington's black and mulatto elite. Based upon his experiences in this special world "midway between the white and Negro worlds,"[158] Toomer claimed that he developed his famous "racial position" in 1914, when he says he first defined himself as an "American, neither white nor black," just a year after declaring himself to be a Negro in his first draft registration. But given the fact that his parents and grandparents identified themselves and Toomer (in the 1900 and 1910 federal censuses) as black, it is apparent that Toomer's feelings about his racial identity were anomalous within his own family."[159] It is important to stress that the first short story Toomer ever wrote, "Bona and Paul," composed in 1918, takes passing as its central theme, and that this deeply autobiographical story reflects Toomer's early preoccupation with his racial identity.

Equally important, Toomer's assertion that "Kabnis is me," in his well-known December 1922 letter to Waldo Frank concerning his relationship to a character of mixed-race ancestry who is deeply conflicted about his Negro ancestry, is further evidence of his ambivalence regarding his racial identity. This ambivalence about his black ancestry is also reflected in the controversial launch of *Cane*, specifically his conflicted, indeed angry reaction to Waldo Frank's introduction, and later his refusal to cooperate with Horace Liveright, his publisher, in "featuring Negro" in the marketing of *Cane* in the fall of 1923. Indeed, he all but said to Liveright: "I

158. *The Wayward and the Seeking*, 84.
159. Ibid., 93.

was not a Negro."[160] According to Darwin Turner, Toomer, in his correspondence with the writer Sherwood Anderson just a year before the publication of *Cane*, "never opposed Anderson's obvious assumption that he was 'Negro.' In fact, Anderson began the correspondence because Toomer had been identified to him as a 'Negro.' "[161] Toomer's contradictory stance vis-à-vis Liveright and Anderson reveals the depth of his anguish about his race in the weeks before the publication of the work that would link him to a literary tradition from which he would flee.

We also must recall Toomer's anger with Alain Locke for reprinting excerpts of *Cane* in *The New Negro* in 1925 (he was silent regarding Locke's decision to reprint "Song of the Son" in the 1925 Harlem issue of *The Survey Graphic*), a reaction that smacks of denial and ingratitude, given Locke's early and consistent support of Toomer while he was still living in Washington, D.C. And then in 1934, almost ten years after the publication of *The New Negro*, Toomer, most improbably, observes to the *Baltimore Afro-American* newspaper that "I have not lived as [a Negro] nor do I really know whether there is colored blood in me or not."[162] During this same period, Toomer refuses to contribute to Nancy Cunard's anthology *The Negro* (1934) stating that "though I am interested in and deeply value the Negro, I am not a Negro."[163] This claim stands out as particularly disingenuous when we recall Toomer's week-long trip with Waldo Frank in the fall of 1922 in Spartanburg, South Carolina, where they masqueraded as "blood brothers," that is, as Negroes.[164] After serving

160. Ibid., 127.

161. Ibid., 11–12.

162. Barbara Foley, "Jean Toomer's Washington and the Politics of Class," *Modern Fiction Studies* 42.2 (1996): 289.

163. Ibid., 313.

164. Kerman and Eldridge, *The Lives of Jean Toomer*, 89.

as Frank's "host in a black world,"[165] Toomer returned to Washington, and for two weeks worked as an assistant to the manager of the Howard Theater, a theater that served the capital's African American community, and where he gathered material for such stories as "Box Seat" and "Theater." These shaping experiences in the black world, among many others, call into question Toomer's odd claim in the *Baltimore Afro-American and to the anthologist Nancy Cunard that he was not, and had not been, black.*

At this juncture, it is useful to return to Elizabeth Alexander's "Toomer," the splendid poem that opens our introduction and that also evokes Toomer's shifting, complex, contradictory stance on race: "I wished / to contemplate who I was beyond / my body, this container of flesh. / I made up a language in which to exist. / . . . Oh, / to be a Negro is—is? / to be a Negro, is. To be."[166] Alexander's key line is this: "I made up a language in which to exist." In this insightful line, Alexander captures not only Toomer's definition of race as a social construction, but also his anguished effort to liberate himself from his apparent anxiety and ambivalence about his black ancestry.

Notwithstanding Toomer's definition of himself as an "American, neither white nor black,"[167] at crucial stages in his life he self-identified as Negro: as a young adult in 1917 at the age of 23, Toomer self-identified as Negro; again in 1942 as a mature adult at the age of 48, Toomer self-identified as Negro. While the registration cards, the census data, and marriage certificate are contradictory, there is, nevertheless, a pattern. It is our carefully considered judgment, based upon an analysis of archival evidence previously

165. Ibid., 90.

166. "Toomer," from *Crave Radiance: New and Selected Poems 1990–2010.* Copyright © 2010 by Elizabeth Alexander. Reprinted by permission of Graywolf Press and the author.

167. *The Wayward and the Seeking,* 93.

overlooked by other scholars, that Jean Toomer—for all of his pioneering theorizing about what today we might call a multicultural or mixed-raced ancestry—was a Negro who decided to pass for white. Here we respectfully disagree with Toomer's biographers Kerman and Eldridge, who claim that Toomer never attempted "to 'pass' in a racial sense."[168]

And what is Toomer's relationship to American modernism and the African American literary tradition? Without question, *Cane* is a classic work of timeless significance in American and African American letters. In its pages we encounter again and again the arresting vision of an astonishingly original writer. And what shall be our generation's relationship to this great artist of the Harlem Renaissance and the Lost Generation, who rejected the very book by which he is destined to be remembered? Alice Walker expressed a perspective we would do well to reflect upon. Shortly after the publication of *Meridian*, her magisterial fictional meditation on the civil rights movement, and her own formal response to Toomer's call in *Cane*, Walker concluded: "I think Jean Toomer would want us to keep [*Cane*'s] beauty, but let him go."[169] Walker is probably correct in her assessment of Toomer's own wishes. However, since Toomer's *Cane* is arguably the most sophisticated work of literature created over the course of the Harlem Renaissance, we imagine that future generations of scholars will find his struggle with his racial identity as endlessly fascinating as we have.

168. *The Lives of Jean Toomer*, 115.

169. Alice Walker, "The Divided Life of Jean Toomer," in *In Search of Our Mothers' Gardens* (New York: Harcourt, Brace, and Jovanovich, 1983), 65.

Toomer's draft registration, June 5, 1917.

REGISTRAR'S REPORT

1   Tall, medium, or short (specify which)? _Tall_   Slender, medium, or stout (which)? _Slender_

2   Color of eyes? _dark brown_   Color of hair? _black_   Bald? _no_

3   Has person lost arm, leg, hand, foot, or both eyes, or is he otherwise disabled (specify)? _no_

I certify that my answers are true, that the person registered has read his own answers, that I have witnessed his signature, and that all of his answers of which I have knowledge are true, except as follows:

Howell J. C'Brien

(Signature of registrar)

Precinct **8**

City or County _Washington, D. C._

State _____

JUN 5 1917

(Date of registration)

1930 census.

Form 15-6

DEPARTMENT OF COMMERCE—BUREAU OF THE CENSUS

TEENTH CENSUS OF THE UNITED STATES: 1930

POPULATION SCHEDULE

Enumeration District No. 31 118c

Sheet No. 22A

Supervisor's District No. 21

Enumerated by me on April 24th, 1930, Franklin Howard, Enumerator.

OF BIRTH	MOTHER TONGUE (OR NATIVE LANGUAGE) OF FOREIGN BORN	CITIZENSHIP, ETC.		OCCUPATION AND INDUSTRY			EMPLOYMENT	VETERANS	
MOTHER				OCCUPATION	INDUSTRY	CODE			
New York		56	yo	Attorney	Law	5X94	W yo	NO	1
Minnesota		50	yo	Writer	Journalist	5444	O yo	NO	2
Messay	Hungarian	65 05	1916 Na	yo	None				3
Rhode Island		69	yo	Banker	Bank	8583	yo	NO	4
France	French	18 74	1927 Al	Artist	Painting	5394	O NO	5
France	French	12 12	1923 Al	yo	None	8294	O	6
Pennsylvania		58	yo	Gen Mngr	Steamship O	7580	W yo	NO	7
France	French	17 17	1882 Na	yo	Manager	Hotel	8494	E yo	W	8
France	French	18 12	1887 Na	yo	None				9
Illinois		61	yo	Architect	Building	5394	yo	yo WW	10
France	French	17 12	1430 Al	yo	None				11
Canada		41 43	yo	Sculptress	Art	5394	O yo	NO	12
Italy	Italian	24 24	1900 Al	yo	Bank Repn	Bank	8583	E yo	NO	13
Iowa		56	yo	None					14
Italy	Italian	24 24	1914 Na	yo	Merchant	Dept Products	8391	E	NO	15
France	French	12 12	1929 Al	yo	None				16
Germany		60	yo	None					17
New York		56	yo	Architect	Owner	4993	W	NO	18
Italy	Italian	24 24	1902 Na	yo	Sculptor	Art	5394	yo	NO	19
England	English	60 60	1910 Na	yo	Writer	Author	8494	O yo	NO	20
Germany	German	18 13	1923 Na	Hairdresser	Beauty Shop	8494	NO	1	21
France	French	12 12	1900 Na	yo	Sculptor	Art	5394	O yo	NO	22
So Carolina		18	yo	None					23
Pennsylvania		57	yo	Physician	Practice	9294	O yo	yo WW	24
Rhode Island		54	yo	Lawyer	Gent Practice	5X94	O yo	NO	25
New York		50	yo	None					26
New York		50	yo	Director	Soap works	7319	E yo	yo WW	27
Iowa		67	yo	None					28
Wisconsin		41	yo	None					29
New Jersey		56	yo	Salesman	Auto Sec	6385	W yo		30
Alabama		81	yo	Writer	Free Lance	8494	O yo	yo WW	31
France	French	12 12	1894 Al	Novelist	Inspection	9991	O yo	NO	32
France	French	12 12	1905 Al	yo	None				33
France		60 12 0	yo	Scholar	Carpentry	9591	W yo	NO	34
France		52 12 0	yo	None					35
Kentucky		64	yo	Promoter	Independent	9953	O yo	yo WW	36
Vermont		59	yo	None					37
England		65 04 0	yo	Merchant	Silks	8491	O yo	NO	38
Ireland		56 04 0	yo	None					39
New York		50 07 1	yo	Writer	Free Lance	8494	O yo	yo WW	40
Louisiana		73	yo	Writer	Free Lance	8494	O yo	NO	41
Pennsylvania		77	yo	Lawyer	Practice	5X94	E yo	NO	42
New York		60	yo	None					43
Massachusetts		53	yo	Advertising	Magazine	6153	O yo	yo WW	44
Missouri		16	yo	None					45
England	English	60 60	1916 Na	yo	None				46
Germany		56 13 2	yo	Stenographer	Public	7193	O	47
Wisconsin		53	yo	Writer	Free Lance	8494	O yo	NO	48
Austria		59 16 0	yo	None					49
New York		56	yo	Millwright	Sawmill	9299	E	NO	50

ENTRIES ARE REQUIRED IN THE SEVERAL COLUMNS AS FOLLOWS:

241

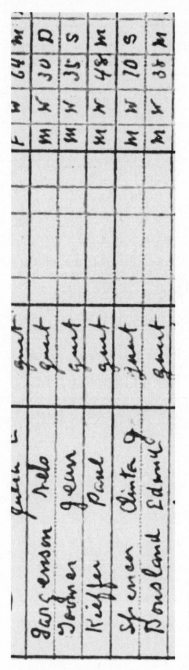

Detail of 1930 census.

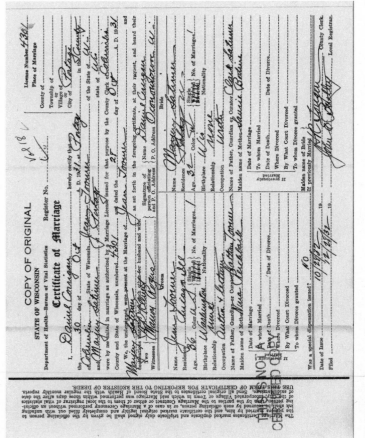

1931 marriage certificate.

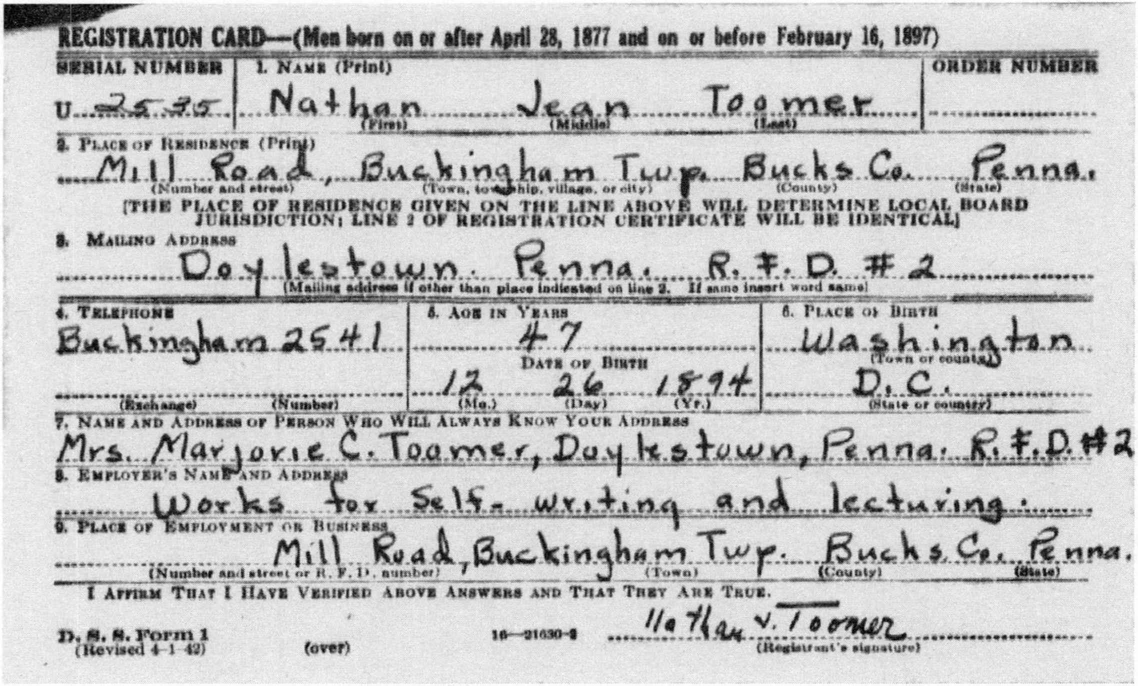

REGISTRATION CARD—(Men born on or after April 28, 1877 and on or before February 16, 1897)

SERIAL NUMBER	1. NAME (Print)			ORDER NUMBER
U 2575	Nathan (First)	Jean (Middle)	Toomer (Last)	

2. PLACE OF RESIDENCE (Print)
Mill Road, (Number and street) Buckingham Twp. (Town, township, village, or city) Bucks Co. (County) Penna. (State)

[THE PLACE OF RESIDENCE GIVEN ON THE LINE ABOVE WILL DETERMINE LOCAL BOARD JURISDICTION; LINE 2 OF REGISTRATION CERTIFICATE WILL BE IDENTICAL]

3. MAILING ADDRESS
Doylestown. Penna. R. F. D. # 2
(Mailing address if other than place indicated on line 2. If same insert word same)

4. TELEPHONE	5. AGE IN YEARS	6. PLACE OF BIRTH
Buckingham 2541	47	Washington (Town or county)
(Exchange) (Number)	DATE OF BIRTH 12 (Mo.) 26 (Day) 1894 (Yr.)	D. C. (State or country)

7. NAME AND ADDRESS OF PERSON WHO WILL ALWAYS KNOW YOUR ADDRESS
Mrs. Marjorie C. Toomer, Doylestown, Penna. R. F. D. #2

8. EMPLOYER'S NAME AND ADDRESS
Works for Self. writing and lecturing.

9. PLACE OF EMPLOYMENT OR BUSINESS
Mill Road, (Number and street or R. F. D. number) Buckingham Twp. (Town) Bucks Co. (County) Penna. (State)

I AFFIRM THAT I HAVE VERIFIED ABOVE ANSWERS AND THAT THEY ARE TRUE.

D. S. S. Form 1 (Revised 4-1-42) (over) 16—21630-2 Nathan J. Toomer (Registrant's signature)

Draft registration, April 24, 1942.

REGISTRAR'S REPORT

DESCRIPTION OF REGISTRANT

RACE		HEIGHT (Approx.)		WEIGHT (Approx.)		COMPLEXION	
White		5 ft. 10"		178		Sallow	
		EYES		HAIR		Light	
Negro	X	Blue		Blonde		Ruddy	
		Gray		Red		Dark	
Oriental		Hazel		Brown		Freckled	
		Brown		Black	X	Light brown	
Indian		Black	X	Gray		Dark brown	X
				Bald		Black	
Filipino							

Other obvious physical characteristics that will aid in identification.............

I certify that my answers are true; that the person registered has read or has had read to him his own answers; that I have witnessed his signature or mark and that all of his answers of which I have knowledge are true, except as follows:

Edith P. Rider
(Signature of registrar)

Registrar for Local Board.......... 34   *Phila*   *Pa.*
(Number)   (City or county)   (State)

Date of registration 4/27/42

245